I0831975

On the Right Track

Also by Jerry Labriola

—Murders at Hollings General

—Murders at Brent Institute

—The Maltese Murders

—The Strange Death of Napoleon Bonaparte

—Scent of Danger

—Object of Betrayal

—Deadly Politics

—Global Shadows

—Diamonds and Pirates

—Dangerous Triangle

—The Blue Baron Mystery

—The Saga of Hodge

—Spying for Keeps

—Discovery

Coauthored with Dr. Henry Lee

—Famous Crimes Revisited

—Forensic Files

—The Budapest Connection

—Shocking Cases

On the Right Track

A NOVEL

By

JERRY LABRIOLA, M.D.

STRONG BOOKS

Strong Books
P.O. Box 715
Avon, CT 06001-0715

First Printing

ISBN 978-1-928782-76-6

Library of Congress Control Number 2019950766

Published in the United States of America by Strong Books, an imprint of Publishing Directions, LLC

Printed in the United States of America

Dedicated to Xavier, a joy of all joys

ACKNOWLEDGMENTS

My sincere thanks to all the
personnel at STRONG BOOKS

NOTE

— To avoid the complexities of different languages spoken, all are delivered in English.

— Names of the main characters are figments of my imagination.

— Since there are numerous meetings among characters, all formal introductions and handshakes have been minimized in number.

— Some parts of this book contain paragraphs taken from other books I have written. There are just so many ways to state the same things.

PREFACE

The following sources have been most helpful. Some descriptive materials have been taken from them — with minor modifications. Much credit is due their authors. Apologies are extended for the accidental omission of some sources.

BBC Reports
INTERPOL
Looted Art
Central European Waterways
ABA Journal
The Lee/Labriola Books
Wall Street Journal
Travel Planner
From PlanetWare
Travel and Leisure
Search for Missing Art
French Connection
Paris
Lonely Planet Review
Peter's Paris
French Academy of Sciences
Les Invalides
Terrorism
Notre-Dame of Paris
Eiffel Tower
Champs Élysées
Nazi Plunder
Pilgrim Monument

New York Times Encyclopedia Britannica
The 20th Century
The Secret History of World War II
The World of Spies
The British World
The National World War ll Museum
Biography of Juan Peron
History of Switzerland
Sicilian Mafia
Vichy, France
Cordoba, Argentina
Switzerland During the World Wars
Wikipedia

PART ONE

Chapter 1

New Haven, CT

April 1

Rick Chandler was a freelancer of sorts, and it was over a month since he had volunteered his time and effort to a worthwhile cause. Back then and further back still, he often worked closely with international police authorities in addressing local problems. This time it arose as a result of a comment from his closest friend, Francis Moreau.

At home in his kitchen, Rick removed two eggs from their container, cracked them open into a frying pan and lit the burner. The phone rang in the next room and he ran to answer it. It was Fran calling from his home in nearby Stamford.

"I've been talking to people," he said, "and more than one has implied you could be of service once again. Involves a little travel. You interested in hearing about it?"

Rick had thought he'd be taking a longer breather, yet for some unknown preordained reason, he couldn't unglue himself from another challenge. This was his immediate thought anyway, and he felt not the least bit uncomfortable in keeping Fran waiting for an answer. Over the years, neither one of them even bothered to explain, for each one knew very well how serious their questions and answers were. This time around was no exception.

Then Rick smelled something burning. "Hold on a minute," he screamed, and raced to the kitchen stove. There, he found both eggs burnt to a crisp. He pulled the pan to the side, turned off the burner, and rushed back to the phone, grabbing its dangling mouthpiece and apologizing. "Sorry about that, Fran, but I just roasted some eggs. I should have known better."

"I'll bring you a dozen someday, but for now I have a challenge involving a little travel. You could do plenty just by concentrating on a few cities, not like before. That was too much. Interested in hearing more?"

Rick was more concerned about the eggs he'd wasted and didn't mind any kind of delay. He felt as though he'd never cooked before, but dismissing that thought, he turned and walked over to the sink. He emptied the pan and watched the burnt eggs disappear down the drain. He almost saluted them.

Returning to the phone, he finally asked, "Doing what?"

"Art work and other valuables are being stolen all over the place. They tell me it's grown into an epidemic. Why not help out? Sounds perfect for you."

"Doing what?"

"Find out who the crooks are."

"And?"

"Have them arrested and get the stolen stuff returned. We obviously can't locate all the pieces, but one or two could get the ball rolling."

"Meaning?"

"Meaning two things. One – word would get around, and two – the perps might band together, thinking it was the best thing to do, but not realizing that we might implicate a bunch at a time."

"Hmm … traveling would be where?"

"Scattered everywhere."

"And what are the other valuables?"

If it meant anything, Rick now took a paper and pencil and was ready to make some notes.

"Valuable books, Nazi gold, paintings, ceramics, deeply religious treasures … those kinds of things."

"If I say yes, where would I start?"

"I would guess with international art dealers who might know of suspects from previous thefts. But who knows if even some of the art dealers are on the take? So we'd have to keep our guards up. And you should choose your favorite countries. Because I've heard you speak about it so often, I imagine your first would be Argentina."

"You got it. I've done some work there before – about a year ago – and I know the police chief, Joe Gomez. Smart fellow. I interacted with him for nearly a week. He happened to work in New York City for 12 years or so. He was assigned to the dock there and lived in the Hell's Kitchen neighborhood. He speaks three languages. What I did in Buenos Aires involved some diamonds that belonged to Eva Peron, but at the time I had no inkling of their importance to what we might end up doing now. In other words, were they hers to begin with or were they stolen? Then and now … talk about coincidence."

"I agree that it's an excellent choice, Rick, because so many Nazis escaped to Argentina after the war. Germany must be another country to visit. But what you accomplish in Buenos Aires can set the tone elsewhere."

Rick's smile of interest turned sour. "What's that supposed to mean?" he asked.

"I'm talking about identifying a culprit or culprits in that city, and then arranging for the stolen articles to be returned to their rightful owners. Right away word would get out, and both the dealers and the owners would clamor for attention. But here's an important point. In some cases, you'd be acting as a spy."

"A spy?" Rick flashed a dirty little grin. "You mean I'd have a dagger hidden in my cloak? With that, I could **be** one when we're sightseeing."

"I'm serious, Rick. You'd have a different name, maybe wear a hat, wear glasses, different style of clothes, wear a wig and so on. So you should be both yourself most of the time and sometimes a spy. Spying would be the best way to find out if certain treasures were legally obtained. So in essence, I wrote out five or six things: What treasures? Who's the stealer, if there is one? Have the treasures been recovered? Arrange for the dealer or police authority to do so. Did some looters band together because of duplication of stolen goods and exchange if necessary … and because of warnings that police authorities were closing in. By that time it's possible your name would get around, and that's when things could get dangerous."

Rick arched an eyebrow. "You make it sound so easy, Fran. I mean 'identify' treasures? That's an unlikely scenario in the time we'd be spending all over the place. And the thought of being a spy makes me remember something." He said he once read several articles that indicated most spies know the identities of other spies, especially if they were involved in the investigation of criminal activities. "In fact, I have a stack up there on a bookcase. Never thought cloak and dagger info would be useful. To me, anyway. I'll get some and read a few for you, so don't hang up."

By now, Rick's bringing up the idea of certain spies knowing the identity of others had made some kind of unexpected headway. He went to the bookcase, rose to his tiptoes and located the stack without even searching for it.

He returned to the phone and said, "You still there?"

"Yes, I'm willing to listen, and then you've got to give me an answer to what I've laid out before you."

Rick avoided an answer and instead said he'd pick and choose:

> The demands of operators in the field of spying include the making of disguises and the forensic documentation for foreign operations.
>
> Spying focuses on non-public information gathered through covert means.
>
> What are spies looking for? Gaining information about military secrets, industrial secrets, political secrets, and secrets about stolen goods.
>
> How do they do it? The methods used often involve the latest technology, which can help the spy eavesdrop, tap telephone calls, and communicate secretly.
>
> A spy who knows the identity of another one never deterred either from being effective.
>
> Caroline Butler said it best when she wrote: A cloak is a long loose coat, and a dagger is a small sharp knife used as a weapon. But figuratively, "cloak and dagger" has the same feel as the expression "smoke and mirrors" in that they both conjure up images of espionage, secrecy and deceit.

"And?" Rick asked.

"And what?"

"You listened?"

"I listened. All was well put. But what about . . . ?"

"I know, Fran, I know. Two last questions: When would we start and who tells us where we start?" By now, he was embracing his words with broad, sweeping gestures.

"I'd say tomorrow and I'll accompany you as always."

Rick lived in New Haven not far from Yale where he majored in psychology and also developed a working knowledge of Spanish, French and German, especially German. But the idea of becoming a spy raised fears he was certain all spies faced – that of being "out spied". A case of espionage ... counter-espionage ... and back to espionage.

His wife, Angela, and Fran's wife, Janet, had just left for the Chandler's summer cottage in Maine where they planned on spending an indefinite period of time. Rick opted not to join them, preferring to spend some time alone working on his latest book. He even kept the latest pages of the manuscript in a thick briefcase, which he kept nearby at all times. When away from his travels, especially during the summer months, he spent most of his time on his writing. The books always dealt with forensic science and law enforcement. Currently, he was writing his sixth one. In two of them, he had written about Sacco-Vanzetti, Charles Lindbergh, Sam Sheppard, and Phil Spector. During the school year, he taught a forensic science class at Quinnipiac University and had an arrangement with President Jones whereby he was allowed time off if international projects arose. It so happened that Rick had once helped the president in locating his missing jewel piece.

Fran enjoyed time alone too, although he was employed at the U.N. in New York where he served as a computer consultant. It was not far from the Cornell Hospital where he volunteered weekend time wheeling discharged patients to relatives' cars.

Rick also taught a karate class at Quinnipiac, having gained black belt status and especially atemiwaza expertise. He could kick an adversary to cause injury, paralysis or even death. He'd never resorted to it but felt confident it could come in handy if necessary. So with disguises, his two guns -- a Beretta Cougar .45 and a Heritage Stealth 9 mm -- and with basic karate moves, he felt fairly well equipped to face any personal threats.

Six years ago, both his parents were killed in an auto accident and he inherited a vast amount of money from them. He was thus prepared to offer his services for worthwhile causes without payment of any sort. He proudly considered himself a "do-gooder" and the joy he always experienced was payment enough.

"You said we'd start tomorrow," Rick continued. "But needn't you show up at the U.N.?"

"Nah ... as you know, my work there is on an on-call basis and I just wouldn't be around if they called. Kinda loose, eh? But I'm pretty well heeled too. As for who tells us where to begin, I turn to the U.N. again. It has connections with INTERPOL and people there can tell us."

Fran had once informed Rick about the nature of INTERPOL:

> It stands for International Criminal Police organization -- an entity that facilitates worldwide police cooperation. It functions as a network of criminal law enforcement agencies from different countries and has 194 members.

"Well, I'm ready, willing and able," Rick said. "With our wives away for who knows how long, the timing couldn't be better. You know, Fran, this might be different. I'm all for taking our time and combining the recovery work with sightseeing."

He was determined to sightsee for a change because he had written about many far-off places but had never visited many in person. Buenos Aires and some brief work in Switzerland were exceptions. "And I'd like to label what we'll be trying to accomplish as PURPOSE. In each city that will come first and our sightseeing will follow. So it's PURPOSE and SIGHTSEEING in that order."

"Good. I'll follow through with INTERPOL and we'll take it from there. I'll get back to you."

As soon as they hung up, Rick phoned another close friend and advisor, criminalist Paul D'Arneau. Paul lived in East Falmouth on Cape Cod but worked three days a week at the Yale Library as an administrative assistant. He and Rick stayed in close touch and often sought each other's advice on investigative matters.

"Paul ... it's me."

"Hey, Rick. What's happenin'?"

"It's a long story and I'll wait to explain when we have lunch together. But the short of it is that I've volunteered to do my thing in a number of countries – helping to locate looted valuables like paintings and gold and books and jewelry. I'm told it's become an epidemic and I'm wondering if you can alert a key histarian or two, so I might call on them if necessary. Just like other times. You know, `histarian' not `historian'. I haven't had a need for their services for at least three or four years."

"I'll alert them. Absolutely. Turn to them if you need help, but by all means let's still keep their existence a secret. As you said ... just like other times."

Rick could tell that Paul was rummaging through his satchel for a description of histarians and could hear him straightening out a sheet of paper.

"Here, let me refresh your memory," Paul said. "This says it better than I can say it off-hand."

> Histarians are individuals, male or female, who are located in practically every region of the civilized world and can provide information that cannot be obtained any other way –very few people know of their existence. They give out facts only to other histarians or to those who come highly recommended. Very often they provide insights that are contrary to what history has recorded so they are properly named. Not "contrarians" but "histarians".

> Most of them like to remain anonymous. They never offer a definitive opinion without first checking with others of their kind … they are constantly doing so … that is, checking or verifying in addition to delving into things with their own critical eye.
>
> Some claim they have mystical powers, but they have nothing of the sort – they simply do exhaustive research – "private collections from private collectors" they call it. Their information sources are never revealed, but their conclusions always turn out to be right. It's superfluous to say – but totally right and totally accurate.
>
> They have sort of a code they live by – "canon" might be a better word: never give out information unless you'd die over its accuracy. So they rely on solid facts, not on opinion … although they will express an opinion of other histarians, usually more than three or four. Four is the general rule.
>
> Finally, they have all sworn never to give out much by telephone or over the Internet – only in person.

"Ring a bell?" Paul asked.

"Loud and clear. Thanks."

"While we're at it, Rick, two or three other things. Number one: remember way back I once had a theory that some cruise ships might be transporting stolen goods? And, that years and years ago, Argentina's Eva Peron might have been involved and that prostitution may be playing a role? So maybe you should check with a cruise line – and even with Argentina about it all.

"Number two: about your transportation needs. Not any different from the last time you did some work in Argentina. Joint Base Cape Cod – JBCC out of Hyannis on the Cape. They're still available for flight on a moment's notice. Anywhere. Anytime. For as long as necessary. They have that light plane manned by Ansel Stewart. As you know, he lands the plane wherever you go and then makes himself scarce until you contact him when you want to move on. He could do the same for you again … I mean when you want to leave for another city or until you want him to drive during your sightseeing. Remember? He'll have a car already rented and he'll give you that small device to contact him. Occasionally, you might want to join other sightseeing people on a bus, or for anything that's long distance, you can take a tram or a train.

"Ansel even dispatches a limo to and from my Falmouth home whenever necessary. I'm sure he'd do the same for you in New Haven. I'll phone him today and if you don't hear back from me within the hour, all's clear. You still don't have to pay anybody and why not remains a secret. Another secret? You can still be armed with revolvers while on board the plane.

"Finally, number three: I think the Mafia is as important for you to look into as anything else you investigate. I know a thing or two about them, but not as much as an old friend and former mafioso. Incidentally, Mafia kinship groups are called 'mafiosi', and a Mafia member is called a 'mafioso.' And as long as we're at it, the boss of a Mafia syndicate is called a `don'."

Sure knows his stuff.

"What I really want, Paul, is the name of a … uh … mafioso who'd be willing to speak to me if I needed help."

"I think one or two would be. I could find out. This guy. … who's not as high up as a don … he lives in Chicago now, but comes from Italy. His name's Fabio Calderone. In Italy, he was once an expert on front organizations before voluntarily stepping aside. Got weary of it, I understand. You know, Rick, when you come right down to it, there are decent mobsters and dangerous ones, and the decent ones won't hurt you. I once had some dealings with Fabio and can honestly say that he's a decent one. Resurrected himself somehow, and now he's completely clean… Anyway, I'll find out."

Rick was making notes in his pad. "Great," he said, pounding the air as an expression of appreciation.

"I'll be around," he finally said, as he received the name of a New Haven histarian: Lance Beck.

Chapter 2

Rick was a strapping six-foot-two whose shoulders seemed to follow the pace of his utterances: slouching, tightening, straightening. As a fifty-two year old, his hair showed little in the way of aging except for thin streaks of grey within fluffy sideburns. He hated haircuts, so he kept his hair long and full but neatly combed back. Usually clean-shaven, he had a generous smile, showing teeth that were even and bright. But it was his piercing brown eyes that captivated most observers. In conversation, he kept them steady, like a chipmunk stalking a runaway.

As for the Chandler home, it was sandwiched among similar ones on a road leading to the Yale Bowl. Minus a front yard, it was of a compact Neo-French design with a steeply pitched, hipped roof. It featured single story facades that were asymmetrical while doors and windows were arched upward, extending through the cornice line. Angela called it a "small house that lives large." But it wasn't small at all … maybe medium small … or medium large.

If its exterior were considered simple, its interior was complex. It had numerous rooms, perhaps nine or ten, and all on one floor. The master bedroom was the largest with a mattress that was king-sized and furniture that Angela had picked out. The room had small, high windows that she felt had created a void on the wall so she purchased a custom platform-style bed with an oversized headboard. And the room had a sofa with piping and rolled arms that included two accent pillows. There was also a purple console that was part of a collection of richly-hued Art Deco style furniture.

She had brightened the living room by displaying hanging wicker and rope accents along with faux flowers on a coffee table. The table spanned the length of another sofa that contained green and white throw pillows.

The kitchen included pine cabinets, some fitted with leaded glass and restored brickwork. White stone countertops and stainless-steel appliances were also new. Angela was proud of the kitchen's clean lines and lack of ornamentation.

Rick never complained about not having a say in any room's decor for he had his way across the hall in a small study that was lined with bookcases containing a thousand-plus books. His desk was just as overflowing and was surrounded by a computer, copier, printer, small tables, a hodgepodge of cabinets, a TV set and a remote control telephone.

It was nearing 9 a.m. when he looked out a window and saw that a storm was upon them, its rain pelting down in torrents, the sound of leaves being torn from their branches, their U.S. flag blowing in the stiff breeze. The window wasn't closed tightly so he could both smell and taste the humidity.

Not long before, when there was a torrential downpour during one of his forensic science classes, a student rose and asked about a possible changing face of crime. It led Rick to think about that winter afternoon as he now set about continuing with his book number 6. With the manuscript before him, he felt energized and typed at his computer:

> One in the audience asked if there was a changing face of crime or was it just hearsay. And the Lieutenant answered:
>
> Strange you should ask. I just finished with that very subject in the book I'm writing and here's what I've written so far. It's in the form of an essay:
>
> The mystery of the last several years is: what caused the rash of mass shooters in our country? Not so mysterious is that although crime rates, including most murder types, have dipped, America has been accosted by a changing face of crime that

defies easy explanation.

A motive-of-the-month mentality has sprouted nationally. There are those who speak of an "angry white man syndrome." Still others blame family alienation; or television, movie, and video game violence; or copycat crime; or drugs; or increased bitterness of the urban underclass. Yet, killers from suburbia have dominated the news lately. And if all these aren't enough, there is still the timeworn list of power, sex, money, poverty, and child abuse.

The mass murderer, as a horrified nation has read too often lately, enters a public or semipublic place, like a school, post office or business, and opens fire. Sociology and psychology experts state this kind of killer differs from, say, serial or spree killers in that the mass murderer does not expect to get away with his crimes, whereas the serial killer does, and the spree killer hasn't even gotten that far in his thinking. The mass murderer is mission-oriented and is making a statement so important to his psyche (or in his beliefs as in the case of a determined terrorist) that he doesn't plan on coming out alive. Such is the weight of his warped motive. John Douglas in *The Anatomy of Motive* put it this way: "It's as if each of them is writing a novel about himself in which the final chapter is [his own] violent death."

If the entire human species were a single individual, that person long ago would have been declared mad. The insanity would lie not in the anger and darkness of the human mind -- though it can be a black and raging place indeed. And it certainly wouldn't lie in the goodness of that mind–one so sublime, we fold it into a larger place called the "soul". The madness would lie instead in the fact that both these qualities–the savage and the splendid–can exist in one creature, one person, often in one instant.

We're a species that is capable of almost dumbfounding kindness. We nurse one another; romance one another; weep for one another. Ever since science taught us how, we willingly tear the very organs from our bodies and donate them to one another. But at the same time, we slaughter one another.

The past 20 years of human history contain untold horrors: in Mogadishu, Rowanda, Chechnya, Baghdad, Afghanistan, Pakistan, London, Madrid, Lebanon, Israel, New York City, Oklahoma City -- at Columbine High School, at Virginia Tech, at Fort Hood, Texas, in Newtown, Connecticut -- all of the crimes committed by the highest, wisest, most principled species the planet has produced. That we're also the lowest, cruelest, most blood-drenched species is our shame -- and our paradox.

What does, or ought to, separate us is our highly developed sense of morality, a primal understanding of good and bad, of right and wrong, of what it means to suffer not only our own pain – something that any organism with a rudimentary nervous system can do … but also the pain of others. That quality is the essence of what it means to be human. Why it's an essence that so often spoils, no one can say.

But isn't there more to be considered here? What about other bizarre and outrageous patterns of behavior in our society: a laissez faire approach to star athletes with substance abuse habits; scandals at the highest levels of corporate America; corrupt politicians; the embarrassing peccadilloes of a former leader of the free world. In a sense, too free, at least in this part of it. And therein lies the rub.

It is a question of freedom -- in the home, at school, in the church or synagogue, in the entertainment business. And a question of balance. Freedom must be paired with responsibility, for without it, unbridled freedom becomes license. The dilemma then is to preserve freedom while not allowing it to empower willy-nilly -- to spawn those who would run amuck, or to foster the notion among some that they are above the law.

Lest readers conclude that an attempt is being made here to link all the above examples to a murderous mind, one need turn again to the experts who claim that future patterns of behavior are laid down in one's early formative years and can lead to varying mindsets carried through adolescence and into adulthood. But the spoiled brat or the corrupt politician or the athlete who craves more kicks than applause is not to be confused with a school sniper or out-of-control Rambo. They are all products of early impressions, and why one veers down route A and another down route B is open to speculation. Yet one thing appears certain: the information children receive and absorb early on -- from parents, teachers, preachers, and the like -- may influence the route taken. And the information may range from casual remarks, through serious advice, to the behavior patterns of the grownups themselves. Or if these and other authority figures shun or become shunned, for whatever reasons, the child may eventually turn to peers similarly treated or, worse still, to angry gangs.

Where does this all leave us? When we speak of parents, teachers and other authority figures, we

> speak of the guardians of our institutions. Their perceived laxity has been matched by the laxity of the public at large. People may be temporarily shocked or chagrined by what they observe but, nowadays, they seem quicker to rationalize or even to forgive. In a strange but not intentional way, they may thus be propagating antisocial behavior. And worse.
>
> In order to gel that most time-honored virtue -- responsibility -- should we not rediscover the enduring worth of those institutions that have always stood stubbornly for all virtues, and thereby give balance to the freedoms we all do and must enjoy? Virtues like love and loyalty and tolerance. Clearly, these underpinnings of our civilization are now much less to be taken for granted. Recent history teaches us that. The changing dynamics of personality coupled with the pace and pressures of the times are such that no institution can be considered invulnerable anymore. And those in authority must recognize the influence they have on future generations by the power their words, by the example of their own behavior, and by the effect of both on their children.
>
> And so ..

The phone rang and Rick answered it. It was Fran calling.

"What took you so long?" Rick asked. It had been only 15 minutes since they had last spoken.

Fran ignored the comment and said, "I've heard back from INTERPOL. A guy named Andy Jenkins, and yes, the various art dealers, should be contacted wherever we go. As for countries, it's up to us to decide, and one dealer can contact another one in our next country. But just like we thought, Rick, we should be careful because maybe not all of them can be trusted. Some might be on the take themselves. He also got into terrorism, saying that many terrorist groups band together -- those that have an interest in stolen art. So do Mafia groups. Some sell the stolen objects to other criminals, or they somehow use the objects as ransom for various crimes. He went on and on about terrorist groups and listed some: ISIS, radical Islam, those in Syria. It's not related but he even mentioned the 9/11 attack here in our country. … 2,752 being killed at our trade center. Jenkins ended the conversation by saying that it usually takes a week for a deal to be done and that we must follow up by contacting the original owners."

"In person?"

"No, maybe by the Internet. And he stressed that he'd be available 24/7 if we need help of any kind. Nice guy."

"Good work, Fran."

"Thanks. So we start tomorrow?"

"Tomorrow. The JBCC out of Hyannis. I've told you about them before. A plane will land here in New Haven. Can you drive here from Stamford?"

"I'll make it my business to."

"Okay. Now before we hang up, let's go through how we handle PURPOSE in each city. Offhand I'd say that my sightseeing would really dictate which cities we should visit -- like Buenos Aires … Zurich … Paris … Hamburg … Rome … London … Lisbon … Madrid … Budapest and … say … Bucharest. They're the places I'd like to see up close and not necessarily in that order. Except, as you know, Buenos Aires should be first. In each city, we'll check with a key art dealer or the city's police chief. I don't think we can actually identify objects that were stolen, but that shouldn't be our intent anyway. If we can, in the short time we're there, that's great, but our major strategy is to have the dealer or chief notify the media that we're there … and **why** we're there. Newspapers, TV and so on. Culprits will notice and maybe stop what they're doing. Or even give up what they've stolen because the heat will be on. News travels fast and culprits in other cities and countries will also take notice. And hopefully many will panic. I know we could just telephone them about notifying media outlets, but in person is more definitive. And besides, we'll be there to sightsee anyway."

Rick could just imagine Fran's look of uneasy puzzlement.

"Your name will get around, Rick. You realize that, don't you?"

"Yes, but I'll be ready. I've faced it before."

Chapter 3

April 2

Dawn came quickly the next day … a wash, a glow, a lightness, and then an explosion of fire as the sun arose in full force. Rick witnessed it as he arose early after a terrible night trying to sleep. He decided to read up on some stolen art particulars in a few old newspapers and to consult with what he could find on his computer. He made both mental and written notes such as:

> Some antiquities are rumored to be cursed. But those stolen and sold do leave a trail of lawsuits – and sometimes bodies -- in their wake.
>
> The looting and illicit export of art treasures is not a new problem. It's happened whenever there have been armed conflicts during which victorious troops plundered churches, temples, and other buildings. Germany carried out massive looting in World War II.
>
> By the start of the 21st century, the trade in massive antiquities had become so huge it was worth billions of dollars each year and was the biggest international crime outside of drug and arms trafficking.
>
> When a piece is stolen, the consequence for scholars is tragic, because essential information about the piece -- where it was found, what else was with it --may be lost forever.

In recent years numerous American museums -- including the Metropolitan Museum of Art in New York, Boston's Museum of Fine Arts and the Getty in Los Angeles -- have been forced to return antiquities to their host countries. These include the famed krater (wine bowl) dating from 515 BC.

Probably the most dramatic case of looted antiquities concerns the notorious Sevso treasure, a magnificent cache of late Roman silver dating from the fourth or fifth century AD and comprising inlaid platters, ewers and bowls, which was unearthed in the 1970s. The finder was later found hanged in a cellar and two of his friends died under unexplained circumstances. The silver -- contained in a giant copper cauldron that he had buried in the cellar -- had disappeared.

Last year, Syria returned relics to Iraq; France returned items to Burkina Faso, and Denmark repatriated relics to China. Both Italy and the Vatican returned parts of the looted Parthenon to Greece.

Also last year, in the Ethiopian town of Axum, tens of thousands of jubilant people turned out for the unveiling of a treasured obelisk that was taken by Italian troops in 1937 but returned after lengthy negotiations between Rome and Addis Ababa.

Swiss Accused of Keeping Holocaust Funds. During World War II, European Jews were victimized twice. Not only were they victims of the Holocaust, but they were also victims of Nazi officials who stole from them. Homes were invaded and stores plundered. The trains came into Auschwitz, a concentration camp in Poland, and as

> the people stepped off the train, not only were they separated from their families, but they were ordered to place their belongings into baskets -- clothes in one, books in another, jewelry in another, gold in another. Everything was separated. From wedding rings to gold fillings from teeth, the Jews' possessions were then melted into gold and sent to Switzerland, where Germany acquired hard currency to carry on their war effort. As the Nazis swept across Europe, they confiscated gold from each country they invaded. The money contained in the Swiss bank accounts from both the central banks of Europe and Holocaust victims is said to be billions in dollars. As the Nazis shipped valuables to Switzerland, they made extensive use of the safe deposit boxes there. American documents have related that there are hundreds of millions of dollars in bank vaults, composed of jewelry, securities, artwork assets, and valuables. Some of it was returned ... most was not.

His phone rang. It was Paul calling. He said that he checked with Calderone and that he had expressed his willingness to assist whenever Rick decided to take on the Mafia situation. And even before then.

Rick responded: "As a former Mafioso, he could be asked to lead us to any important Mafia meetings. There might be big ones in the future."

- - - - -

Rick remembered his last flight to Buenos Aires. It took ten hours and he was unable to nap during any of it because his thoughts were scrambled and he couldn't get rid of them. He even neglected sliding his window shade shut, not caring about the light shining in his eyes from time to time. But all the while, he tried to minimize the problem, and although he had grown tired of its recurrence during other flights, he scolded himself.

Live with it!

As before, they landed at the EZE Airport. Rick had phoned ahead to be sure Joseph Gomez was still the police chief, and Ansel had phoned ahead to rent a car. The three men registered at the Claridge Hotel. Rick and Fran would occupy one room with twin beds and Ansel would be in the room across the hall. He had been with Rick during a last visit there and knew exactly where the Police Department Building was. He said to call him when they were ready to leave and pulled up in front of the building at 9:30 a.m., Buenos Aires time.

"You want me inside with you?" Fran asked, "or should I stay with Ansel?"

"No, stay with me. You look like my bodyguard."

In fact, Fran did. At six-three, he was a shade taller than Rick, had wavy brown hair parted in the middle, dark eyes that seldom blinked, and a wiry mustache. If others in his presence were to laugh, he only smiled. In fair weather, his shirt was always collarless and sleeveless -- displaying biceps thicker than Rick's. And in the center of his right forearm was a tiny tattoo of the American flag.

Three years younger than Rick, they had been friends for years. Throughout those years they had often gone out to dinner with their wives. Rick was impressed with the Moreaus and especially with Fran's upbringing. He grew up on a large farm in Eastern Connecticut – Griswold – became a scholarship student at Yale and served in the U.S. Navy for four years. He came upon his wealth by inheriting most of it from his divorced and deceased father, Henry, who had sold the farm shortly before his death.

As for an initial phone call to Gomez, Rick said he wanted to get the chief's take on a variety of subjects, including stolen art, Evita, prostitution and cruise ships, and that it would all be better to do so in person. Sightseeing was also briefly mentioned, as were nine cities he wanted to visit with other officials.

"I hope you understand, Joe."

"Yes, so do come ahead. I just pray your trip proves worthwhile."

- - - - -

In a small waiting room, Rick announced their arrival to a male receptionist. He was as tall as Rick and was immaculately dressed: dark blue jacket, lighter blue vest, blue and white bow tie, silver key chain.

"Oh yes," he said, "you're expected. He said you wanted to discuss a couple of things with him. Do have a seat while he finishes up with another visitor. Won't take long."

"You're new, I see," Rick said. "What happened to Juanita? Was that her name?"

"Yes … Juanita. And I'm Carlos. She decided to retire. I'm just filling in until Joe hires someone else."

They sat down and once again Rick admired a large photo of the sweep of coral colored roses alongside the building's entrance. Still savoring their aroma, he then noticed a stack of handouts on a small desk beside his chair. He picked one up and saw that the writing on both sides was in Spanish.

Why are there more Spanish-speaking people who also understand some English? Why are they greater in number than the reverse?

He understood most of what he read:

The massive crowd waited plaintively. … refusing

to believe that their beloved Evita could be gone from them forever at the age of thirty-three. To Argentina's poor, she was thought to be saint-like, but to the elite, she was more like Satan incarnate.

She was one of the most complex, paradoxical and enigmatic women in history who, more than once, embodied a litany of opposites: earthy/ethereal -- sacred/profane -- good/evil -- puritanical/promiscuous.

Fueled by a desire "to be someone", a yearning stoked by a childhood poverty and shame, she hungered for the respect and acceptance denied her as a child of illegitimacy when such an enigma held grave societal consequences.

Early on, while working as an actress, she was Eva Duarte. She met and married General Juan Peron, the future president of Argentina. As his wife, she afforded great respect and wielded much power, a perfect position from which to avenge the many deprivations and humiliations she had suffered at the very same hands of those she now ruled. It is difficult to reconcile the disparate Evitas that seemed to inhabit her being.

Her complicity in offering asylum to the heinous Nazis, a commiseration born more out of greed than a shared ideology, contrasted dramatically with the unabashed tenderness and utter lack of concern for her own health, when allowing a tubercular to kiss her face, or when comforting a sick or orphaned child.

Her charitable foundation granted favors for the needy and built many hospitals. Yet, as she championed these very human causes, her detractors point out that she simultaneously helped herself to vast sums of money and precious gems -- obviously not having a conflict of conscience and ambition.

She envisioned one day being VP on her husband's presidential ticket, a position that would enable her to satisfy her fever for power.

But then, the first signs of illness were evident in 1950 when she fainted at an official function. From that point on, uterine cancer, surgery, and radiation dominated her life, although she continued a grueling public schedule.

She died in 1952, and for the next 14 years her well-embalmed body was transferred from place to place -- including Spain. Finally, in 1976, she was entombed without fanfare inside the Duarte family mausoleum in the Cementerio de la Rocoleta, Buenos Aires' preeminent cemetery. Her gravesite, on which a plaque is inscribed with the words, “Don't Cry for Me” in Spanish, is positioned among the most famous names in Argentina's history. It is a peculiar irony that her body now lies eternally surrounded by the country's elite, the very people she so hated in life.

The myth of Evita persists until today, kept alive by a spate of books, a play, a movie, a song and by an enduring interest in this passionate woman who lived a short life of stunning contradictions and loomed larger than life.

The world's attention she captured during her lifetime is now eclipsed only by the iconic status she has realized since her death.

Rick ratcheted up his resolve as he focused his mind on the

phraseology he'd just read: " … she simultaneously helped herself to vast sums of money and precious gems -- obviously not having a conflict of conscience and ambition." He slid the handout into his briefcase.

Ten minutes later, the main office door opened and the chief appeared. Rick bounced up, shook Gomez's hand firmly and said, "It's been awhile, Joe, but good to see you again." Gomez concurred as Fran was introduced and they, too, shook hands.

"Big guy you have out there," Rick said. "Kinda formal – maybe even stoic. Says he's temporary."

"No, he thinks he is, but he's here to stay. Anyway, I hope so. Comes from royalty. .. way back. He represents me anywhere if I'm tied up. For years his family has run a self-defense studio in Zurich. He says he wants to spend more time there."

"As a student or a teacher?"

"Student. He's still learning."

The chief looked just the same as he had a year ago: tall, in shape, a bit gray at the temples. His blue uniform was still over-brimming with gold and silver badges, and he spoke more like a Brooklynite than an Argentinian.

It had nothing to do with the upcoming discussion, but Rick hunched his shoulders and reached down to pat his ankle to make sure his guns were in their holsters. They were. He saw that Fran, while observing him, also hunched his shoulder – obviously to ensure that his .22 mm was there. They gave a slight nod in unison.

They were ushered into the office and the three men sat around a buffet with walnut veneer, a marble top and brushed hardware. Both impressed and curious, Rick asked if the buffet represented the chic yet comfortable style of midcentury French and Italian furniture.

"That's right on the nose," the chief said.

Rick then continued: "Joe, we won't take up much of your time, or ours really, because I know how busy you usually are, and in our case we wanted to meet with other officials in some other cities -- nine more to be exact -- and I think I named them for you on my call here. I know them by heart and just to review, they're Zurich, Paris, London, Rome, Hamburg, Lisbon, Madrid, Budapest and Bucharest. But you're number one. The other things I named were four in number: looted treasures, Evita, prostitution, and cruise ships." With pauses, inflections and a hard stare, Rick continued on as though the chief was an integral part of destiny. And the chief's stare back was just as hard.

"So let's take the four one at a time," Rick said. "Make sense?"

"Yes, it does … and I'm all ears."

"Okay. First of all, regarding what we're labeling PURPOSE. Could you notify all local media outlets that we're here and why? Concerns the looting of treasures, if you remember. This might cause a stir. In other words, some of it might come to a halt or even better than that, some items might be returned on the q.t."

By now, Joe was making notes on a paper tablet. "Certainly," he said.

"Secondly, could you check on whether or not Evita was dealing with stolen diamonds and somehow with Switzerland? Was she and that country somehow in cahoots over them? But who cares … years later. … whether or not her diamonds were stolen? The answer is Switzerland. That country's possible involvement might still exist today."

"Third, the role of prostitution. Is it being used to cover up treasure stealing?"

"As I told you way back, Rick, it's legal throughout our country, but organized prostitution isn't. Like brothels, or pimping or prostitution rings. Usually your ordinary whore becomes a whore because she needs the money for survival. But regarding the other countries you're going to? I wouldn't be surprised if they have prostitution rings in all of them. And the way it works is if you're on to them in one country, like here, they band together and warn other countries, just like your first challenge …

uh … looted treasures. Another way of putting it is … when the going gets tough, so do prostitution rings. On an international scale."

"I understand. Finally, should we visit some cruise lines and talk to the captains? I hear some ships might be transporting stolen items. To where and why, I can't imagine. And prostitution acts as an incentive for the ships to do so.

"That sums it up, Joe, except for two last things. First, just reeling this off in my mind earlier changed my outlook about personally visiting nine more countries only for our PURPOSE. Instead, would it be asking too much if you could call your counterparts in the nine other cities and ask them if they could handle much of what I just covered? In other words, duplicate what you're agreeing to do here in Buenos Aires? Have *them* do it. And the second has to do with my possibly lecturing in some of the cities."

"Lecturing?"

"Yes. I've given this plenty of thought. I feel guilty about taking and not giving. Could you also ask the chiefs in four of the cities … I'd prefer Zurich, Paris, Lisbon and Budapest … if they could arrange for me to give a lecture at their best universities? I'd be willing to do so. I understand that many people in those cities understand and speak English, especially the younger folks. I'd speak about certain cases that deal a lot with forensic science even though they're old cases. Two of my private investigator friends gave these talks … I forget where … and they gave me a copy of their full texts which I could read and not just wing it, although I could make a modification or two. They collaborated on what they gave me. The cases are O.J. Simpson, Charles Lindbergh, Sacco-Vanzetti and Phil Spector. Plus there's the one I coauthored with Dr. Henry Lee. As I said, they're filled with forensic science matters and hell, I lecture on them at Quinnipiac, so why not in some foreign cities? Therefore, I wouldn't only be sightseeing but also be giving lectures. My 'taking' would be seeing the sights, and my 'giving' would be the lectures. Finally, I printed out a short version of my bio that you could read to the professors at each university. It's here in my briefcase." He located the bio and handed it to the chief.

"Could you read the bio to them real slowly so they could copy it down? And I'm sure you can tell that I've rehearsed everything I want to say to you, or should I elaborate?"

Gomez's answer was immediate. "No, no need to, Rick. I understand what you're getting at. I'll do it all and get back to you .... maybe before the day is over. And just so you know, I followed all four of those cases when I lived for a dozen years in your country. O.J. and Spector were in the 1990s and although the other two were in the 1920s, they were highlighted later."

"Even Sacco-Vanzetti?"

"Yes. It's long but it has many angles and layers. As you know, the whole case lasted ten years."

Rick felt like the entire conversation was among the best he'd encountered and wanted it to continue. "Maybe have them get back to you after they've contacted the media outlets," he said. "And when you've heard from all of them, could you contact me? My cell phone is augmented to make and receive calls from anywhere. And I'd also need to know the names of the universities and the professors to see." A pulse fluttered in Rick's neck as he added, "I sure hope I'm not being too demanding, Joe. I really do."

"No, you're not, so don't worry about it. I'll follow through as best I can. I've got your land phone and cell phone numbers. Just remember: I have many friends all over the world - - - police chiefs. We do favors for one another and compare notes all the time. If a chief isn't readily available, I can always speak to a sergeant-at-arms who'll relay the message. So, it's a given, Rick. I've got to praise you for such undertakings. "

Gomez's last comments pumped Rick and Fran up simultaneously. They both thanked him with a hand held over their hearts.

"Excellenté," Rick said. "That means we can spend more time sightseeing. Beginning today, really, and guess what?"

"What?"

"I'm sticking with the cities I'd planned on visiting because they're so etched in my mind."

Chapter 4

On the way to Buenos Aires, Rick had warned Fran that much of what was ahead would be the same in all nine cities: walking past known and unknown landmarks; entering ones that had doors to enter; eating at impressive-looking restaurants; and taking bus or van tours.

"Think about it, Fran. If I were to write a book about what we're about to do, I'd call it a travelogue, not something else."

"But there's a lot of traveling in your books, too."

"I suppose you're right. Can't get traveling out of my mind, I guess."

Ansel did the driving. He even accompanied them during some walks, leaving the car behind and returning to it when it was needed, and he was often asked to use Rick's camera to take pictures of the two men. In appearance, Ansel was the perfect man for the job he had with JBCC … short, young, reserved, but most of all, inconspicuous. He was born on Cape Cod and, quite by accident, landed a job at the airport in Hyannis. He was helping his mother climb into a plane, was mistaken for an employee and moved to a larger plane to assist other passengers. Management was so impressed with his inconspicuous conduct that he was hired for his present position. That was eight years ago.

- - - - -

Monotony aside, Rick intended to read every handout, every circular, every poster note that they came across – short or long.

Now's my chance to digest everything 1 can.

He would read not only those in English but also those in Spanish, French and German (as best he could).

They began their sightseeing in Buenos Aires, walking through a huge and busy port, noting mammoth machinery used to move humongous containers. The sun was warm, a slight wind causing clouds to move about or to come and go. While still at the dock, they climbed into a tour bus and, along with other passengers and a standing guide, began a lengthy tour of noted landmarks. There were a number of stops. First at the Recoleta Cemetery with its maze of mausoleums. It was where Evita's body was placed, according to the guide. Most of the passengers stepped off the bus to get a closer look. Rick noticed symbols on the pavement that represented bodies of soldiers. He also noticed something else. Atop a metal post that was attached to the sidewalk was a printed message under glass. At eye level, it read:

> Two points must be made.
>
> (1) There aren't many cities in which a graveyard should be on your sightseeing list, but Buenos Aires is one. The Recoleta Cemetery contains row after row of elegant and elaborate commemorations of those who have passed on, each mausoleum competing with the next in style and scale. The result is an amazing collection of architectural masterpieces, linked to names that make up a "Who's Who" of Argentine history-makers -- among them Eva Duarte de Peron and world heavyweight boxing champion Aluis Angel Firpo.
>
> (2) Argentina is the eighth-largest country in the world, the second largest in Latin America, and the largest Spanish-speaking one. It is divided into seven

> geographical regions: Northwest Puma, Mesopotamia, Gran Chaco, Sierras Pampeanas, Cuyo, Pampas and Patagonia.

They passed by the funnel-shaped bay called the Rio de la Plata; over broad avenues; numerous parks and plazas; many museums and libraries; and the Pink House, which is the equivalent of Washington's White House. Then they slowed down at the Plaza de Mayo and Casa Rosa where Evita reportedly spoke from a balcony. Rick couldn't help but recall seeing the movie starring Madonna: *Don't Cry for Me, Argentina.* The guide's mentioning Evita reminded Rick of another article about her and her husband. It was given to him some time ago by another treasure hunter friend, David Brooks, and it was in his briefcase. He recalled that the article duplicated some of what he had already read in Joe Gomez's office but he didn't care, for it also dealt with Switzerland, which was next up in their travel plans. Sitting on a bench, he said to the others, "Go ahead, just drift around. I'll catch up to you in a few minutes. I have an article I'd like to review." He found it in the briefcase:

> Juan Domingo Peron spent most of his youth in the region of Patagonia. He graduated from a military academy and by now (1944), has become Vice-President of Argentina.
>
> Strictly speaking, throughout his career thus far, most observers feel his political skills outweigh his military skills. Not long ago, he stayed on good terms with Jews and Nazis but this has changed as the war is nearing its end.
>
> Six years ago, he went to Europe simply as a military observer, spent time in Italy, Spain, and Germany and while in Italy, became impressed with Benito Mussolini. It is not clear why he chose these countries, but they so happen to form the Axis alliance in Europe. Some of its leaders have come to be known as war criminals and have sentenced many innocent citizens to death. Those who escaped such cruelty sneaked away to Argentina and to other

> South American countries. Why here, you may ask. Three reasons are given (and rather weak ones) One – our country was colonized by Spain. Two – Spanish is our official language. And three – much of our population is of Italian or Germen descent.
>
> Meanwhile, Peron has been associating with one Eva Duarte, and the general consensus is that their marriage is not too far off. She has had a successful career in radio, movies and the theater and soon won the affection of the Argentine people. Born in 1919 as an illegitimate child, she became a prostitute in order to survive and to obtain those roles. She also became a mistress to army officers. And due to her ties with prominent Nazis, it is alleged that she paved the way for the prevalence of Fascism across Latin America.
>
> Known as Evita by her adoring followers, it is alleged that because of those ties to Nazis, Switzerland would come into the equation. She and a longtime friend and a Swiss diplomat were to arrange a relationship between the Central Banks of Argentina and Switzerland, business contacts that would eventually advance both Argentine commerce and the relocation of Hitler's henchmen. The bottom line is that her flirtations with the Nazis will no doubt facilitate a formal Swiss-Argentine-Nazi collaboration. And there is no doubt that when she and Juan Peron marry, they will in effect become Argentina's "Populist Power Couple."

Rick scratched his head as if there were a tangle of cobwebs inside. He removed the handout from his briefcase, found the sentence he had in mind and read it again as he done once before.

" … she simultaneously helped herself to vast sums of money and precious gems … not having a conflict of conscience and ambition."

Says it all.

They next came to La Boca, the city's colorful Italian quarter. The passengers exited the bus and Rick again came upon a post that was not far from the bus, and he read the message there:

> Another section of town that stimulates the senses is right here – La Boca. You are at the mouth of the Rio Plata. A former warehouse district, this sector of Buenos Aires is a bit funky, decorated with brightly painted, tin-roofed wooden houses that serve a deservedly dual role: as backdrops for local painters working on, exhibiting and selling their innovative work, and as colorful backgrounds in the paintings themselves.

Rick suddenly realized that he had left his briefcase behind and turned to re-enter the bus. At that point, a shot rang out, its bullet piercing a bus window several feet from him. While others scattered, he ducked and at the same time withdrew the Heritage Stealth from his ankle holster.

"Here we go!" he screamed to Fran who was racing over, his .22 mm in hand.

"See, I told you so," Fran whispered. "You all right?"

"All right. The shot came from that car that's speeding away. I can't tell its make.

"You know, Fran," he said, returning the gun to its holster, "that shot missed by so much, I think it was meant as a warning, not as a kill – if it was meant for me in the first place. But regardless, all the more reason to keep our guards up as we carry on."

Rick kept his gun pressed against his upper thigh as he walked haltingly back to the bus. Once seated, he returned the gun to its holster and wondered why there had been no comment made by other passengers, the driver or the standing guide. Finally, one woman wandered over and, putting a reassuring hand on his shoulder, asked, "That wasn't meant for you, was it?"

"Gosh, I hope not," he said. "I think it could have been a stray bullet of sorts."

"What about the car, though?"

"The car? Maybe the guy was cleaning his gun when it accidentally fired. He then panicked and the car took off."

After the woman shook her head and left, both men wiped sweat from their necks as the bus set out for Dorrego Square in the San Telmo district where the guide said its pricey junk and most antique treasures were made and purchased in Europe before the 1940s. Their attention was minimal as they observed white statue-mimes, musicians and tango dancers, all within a flea market that lined the perimeter. The driver seemed to be hurrying away from the shooting incident but did finally slow up and stop at the next post message. Rick had expected to see a post wherever they stopped and to beat everyone else to it. He did and read the following:

> In a compliment to both cities, Buenos Aries is frequently dubbed the Paris of South America. The comparison stems from the decidedly European flair found in the food, the cafés and the chic boutiques. It shines out of the city's noble architectural beauty and sings from its sophisticated cultural attractions. Yet look deep into this highly polished veneer and you will find that Buenos Aires – like its signature dance, the tango – has a wild Latin passion bubbling just below its stately surface.

Better yet was the impromptu performance they caught in Dorrego Square – an interpretation by young, gorgeous dancers who literally took to the streets to flaunt their prowess. After their strenuous and sensuous workouts, each couple passed the hat and collected a small fortune. Then, what started as a drizzle, turned into a soaking rain.

I'm so tired of rain.

It was cool but not cold. Yet in spite of the change in weather, they took a long hike to the Teatro Colon opera house for an interesting tour, including a walk-on stage. On a wall just outside its entrance was the following:

> Another architectural masterpiece linked to history is this awesome Teatro Colon where, for instance, Maria Callas and Enrico Caruso appeared repeatedly. Outstanding acoustically and famous for opera, it is also an architectural incongruity. The building is ltalianate, but the decor is French. The auditorium imitates a scintillating wedding cake, done in gilt and red velvet. Let us give you a tip: if you can't get a ticket to this world renowned theater (it is often sold out), take a behind-the-scenes tour instead. It is well worth it.

But they were allowed in, and it was indeed beautiful and ornate with lots of reds, gold and marble and a large display of musical instruments.

They next walked through a detour into La Galleria – long and wide – past a posh and huge mall. Then back to their hotel where at its entrance twilight was dissolving onto the dark shingles of its roof. Inside, they had drinks and dinner in the lobby bar and restaurant. After a last drink and a lull in their conversation, they finally dropped into bed at 10:30.

- - - - -

They didn't start the next day until late afternoon, choosing instead to relax, watch TV and nap. Around 5:30, they were taken by van (with others from different hotels) to La Ventana for a spectacular night. There were juicy steaks to eat and an unbelievable show. Seven elderly gents in tuxedos played concertinas, violins and piano. Plus singers, more dancers and an amazing rendition of "*Don't Cry for Me, Argentina*" and the haunting melody, "*La Cumparsita*". On the ride back to the hotel, they had a discussion about the meaning of "cumparsita". It was still only 8:10 when they were getting ready for bed and Rick's phone rang. It was Chief

Gomez.

"Hello, my friend," he said. "Good news. It was early morning in most cities, but I reached all the chiefs and every one of them said he'd follow through. Now – you got pen and paper handy?"

"Yes, I do." Rick couldn't wait to write down what he anticipated was about to come.

"The universities and professors to see: In Zurich -- The Federal Institute of Technology. Franz Kauffman. In Paris -- Sciences and Letters Research University. Charles Lerferve. that's L – E – R – F – E –R – V – E. In Lisbon -- University of Lisbon. Alberte Breno. In Budapest … .Corvinces University. John Weedon. Got it all?"

"Got it."

"And two other things, Rick: One, I read each professor the bio of you, and two, I think it best if you first spend two days for your scouting around the cities; then a day for your lecture. And repeat the process three more times. So it's two – one; two – one, and so on. That amounts to 12 days. About right?"

Rick was counting on his fingers when he answered, "Forget the 'about', Joe. You know, you're astonishing. If there were a stronger word, I'd use it."

- - - - -

When checking out of the Claridge the next morning, Rick paid for their stay with an L.L. Bean Mastercard and indicated to the other two that the same would apply at all future hotels.

Chapter 5

Switzerland

April 4

The next morning, the three men arrived at Switzerland's Zurich Airport and then registered for the second floor of the Marriott Hotel, a short distance away. Rick had stayed there once before. Their rooms were not completely ready so they gobbled down a quick breakfast in the lobby restaurant. But their rooms were still not completely readied .... a maid indicated 15 more minutes .... so to kill the time, they bunched together and read a long, three-piece statement that was printed on a bulletin board near the reception desk. Rick remembered skimming through it some three years before, but this time he read every word:

> Welcome to Switzerland! To acquaint you with its characteristics, the following has been taken from the booklet, *Central European Waterways*, by Vantage. Some of the booklet's renditions have been eliminated. Our goal is to give you the essentials.
>
> Each of Switzerland's eight regions has its own history. Landscape, cuisine, architecture and even languages become changed as otherwise invisible borders are crossed. A landlocked country in the cultural and geographical heart of Europe, Switzerland has a distinct character and dynamism. While the country is admired for the beauty of its

Alpine environment, its people are respected for their industry and technical ingenuity, as well as their social responsibility and direct democratic system of government. It is one of the world's richest countries, located in the Alpine region of central Europe. It covers some 15,950 square miles and is inhabited by 7.5 million people, 22% of whom are non-Swiss. It borders Germany to the north, Austria and Liechtenstein to the east, Italy to the south, and France to the west and northwest. The mountainous country has engendered a robust spirit of independence and enterprise and a zealous work ethic in its population.

Though divided by religion and with diverse cultural roots, the Swiss are remarkable for their strong sense of unified nationhood. Its national character has also been molded by its neutrality. Having avoided many of the major conflicts that shaped the culture of other European nations, it stands slightly removed from the wider world. Although it is a neutral country, it maintains a citizen army to defend its borders. National service is compulsory. However, except in time of war, the Swiss army has no active units and no top general, although regular training takes place. The last mobilization occurred during World War II. Today, the only Swiss mercenaries are the Swiss Guards who defend the Vatican and act as the papal bodyguards in Rome. Switzerland maintains the European headquarters of the U.N. and the world headquarters of the International Red Cross based in Geneva, and sees its role in international affairs as a largely humanitarian one.

Regarding the famous Swiss Alps, at altitudes above 9,800 feet, mosses and lichens cover a

> desolate rocky landscape, above which are snowfields, glaciers, and permanently snow-covered peaks. Forests are closely monitored and protected. Clearing hillsides, which increases the danger of avalanches, is forbidden. Also, most Alpine flowers are protected and it is forbidden to pick them. Edelweiss, the symbol of Switzerland, grows among rocks at altitudes up to 11,500 feet.
>
> The country is divided into 26 cantons or territorial districts, and three main linguistic regions. The German language predominates (75%); then French (20%) and Italian (5%). A small number speak English. As for religion, 46% of the population is Roman Catholic; 40% Protestant; and 6% practicing Jews and Muslims.
>
> In 1798, having conquered northern Italy and wishing to control routes between Italy and France, Napoleon invaded Switzerland. Then for fifty years, even beyond his fall in 1815, internal religious hostilities transformed what had been until then a loose confederation of cantons into a union ruled by a federal assembly in Bern, which was chosen as the Swiss capital.

At about this time, Fran and Ansel looked at each other and then backed up and retreated to a nearby bench. But Rick kept reading.

> In the early 1930s, Switzerland's pacifistic stance and democracy were threatened by Nazi and Fascist sympathizers among its population. Later in that decade, as war seemed imminent, its economy accelerated, fueled partly by the booming army industry in which the country was involved and by the fact that Swiss banks played an important role in international finance. In the next decade, with Nazi Germany to the north and east, France under German occupation to the west, and Fascist Italy to

> the south, Switzerland was surrounded. Invasion seemed inevitable, but it never took place as the country demanded its neutrality. It was not directly drawn into World War II but played a part in the conflict. It acted as a secret meeting place between leaders of the Allied and Axis powers and set up anonymous bank accounts for German Jews. Swiss banks also provided currency for the purchase of military equipment and exchanged large amounts of gold that were pillaged by the Germans for currency needed by the Third Reich. Unlike all other European countries, Switzerland remained untouched by the upheaval of war and detached from the postwar new world order.
>
> With respect to gold, the country was rocked by the "Nazi Gold" scandal when it was alleged that Swiss banks were holding gold looted by the Nazis and the assets of Jews who had perished in the Holocaust. Under strong U.S. pressure, Switzerland agreed, in August 1998, to pay $1.25 billion in compensation to families of Holocaust victims and to certain Jewish organizations -- leaving a severe impression on the national psyche.

Rick then joined the others and commented: "Boy, that's one for the history books ... almost takes the place of sightseeing. But let's get going. I hope I'm up to the lecture."

After a quick settling in at their rooms, they left the hotel and took the short walk to the university building. It stood four stories tall, had a tower shape, and featured lime brick walls and dark green-stained timber boards. Out front, Rick was impressed with the odor and color of a variety of flowers that lined its entranceway. Inside, they were given directions to Science Professor Kauffman's office. There, after some initial cordiality, he indicated that at ten o'clock, students would be assembled in the auditorium one floor below. He stressed that they were special students who were well versed in English; they'd been trained in it since childhood since English is the usual language in banking.

It was 9:40, so he showed them around: a massive library, three massive laboratories, a massive meeting hall and several smaller rooms that seemed to be reserved for private conferences. At 9:55, they walked through a door at the foot of the auditorium. It was filled to capacity - - - 400 or so students. The four men – Rick, Fran, Ansel and the professor-- were met with loud applause even before Rick was introduced.

> *But why is there a much longer intro than the one Gomez read to me?*

That completed, the professor motioned for Rick to replace him at the podium. Rick thanked them all for coming and, after locating a folder in his briefcase, he opened it and spread out papers before him. Then he continued:

"I'll be giving lectures at universities in three other countries. I'll pretty much read from notes so that I'll be as accurate as possible. This might take some time … I hope that you can take it and that not too many of you will fall asleep."

The degree of laughter that erupted equaled that of the preceding applause. Rick tried to hold back on his own laughter but without much success.

> The subject matter will be different at each location, but here I'll talk about O.J. Simpson. His case, involving a double homicide, started in 1994. Some of you may be familiar with the case; some may not, but I hope you all will appreciate the forensic science particulars.
>
> First an historical summary. Then I'll follow with key personalities, the crimes themselves, the trial, the evidence, closing arguments, and the verdict.
>
> An African-American football hero, O.J. was a running back at the University of Southern

California, and in 1968, he was named the Heisman Trophy winner, emblematic of college football's most outstanding player. He went on to professional stardom with the Buffalo Bills In 1985, his first year of eligibility, and his name was enshrined in the Professional Football Hall of Fame. After retirement as a player in 1979, he maintained celebrity status as a television network sports commentator and a highly successful pitchman. He was also a movie actor, appearing in roles opposite the likes of Paul Newman and Steve McQueen. Over a high-profile career, the "Juice" had established himself as an American idol, respected by an adoring public who had seen him running through defensive lines, leaping through airports in TV commercials or hamming it up in three *Naked Gun* movies.

At 47, O.J. seemed to have it all. And then came the fall. The time was 1994 when, at home, former president Richard Nixon and former first lady, Jacqueline Kennedy Onassis had just died. Abroad, Nelson Mandela had been sworn in as South African's first black president, and the Channel Tunnel linking England and France took its first passengers. The place was Los Angeles, the city where a black motorist named Rodney King had been beaten by police officers a few years earlier, and where blacks rioted in Watts more than a generation before.

Rick took a sip of water from a glass on a side table and in doing so, looked up and saw that many in the audience were leaning forward in their seats and taking notes. He smiled and returned to his papers.

On June 12, Simpson's former wife, Nicole Brown Simpson, 35, and Ronald Goldman, 25, were savagely murdered ... stabbed repeatedly. This all took place near the front gate of her Bundy Drive condominium in the Brentwood section of Los Angeles. Simpson became an early suspect, but it wasn't until five days later that the possibility of his involvement became evident when a white Ford Bronco led police cars and a fleet of TV news helicopters in a slow, 60-mile chase across the southern California freeway. O.J. was in the car, which was driven by his boyhood friend and ex-football teammate, A.C. Cowlings. Simpson rode in the back seat pointing a gun at his head. The improbable drama was viewed by a national TV audience of an estimated 95 million people.

Earlier that day, O.J. had failed to appear for arraignment on charges of double homicide. When the Bronco eventually pulled into his Rockingham estate, he was taken into custody, and the much-admired face of a confident, smiling O.J. Simpson had been transformed into a somber television image of confusion and darkness. He had been stripped of his superstar mantle and cloaked beneath the weight of a new and unseemly role: murder defendant.

More than a year after jury selection began, and after a sensational trial that covered 133 days of televised courtroom testimony, Simpson was acquitted of all charges. Fifty thousand pages of transcript, 126 witnesses and 857 pieces of evidence were produced. The verdict rendered by a predominately African-American jury was met by a public reaction clearly split along racial lines, and many observers feel the outcome dealt a serious blow to race relations in America.

Millions of viewers tuned in to watch a falling star on a collision course with the so-called "mountain of evidence" amassed by a resolute prosecution team. Part melodrama, part soap opera, there was a little for everyone. And the daily spectacle, along with its coverage by news anchors, pundits and spin doctors, all combined to transfix a nation.

Moving on now to key personalities. First, with respect to Nicole:

O.J.'s first marriage to his teenage sweetheart, Marguerite, ended in 1979, the same year he retired from professional football and the same year their two-year-old daughter, Aaren, accidentally drowned in a swimming pool. The couple's union produced two other children, a son, Jason, and a daughter, Amelle. She would later become an important witness in defense of her father.

Nicole Brown first entered Simpson's life in 1977 when she was 18 years old. He was still married to Marguerite, but the knot was unraveling.

Simpson's new love was born in Frankfort, Germany, to a German mother and a U.S. military serviceman, but she was raised in California. A stunning blonde, she was elected homecoming princess at Dana Point High School, south of Los Angeles. After Simpson divorced, Nicole moved in with him and they married in 1985.

Their daughter, Sydney, was born the next year and a son, Justin, followed two years later. The children were living with Nicole at the Bundy Drive condo at the time of the crimes. Until their divorce in 1992, the beautiful Caucasian and the handsome

African-American occupied a mansion on Rockingham Avenue, in the tony Brentwood section of West Los Angeles. Their marriage appeared to transcend interracial considerations. Nicole seemed happy, just as she did in the months before her murder when she could be seen tooling around in her $90,000 white Ferrari with its license plate L84AD8, “Late for a Date".

But throughout their marriage, there were signs of serious trouble, and the veneer of glitz, glamour and marital paradise gave way to public revelation of an abusive relationship. Police had responded a reported nine times to calls alleging domestic violence, an issue that was to become one of the cornerstones of the prosecution's case in the trial. Two 911 calls were made in 1993 – after their divorce -- and released as a tape by the L.A. Police Department two weeks after the double murder. The calls were less than a minute apart and occurred during one of their reconciliation attempts when she lived in a rented home on Gretna Green Way, six blocks from Bundy -- which was the eventual crime scene. O.J. had come upon a photo album of Nicole's boyfriends and became enraged. Later, during the trial, the tapes would frame the picture of O.J. Simpson as a violently jealous stalker.

The 911 tapes represented the most dramatic examples of domestic violence since an early morning incident on New Year's Day in 1989 when Simpson severely beat his wife and was ordered by the court to undergo therapy. Pictures of her face showed that it wasn't just a slap. She looked like a badly beaten boxer after the last round of a boxing match. Swollen, bloody and so on. Anyway, he complied regarding the therapy. Both pieces of evidence were introduced by the prosecution at a preliminary hearing and again early in the trial to demonstrate Simpson's volatility, to document his abusive behavior and to establish that he was capable of stalking and eventually killing his ex-wife.

When he wasn't engaged in reconciliation with Nicole, O.J. dated several women -- like one Paula Barbieri, a 20-year-old Caucasian model. She later denied rumors that they had been romantically involved. In contrast, Nicole didn't form a public romantic relationship with anyone else after the end of their final attempt at reconciliation -- a month before her murder.

Next, Ronald Lyle Goldman. The brutal murder of this 25-year-old was a classic example of a person who was at the wrong place at the wrong time. He'd struck up a relationship with Nicole six months before, but there was no evidence they'd been linked romantically. Tall, handsome and fun-loving, he aspired to become a model. He was a waiter at a nearby fashionable restaurant, the Mezzaluna, where on the night of the crimes, Nicole had hosted an evening dinner party commemorating Sydney's performance in a dance recital at the Paul Revere School earlier that day. Significantly, 0.J., who was at the recital, wasn't invited to the dinner. But Nicole's parents were. At 9:30, her mother, Juditha Brown, phoned the restaurant to inquire about her reading glasses, which were apparently lost. The glasses were found by an employee and placed in an envelope. A few minutes later, Nicole called Goldman, who was preparing to go on a date with a female co-worker. He agreed to deliver the glasses to her condo. He canceled the date and arrived at Bundy only to become a victim in the double tragedy.

> Then there was Brian "Kato" Kaelin. As a tenant at Gretna Green Way, he was offered a room when Nicole moved to her Bundy condo in 1993. He was considered no more than her baby-sitter, confidant and good friend. But regardless, O.J. prevailed upon the blond Hollywood bit player to move into guest quarters at his Rockingham estate, rent-free. O.J. had evidently convinced him that it would be inappropriate for a single man to occupy the same condo with a recently divorced woman.
>
> Kaelin later testified at the preliminary hearing and the trial. With his shaggy hair and jeans, he combined nervousness, a halting delivery and definitely humor -- to bring out some loud laughter from the people in the courtroom, even at times, from O.J. himself. In the long run, his value as a prosecution witness may have been overestimated.

Next we have Robert Kardashian. He was one of Simpson's oldest friends, and he continued to be his closest advisor during the trial. After it was over, their friendship dried up. He was a business entrepreneur and selected O.J. to be an usher in his wedding. It was at his house in Encino that O.J. sought refuge after Nicole's funeral. It was from that house that he left with A.C. Cowlings on the famous slow pursuit. And it was Kardashian who produced the so-called suicide letter just prior to the Bronco chase. Here are some excerpts from that handwritten letter. They're in my notes:

> To whom it may concern: First, everyone understand. I have nothing to do with Nicole's murder. I loved her. I always have and always will. If we had a problem, it's because I loved her so much.
>
> Unlike what has been written in the press, Nicole

> and I had a great relationship for most of our lives together. Like all long-term relationships, we had a few downs and ups. I took the heat New Year's 1989 because that was what I was supposed to do. I did not plead no contest for any other reason but to protect our privacy and was advised it would end the press hype.
>
> I think of our life and feel I've done most of the right things, so why do I end up like this? I can't go on. No matter what the outcome, people will look and point. I can't take that. I can't subject my children to that. This way they can move on and go on with their lives. Please, if I've done anything worthwhile in life, let my kids live in peace from you, the press.
>
> Don't feel sorry for me. I've had a great life, great friends. Please think of the real O.J. and not this lost person. Thanks for making my life special. I hope I helped yours.
>
> Peace and love, O.J.

Now onto Faye Resnick. She was labeled the "mystery woman" by the media. She was Nicole's best friend, sometimes roommate and reportedly the last person to speak with Nicole over the phone shortly before the murder.

> Resnick was rumored to have had close ties with the Westside L.A. drug culture. It was never disclosed why she moved into Nicole's condo on June 3rd -- that was 9 days before the murders -- and stayed until late on June 8th when she suffered a drug overdose and was admitted to a rehabilitation

center. She'd been unemployed for some time and had no assets, so we have to question how she could have supported an expensive cocaine habit over a period of months, if not years. There were press reports that she flew to Europe or South America after the killings and some even believed she was somehow in on them.

There were other suspicious things related to this woman. Her diaries for the six days she lived with Nicole were stolen. She was given a set of keys to the condo, but the set was never located. And then there was that last phone call just before the killings. Was she acting as a go-between -- as an informant for Nicole's time schedule? Some believed that elements of organized crime had arranged Nicole's murder, but why? Again, was Resnick the mob's informant and did it provide her with a steady supply of drugs?

I won't go into details regarding the other key characters. Some of you may know of them:

Lance Ito, the presiding judge.

For the prosecution: Marcia Clark and Chris Darden

For the defense: Robert Shapiro. Johnnie Cochran. F. Lee Bailey. Gerald Uelmen. Barry Scheck. Alan Dershowitz. Dr. Henry Lee, the chief criminalist. Dr. Michael Baden, pathologist.

The detectives: Phillip Vannatter. Tom Lange. Mark Fuhrman. Person who taped Fuhrman: Laura Hart McKinney.

Now about the crimes themselves.

Once again, Rick paused to study his papers in order to keep things straight, particularly with regard to sequence. It became necessary to rearrange them several times before he was ready to continue:

> The sequence of important events that occurred on June 12, 1994, involved 0.J., Nicole, Goldman, Kato Kaelin, limousine driver Allan Park and an Akita dog also named Kato.
>
> Well in advance, O.J. had made arrangements for an 11:45 flight from L.A. to Chicago. On the next morning, June 13, he planned to attend a convention of the Hertz rental car company whose TV commercials featured him hurtling over airport benches. A limousine was scheduled to pick him up at 10:45 p.m.
>
> Earlier, he played a round of morning golf at the Riviera Country Club and, in the afternoon, attended daughter Sydney's dance recital. But as stated before, he wasn't invited to the dinner at the Mezzaluna.
>
> At about 9 p.m., he and Kato Kaelin drove to a Santa Monica McDonald's for hamburgers. O.J. ate his burgers on the way home while Kaelin saved his for later. He last saw O.J. that night at 9:45.
>
> Meanwhile, Nicole's party of ten people dined from 7:00 to 8:30 and, after dinner, she walked with her children to a nearby ice-cream parlor before heading home.
>
> Later at Bundy, several neighbors heard the persistent barking and wailing of a dog around 10:15 or 10:20. One neighbor reportedly saw Nicole's brown and white Akita on the loose at 10:45. Its paws were covered with blood.
>
> At 12:10 a.m., two passersby looked down the

moonlit walkway of Nicole's condo and, through the open front gate, saw a woman crumpled in the alcove at the foot of several steps that led to a landing. Later, police would discover a male body sprawled against a wrought-iron fence to the right of the walkway. The bodies were those of Nicole and Ron. They had, in effect, been sliced to death and were lying in pools of blood.

Throughout the slaughter, the two Simpson children – seven-year-old Sydney and five-year-old Justin – remained asleep in an upstairs bedroom.

At approximately the same time that the Akita was spotted roaming the streets near Bundy Drive – 10:45 -- Town and Country limousine driver, Allan Park rang the intercom buzzer at the gate surrounding the O.J. Rockingham estate. There was no answer. Park had arrived at 10:25, 20 minutes early, and over the course of the next 10 or 20 minutes, he didn't see the Bronco parked on North Rockingham. He stated that at 10:55, he saw a large black man running across the front of the mansion. The lights went on and then O.J. answered the intercom. Six minutes later, O.J. appeared at the doorstop, immaculately dressed and carrying four bags of luggage. The two left for the airport between 11:10 and 11:15 p.m.

Several key points must be added to the time line. One, phone records showed that at 10:03, Simpson called his girlfriend, Paula Barbieri, from the cellular phone in his Bronco. Two, Kato Kaelin would later testify that at 10:52, he heard three thumps on the outer wall of the Rockingham guesthouse. And three, those several neighbors corroborated each other's statements regarding the time of the dog's protracted barking.

Obviously the barking dog and Park's statements would become important to the prosecutors in their attempt to set the time of the murders. They would allege that Simpson killed two people at Bundy Drive at 10:15 and disposed of the weapon and bloody clothes. Then he had sufficient time to drive to Rockingham Avenue to meet Allan Park. Some defenders of O.J. countered with the question of how, after his arrival home, he could have tidied up and presented himself at the front door in just six minutes. And these same supporters asked why Park didn't see or hear the Bronco pull up to Rockingham.

When police arrived at the blood-spattered scene and cordoned off the area, they proceeded to use white towels to soak up the blood in order to allow an easier approach to the bodies. This was considered a huge mistake by top forensic experts, including Dr. Lee.

By 1:30 a.m., authorities were anxious to locate O.J, not only to inform him of the deaths, but also to interrogate him. At that point, he was on the red eye special to Chicago. He was finally contacted by phone at 7:30 a.m. Central Time. He hurried home and was taken to police headquarters for questioning.

At the crime scene, bloody paw prints lined Bundy Drive in front of Nicole's condo. A restaurant menu lay beside her. Near Goldman's body were a bloody, leather left-handed glove, a dark blue knit cap, a white envelope and a pager.

Bloody shoeprints led from her body through the walkway to the back alley. A trail of five blood

> spots lined the shoeprints to the side. Weeks later, bloody spots were noted at the bottom of the back gate. A white Ferrari was parked inside the garage and a black Jeep Cherokee was parked in the driveway. Both hoods were cold.
>
> The point is: had Nicole been expecting another guest or just Goldman? The residence hadn't been ransacked, the stereo was playing, the lights were dim, and candles were lit in the living room and around the tub in the upstairs bathroom. These points were never explained during the investigation.

The amount of time Rick spent leafing through his papers increased. "Sorry," he said, "but this gets more complicated." Most of the students were spellbound, focusing on his every move.

> After it had been determined that the female victim was O.J.'s former wife, Fuhrman, Vannatter, Lange, and Detective Ron Phillips drove to Rockingham in two cars, arriving at 6 a.m. Three hours before that, the L.A. Bureau Chief had phoned to relieve Fuhrman and Phillips of the case. He reassigned it to Vannatter and Lange's Robbery and Homicide unit. Strangely, Fuhrman's name never appeared in the report of the night's activities.
>
> Without a search warrant, he scaled the five-foot high wall and let the others through the main gate. They rang the bell at the front door and received no answer. They walked to the rear of the house toward three bungalows rimming the property just inside a Cyclone fence. They knocked on the doors of houseguest Kaelin and Simpson's 25-year-old daughter, Amelle. Kaelin informed them that during the night at approximately 10:45 he heard three thumping noises on the wall above his bed. Amelle, who lived next door, admitted all the detectives

except Fuhrman. About an hour after arrival there, he decided to investigate a dark, narrow walkway between the bungalows and chain-link fence. On leaf-covered ground, he saw a right-handed leather glove with dark, wet material on it. He later said he believed the material was blood and that the glove matched the left-handed one at the Bundy crime scene. He said he noticed nothing unusual about the leaves or ground in the immediate vicinity. Continuing some distance beyond the glove, he brushed against some cobwebs. Over the next few minutes, he summoned the other detectives back individually to examine the glove.

Vannatter instructed Fuhrman to drive to Bundy to check on whether the glove found there matched the one at Rockingham. Fuhrman complied and discovered it to be a perfect match.

Upon the detective's return to Rockingham at about 7:15, he and the others located several drops of blood on the street near the Bronco, on the driveway, on the cement walkway outside the front door and on the light-stained door inside the house. Fuhrman and one of the others checked the rest of the house and found nothing unusual except a pair of black socks on the floor of the master bedroom.

Detective Vannatter officially declared Simpson's estate a secondary crime scene.

There are some burning questions to consider now:

- - - How do you explain the Rockingham glove still being damp with blood at 6 a.m. if it had been dropped there at 10:45 p.m. the previous night? That was a time span of at least seven hours -- and the clotting time of blood is roughly five minutes.

- - - What was the state's theory as to how the glove got there? Why was there no blood near it?

- - - Why was Fuhrman alone outside the crime scene for 18 minutes? Isn't it equally reasonable that the real killer dropped the second glove outside the crime scene rather than behind O.J.'s house?

- - - If the killer was covered with blood – as he had to be – how do you explain the absence of large amounts of blood either on the way to the car, or within it?

But on the other side of the ledger, so to speak, were there some other allegations? Such as:

- - - Simpson cut his finger during the killings and dripped blood at the crime scene. DNA results pointed to a match with Simpson's DNA. Prosecution scientists claim that the chances of a match with a person other than Simpson would be less than one in 170 million.

- - - Simpson lost his left glove at Bundy during the struggle, then deposited his right glove along the walkway near the guest cottages. Was he hurriedly trying to hide it in the dark?

- - - Blood found in the Bronco established that Simpson drove it from the crime scene.

- - - The barking dog fixed the time of deaths after which Simpson had adequate time to return to Rockingham, dispose of the weapon and his bloody clothes, drop the glove, and meet his limo driver.

- - - Simpson's whereabouts were unaccounted for between 9:40 and 10:50 p.m. on the night of the murders.

When interviewed early on Monday, June 13, O.J. explained that he sustained a cut on the middle finger of his left hand when he broke a glass in his Chicago hotel room. He also agreed to be fingerprinted, to have his injured finger photographed, and to allow the LAPD to draw a blood sample.

That being said, if he had something to hide, why did he allow an interview with police without a lawyer being present? And why would he give a voluntary blood sample and allow his finger to be photographed? Because he wasn't smart?

Now then, we're up to the trial. It appeared that the most important aspects of the case were one, the blood evidence; two, what can be called the "Fuhrman Factor"; and three, the testimony of the defense's chief criminalist, Dr. Henry Lee. Let's begin with the last.

Dr. Lee, the world-famous criminalist, maintained that many of the DNA results had come back "inconclusive" because of an insufficient quantity of DNA in the samples or because of deterioration. And this came about because of mishandling after collection. He also said that it was later revealed that blood was discovered on the back gate of Nicole's condo and on the sock found in 0.J.'s bedroom but not until weeks after the crimes. He would go on to say that three things prompted his later comment: "Something wrong here." One was that some of the blood swatches collected from the crime scene were not dried when placed in paper packages.

A second was that the stains on several items, including the back gate and sock, contained EDTA, a preservative added to collection vials and test tubes to prevent coagulation of blood.

And the third was that the blood from the back gate and sock had much higher concentrations of DNA than that in the blood samples collected on June 13, the morning after the crimes. So why the presence of EDTA and the higher concentrations of DNA?

Next the “Fuhrman Factor". As a prosecution witness, Detective Fuhrman became the best witness the defense ever had! What he said turned out to be the turning point in the case. Simpson's lawyers pounded away at the detective's documented history of using racial slurs and his proclivity to “bag” suspects in any way possible. Listen to F. Lee Bailey's cross-examination of the detective. It's considered one of the classics in the entire history of American jurisprudence because of its brevity, its non-use of notes, and the impact on the case's outcome:

Question: Do you use the word “nigger” in describing people? Answer: No, sir.

Question: Have you ever used that word in the past ten years? Answer: Not that I can recall, no.

Question: You mean if you called someone a nigger, you have forgotten it?

Answer: I'm not sure I can answer the question the way you phrased it, sir.

Question: You have difficulty understanding the question?

Answer: Yes.

Question: I will rephrase it. I want you to assume that perhaps at some time since 1985 or 1986, you addressed a member of the African-American race as a nigger. Is it possible that you have forgotten that act on your part?

Answer: No, it is not possible.

Question: Are you therefore saying that you have not used that word in the past ten years, Detective Fuhrman?

Answer: That is what I'm saying, sir.

Question: So that anyone who comes to this court and quotes you as using that word in dealing with African-Americans would be a liar, would they not, Detective Fuhrman?

Answer: Yes, they would.

Question: All of them, correct?

Answer: All of them.

This exchange set the stage for what was to follow: a series of audiotapes as evidence that would prove to be devastating for the State judicially, and for Fuhrman personally. The tapes and their transcripts were obtained by the defense from Laura Hart McKinney who, at the time of their recording, had been piecing together material for a screenplay about the experiences of female police officers. She'd met Fuhrman in a restaurant in early 1995 and enlisted him to assist in the development of background material for her project. He subsequently met with her over a ten-year period for a 13-hour series of taped interviews.

The transcripts contained 42 instances of Fuhrman using the word “nigger", and 18 instances in which he admitted his participation in police misconduct in order to incarcerate “criminals". Among them were the use of deadly force, beating confessions out of suspects, covering up the misconduct of other police officers, and of particular relevance, the planting of evidence and the framing of innocent people.

Can you imagine?

Here are a few of his recorded statements:

- - - We got all this money going to Ethiopia for what? To feed a bunch of dumb niggers that their own government won't even feed. Let 'em die. Use 'em for fertilizer. I mean, who cares?

- - - I am the key witness in the biggest case of the century. And if I go down, they lose the case. The glove is everything. Without the glove -- - bye-bye.

- - - People don't want niggers in their town. People don't want Mexicans in their town. They don't want anybody but good people in their town, and anything you can do to get them out of there, that's fine with them. We have no niggers where I grew up.

So what does all of this mean? It changed the entire complexion of the case. Fuhrman's credibility was ruined and reasonable doubt was established. And that's all the defense needed.

Two other points are worthy of mention. First, three days after the crimes, Detective Vannatter spent much more time at Rockingham than he had at

Bundy. It was a fact supporting the defense's claim that O.J. was an early suspect. And second, when Vannatter obtained 0.J.'s blood sample, he didn't follow procedure and book it into evidence. Instead, he carried the vial in his pocket for three hours before giving it to a criminalist at Rockingham. And, 1.5 ml were missing.

Now returning to the load of burning questions:

— Regarding the 1.5 ml of missing blood, could it have been spread around as droplets on the Bronco and at Rockingham, and then later added to the sock and back gate?

— Marcia Clark said O.J. drove the Bronco home wearing the murder clothes and shoes. Why was such a small amount of blood found in the Bronco? And only on the steering wheel?

— Regarding O.J. walking upstairs: Why wasn't there any of the victims' blood on the carpeting, light switches or doorknobs? The Rockingham house had wall-to-wall beige-white carpeting.

— If the glove was as described and 0.J.'s sock had wet blood on it, why wasn't there a blood trail from the back fence to the glove at Rockingham?

— What happened to the weapon and bloody clothes?

— Mark Fuhrman had been dismissed from the case, yet he insisted on going to the Simpson estate. Why so, considering the others knew how to get there?

— If O.J. was the killer and didn't want to be detected, why didn't he enter his house from the back?

— Again, Fuhrman had been taken off the case. Why, then, was it he who investigated the Bronco, questioned Kaelin, and allegedly found the glove near the back fence?

— Why were there only five drops of O.J.'s blood evenly deposited on the Bundy walkway? If he'd cut himself during the killings, there should have been more at the beginning of the walkway and less as one got to the back gate. In other words, there shouldn't have been an even distribution, as there was here.

— Why did it take ten hours to notify the coroner?

— Why, following a probably fierce struggle with an athletic Ron Goldman, didn't Simpson have more signs of injury on his body, such as scratches and bruises?

— Simpson allegedly jumped the fence near the guest house in his haste to return home and, at the same time, avoid being detected by limo driver Allan Park, who was out front. The fence is very high and is covered with a large number of vines and other vegetation. Why was there no damage to that vegetation?

— Since O.J. had cuts on his finger, why were there no cuts on the glove itself?

— A second type of bloody shoe print was found at Bundy. Whose was it?

— How could Allan Park not have noticed the Bronco parked near the front gate at Rockingham?

— The blood issue was obviously paramount in the trial. And just to repeat: some believed that the bloody glove on the walkway of Simpson's estate,

> the blood smears on the Bronco, the five blood drops on the walkway from the bodies to the back gate, the drops near the front of Simpson's residence, and the smears on Bundy's back gate and on his sock, which were later examined in the LAPD evidence room, were all planted.

Rick reached over for another glass of water but stopped short when he noticed a man leaning over the railing at the top of the auditorium. He was older than the students, his face was 90% scar tissue, and he was wearing a black cap.

Hardly one of the teaching staff.

But Rick gave it no further consideration. He drank some water and continued with his talk:

> Robert Shapiro was eloquent when he later wrote:
>
> It was not the obligation of the Simpson defense to prove how the blood got there, when it got there, why it got there, whether it was planted there, whether it had been there for some period of time, whether it was contaminated, whether it came from sloppy techniques in the lab, or whether the reference samples of 0.J.'s blood, when they were opened in the lab, spewed out onto other samples. This was not our job. Our job was to ask the questions, point out the improbables. For every item – sock, glove, knit cap, blood – we were able to show doubt, reasonable and real.

And I'll end this talk by referring to the most memorable quote: "If it doesn't fit, you must acquit," by Johnnie Cochran. He was not referring to the gloves but to the knit cap. Here's the quote, ridiculing the prosecution who claimed that the cap was used as a disguise:

> "Let me show you something. This is a knit cap. Let

> me put this knit cap on. You have seen me for a year. If I put this knit cap on, who am I? I'm still Johnnie Cochran – with a knit cap. And if you looked at O.J. Simpson over there –and he has a rather large head–O.J. Simpson from two blocks away is still O.J. Simpson. It's no disguise. It makes no sense. If it doesn't fit, you must acquit."
>
> And O.J., as some of you know, was found not guilty.

"I must thank you all for your attention," Rick said as he reassembled his papers and put them in his briefcase. "You've been a wonderful audience and I wish you all good luck in your endeavors."

The students stood and cheered. Then the four men made their way up three rows of steps and filed out the top three doors. As this was going on, Rick noticed that the older man had disappeared.

He and Professor Kauffman shook hands and exited the way they had come in.

"Great job," Ansel said.

"Very great," Fran added.

"I agree," the professor said. "I hope to see you again."

As they rounded a corner of the building, the man wearing the black cap jumped out from behind a large cart, not five feet away. He was wielding a gun.

"Duck, men, duck!" Rick yelled as he leaped forward and unleashed a karate kick to the man's midsection. The gun went flying. Fran and Ansel pulled Rick away as protection, and the man limped out a nearby side door, but he was fast. They chased after him, Rick nearly tripping over his briefcase. They caught a glimpse of the man making it to a car with a driver in it.

Everything happened so fast that, as the car sped away, there was no chance of catching a license plate number or the make of the car, although it appeared to be multicolored.

Kauffman took Rick by the arm and said, “I'm so sorry this happened here, and I apologize. Would you care to join me in my office? We could all calm down in there. Maybe have some coffee or a glass of wine.”

“It's not your fault, professor, and no, we’d better get going. Our schedule is kinda rigid.”

“But we'll keep in touch?”

“That we will.”

Kauffman stated he was still frightened, but he didn’t look it.

Rick, Fran and Ansel left through the entrance door and looked around at street level as if they were getting their bearings. Rick had pushed the door open with his finger.

“Well men, here we go again,” he said, as he smelled frightened sweat. “That's number two and we'd better expect it in every city.”

He could swear someone had come in behind them, yet hesitated to turn around for fear he would be right. But he did, along with the others. They saw Kauffman waving at them. Each of the men returned the wave.

- - - - -

Heading back to the hotel, Rick said, “You know, I'm beginning to feel guilty about not doing more in locating and returning stolen goods. Is just notifying the media enough?”

“But what can we do in a short time abroad?” Fran asked.

“Oh, maybe see the police chiefs ourselves.”

“In all the cities?”

"In all the cities."

"But even if we spend two days in each city –that is, where you're not lecturing –is that enough time to locate and return?"

"Not really, but we'd be reinforcing what we asked the chiefs to do. And who knows – we might hit upon something."

"Like what?"

"I wouldn't know until we get there. So I think we should spend half our time sightseeing and half in meeting with the chiefs."

Rick lagged behind the other two for a minute, then caught up and said, "Wait. Let's huddle, and please hear me out. I've had a change of heart. It's the two damn men after us … I mean after me. It's obvious that in sightseeing plus lecturing, we're out in the open too much. You may think I've gone bonkers but I'd like to nix them … at least for now. Screw the other lectures and the other cities. Even screw time. Let's spend whatever it takes to accomplish locating stolen art. Actually though, I should be investigating people, not stolen art per se. The people who might be involved in stealing, not the other way around. Think about it, guys: if we make inroads that other people can take – like the police – that's plenty, and we'd be aiming at what we set out to do."

Fran and Ansel were staring at Rick as if he were intruding on the march of history.

Rick continued: "You game with all that?"

They said nothing but gave drawn-out nods.

"Good," Rick said. "The stolen things? Locating some … retrieving some? I think the best way to tackle that is to consult with the histarians and spend some time on cruise ships because they may be transporting some of the goods and even the stealers. And that's where prostitutes come in."

"How's that?" Fran's words were the first he had uttered in the last five minutes.

"We could talk the ladies into working for us. If we make headway, word might get around that we're doing just that. Word that might help us."

Rick hoped that the silence of the other two meant that they were still swallowing all that he had just revealed. Swallowing and digesting.

Near the entrance to the Marriott, he said, "I also want to use some artificial intelligence, or so-called AI."

It seemed to open up Fran's mind. "I was hoping you'd get to that," he said. "It's the wave of the future." He wrinkled his nose as if he were trying to sniff the truth out of what Rick just said.

"And maybe of the present, in our case," Ansel chimed in, the first time in 30 hours that he had offered a meaningful remark.

Rick thought he'd take advantage of their return to a sharing of comments. "You know," he said, "AI has two principle components. First is crime scene reasoning and logic. As applied to us in this search for stolen goods, the act of stealing is the crime scene and the reasoning and logic are what we'll be trying to use. And second, there's the getting into the mind of a stealer. This is the difficult part. I have a copy of what I wrote about AI in my last book. Why not read it? It's not long. We can sit here so we won't have to decide which room to meet in upstairs." He was pointing to a cement sitting area that projected from a sidewall adjoining the entranceway. You two read and I'll rest my eyes, if I can."

He found a folded piece of paper in his briefcase and, as all three sat down, he handed it to Fran. Then, Rick didn't rest his eyes but, instead, began making notes on a pad he pulled out of his back pocket. Fran and Ansel read what he handed to them:

> Artificial intelligence or AI. First of all, what is it? It's intelligence displayed by machines, not by humans. It's quickly becoming part of our information infrastructure. For example, certain recruitment companies analyze video interviews of

> job applicants so the employers can compare an applicant's facial movements and body language with that of their already existing employees. But it can get out of hand, and here's how I can relate it to people like me – in the job I'm in. There's a recent AI study that was supposed to identify suspected individuals involved in violent crime, police harassment and who gets out of jail. However, it failed miserably. It's because the whole machine idea is still in its infancy. And I would say that's enough about that. You get the idea though, right?

"So what did you think?" Rick asked.

"Well ..." Fran said, tilting his head to the side.

"I see. Well, I stated in the article that it's still in its infancy, but who knows. . . maybe it'll get better. And if it doesn't come in handy for us, we'll just chuck the whole idea."

Rick put the article back in his briefcase and said, "Of more importance right now is my speaking again with Joe Gomez."

Chapter 6

Rick had always checked the background of people in his life, but there were two exclusions. His wife was one and number two was Joe Gomez. Despite their years-long relationship, Rick didn't look forward to phoning the chief – not at all – but it simply had to be done. And combining that with his growing disinterest in making long-distance calls to anyone, he sat at his desk and nervously pulled apart a paper clip. He figured it was about noon in Buenos Aires.

"Joe, it's me, the pest," Rick said. "I have something important to say and I'd like your input … if you have the time."

"Wait now," Gomez said. "Are you alright? I mean healthwise."

"Aside from nearly falling apart? Yes, I am. Not really falling apart … ' overwhelmed' is a better way of putting it. And I could use your help."

"Okay. Sure. And you're not a pest. Call any time."

"Thanks, Joe. This is something new and major. The O.J. lecture went very well, but I've decided … no more lectures and no more sightseeing for now."

The long silence that followed was background for a heavy dose of audible breathing, mostly Rick's.

The chief said, "You know, Rick, I'm not surprised. You'd taken on too much. If you went through with all of it, your health would not be okay — as you said it was. Remember? That's what you indicated. In fact, I'd limit what you're trying to find to only one thing — valuable books, for example. Find out if the guilty parties are willing to return books. "

Rick felt relieved both by being able to voice the situation and by the chief's understanding.

"Yes, that's what I indicated. And at the time, I was headed in the wrong direction."

"So what's in your plans now?" Gomez asked.

"Well, first and foremost, could you call the other three professors and cancel my lectures? And also notify your counterparts in the nine other cities that I won't be calling on them?"

"Yes — that's not a problem."

"Secondly, we're not going to be paying much attention to time. That can be a killer. We'll move cautiously and deliberately. Our wives won't be pressing us to return home. Hell, they're up in Maine having a good time, I'm sure. So they'll probably be happy to be alone. Which reminds me: I'd better call my Angela."

"But what will you actually be doing?"

Rick removed the pad from his pocket. "I've written it all out," he said. "I'll read to you what I call our challenges." He relaxed his legs and read:

One – Identify some looted treasures, and I mean some.

Two – Have them returned to their rightful owners and have the looters arrested. Some but not all, obviously.

Three – Have this somehow serve as an example for others who may be contemplating the same behavior. A deterrent.

Four – Prostitutes and cruise ship captains might play an important role.

And Five – Organized criminals, like the Mafia, both help and hurt our cause. *Help* because some looters are competitors. *Hurt* because some are in cahoots with the looters.

"I'm not at all aware yet of how we'll do all of this — and that's why they're challenges and not — what else would you label them … certainties?"

Rick then excused himself, saying he'd continue in a minute. He rose from the desk, moved to a nearby table containing his cell phone, and called his wife in Maine. He deadpanned most of what he said in their brief conversation, but she understood the change in plans.

"Whatever you say, darling," she said, which pleased Rick, especially the "darling" part.

After their brief conversation, he returned to his desk and turned his attention back to Gomez. "And there's one other thing I want to share with you," he said. "I'm thinking of having what I'd call a summit meeting. Why? To iron things out and to fine-tune them. There are so many goings-on to consider."

"Quite an idea," the chief said. "Who would be there?"

"Fran, Ansel, me, you and your Carlos, a cruise ship captain or two, and Paul D'Arneau who's a fellow investigator. He doesn't know about it yet, though I'm sure he'd be willing to participate."

"And where would it take place?"

"Not sure yet, but maybe there aboard the *Seacraft.* Does it still dock in your city on a regular basis?"

"Yes, good choice. But it also docks in your New York harbor, and I'm willing to fly there."

"Good, and when the time approaches, we'll make a decision. I'll be checking with the availability of the others, but it's too soon for a summit, really," Rick said. "Maybe after we finish with a cruise ship."

There was more than a moment of silence before Rick broke it with, "So let's leave it at that and thanks for your time now, Joe."

"You're welcome. Call any time. After hours, my office phone also rings at my home."

Chapter 7

April 5

Rick was elated after the call to Gomez and didn't waste any time in looking up the phone number of histarian Lance Beck, the name that Paul D'Arneau had given him. He dialed it and the two traded some preliminary talk. Rick then gave a shortened version of what he had said to Gomez, after which they agreed to meet in Yale's Sterling Memorial Library the following day at one p.m., Eastern time.

"That's fine," Lance had said. "Looking forward to it."

"Okay. Now when you enter the library, take a right and straight ahead is the Linonia and Brothers Room. It's commonly called the L & B Room. I'll meet you in there."

After those two calls, Rick decided to mollify their effect on his psyche by chiding himself over his now-present mindset. When it came to the conclusion of significant matters - - - good or bad - - - it was a mindset he'd never prevented, never lightly tolerated, and was always predictable. But to those around him at the time, he successfully hid its existence. Except in the case of his wife. Angela always forewarned him that such reactions could even shorten his life and he would always reply, "So forget a casket. Make it cremation."

- - - - -

He and Fran took their own cars to the library and walked into the room at exactly one o'clock. In addition to being expansive and well-lighted, the room was filled on three sides with stacks of books and papers, and down the middle, with row-upon-row of tables. Many visitors were seated randomly and reading newspapers that were fully opened and covered their faces. Except for two, one slightly older than the other.

"Over here," the older one said, obviously trying to keep his voice from sounding like a muffled echo. "I'm Lance."

Rick and Fran approached them as the men rose from one of the tables. Their smiles appeared sincere. All handshakes were firm and sustained. They looked pretty much alike … dark hair, fluffy at the sides; thin-rimmed glasses; attire that was casual but neat: blue sport coat, open collar and light gray trousers. At probably five-eight or so, they were sitting slouched over, thus betraying their short statures.

"Thanks for coming," Rick said. "This shouldn't take long." He put his hand on Fran's shoulder, saying, "And this handsome man here is my longtime colleague, Fran Moreau."

"I brought along a colleague of mine, too – Roger Radford. He's from Hartford and is brand new as an histarian. This is his first case."

"Good luck," Rick said.

They took seats, two across from the other two. Rick removed several papers from his briefcase and spread them out before him. He wasn't sure he'd need them but they contained notes if necessary. He also took out his notepad. Lance already had papers laid out. He also waved a pad and said, "Maybe our pads should meet and not us." He didn't allow time for a reaction from Rick or Fran.

"First of all," Lance continued, "your friend, Paul D'Arneau, told me what you're trying to do."

Then there followed what Rick believed to be the most utter coincidence he'd ever experienced. Lance said, "I spoke with some of my colleagues - - - in person of course - - - and it was unanimous. We believe you should confine your investigation to books, and books alone."

Just what Gomez said!

Rick's hand lacked the energy to make any kind of note, and his pencil had fallen to the floor. If anything, it gave him a chance to think of how to respond. He picked it up and said, “I see.” He then found two copies of his “MAIN CHALLENGES” among his papers and slid them across the table. “Here,” he said, “Do look these over. Take your time. We'll wait.”

Rick allowed two minutes for them to read his notes about the main challenges before them and for himself to gather his senses. But he didn't want to mention the coincidence. Instead, he said, “I would think that what you said could be good for starters, and might even make that list of five shorter.”

“Maybe you're right. And maybe if some perpetrators are willing to give up the books, you'd promise them they wouldn't be arrested and that you wouldn't notify the police. Even more than that, so it would appear to be more convincing, you could ask them who the books belong to. So it would be: return … identify … and no arrest.”

By then, Rick was somewhat reassured and asked, “How could you and other histarians help our cause?”

Lance's answer didn't take long. “I understand we have some information that may or may not be of use to you. It involves addresses–past or current–of bad guys who may or may not still be living. But addresses are the only thing we can provide–not identities–because identities can change so often. Specific addresses of specific houses do not. You see, what was happening made us stop recording names awhile ago. We even destroyed the ones we had. And the reason was that new buyers–all innocent–were threatening legal action unless we backed off. They were apparently afraid of the way their names might be used. It sounds complicated, but we did back off, and that was that. So Rick–addresses yes, if and when you want them; but names–no. And don’t worry about my using a phone to give them to you. I’ll just list them without any elaboration.”

“I get it–and I can call you whenever necessary?”

“Absolutely. As long as my phone works, I'll respond.”

"Since we're at it," Rick said, "there are more questions to ask. What's your regular work?"

"I teach computer science, and my class starts in about an hour."

"Where?"

"At UConn."

"I understand. And do you get paid as an historian?"

"No. And are *you* getting paid for what you're doing?"

"No. Thankfully, Fran and I are well heeled and helping out is enough of a payment. We just consider it as something that has to be done."

Here comes probably the most important question.

"Do people know you're an historian?'

"No."

"But how about those you help? Do they squeal?"

"I hope not. Not so far, anyway. Private collections from private collectors. They so appreciate what we've done for them that they treat it like a miracle - - - one that's never admitted - - - to anyone. That will be the way you'll handle it?"

"Yes. I believe in miracles."

What triggered Rick's last comment was something in his life that occurred when he was in grammar school. As a ten-year-old, he was willing to try anything. The school was separated from a cemetery by a short stone wall. He wondered if he could jump clear of the wall and onto the cemetery's rich green grass. He backed up at least 30 paces, ran like the dickens and leaped over the wall, only to land directly into a wheel barrel half-filled with peat moss. He brushed it easily off his clothes.

It could have been manure.

He called it a miracle and to this day, he believed in them and told Lance why he did.

"You'd better stay clear of wheel barrels, Rick," was Lance's reply.

While they both sorted papers, Rick happened to see a woman standing several tables away. She wore a white hat; a veil covered half her face; and she was aiming a camera in Rick's direction. Within seconds, she hurried from the room.

What is this? Women too?

Rick told Lance about it and was greeted with a shrug. But Rick made a note on his pad. Lance asked his partner if he had any questions and received a "no".

Then in the process of gathering up his papers, Lance said, "I have one more thing to cover with you, Rick. It involves Nazis. I have clippings here from an old edition of the *Wall Street Journal*. They might be of some help to you. It's better that I read a couple paragraphs than to go verbatim, although I reviewed the clippings before leaving my home." He checked his watch. "Shouldn't take long."

There were two paragraphs and Lance read them fast:

> According to Holocaust experts, the Nazis stole tens of millions of books from Jews and other victims. Recently, scholars have focused on 1.2 million volumes the Nazis plundered -- including 500,000 taken largely from French Jewish families and institutions. The Nazis also looted art, grabbing paintings by Monet, Renoir, Picasso and others. This sparked a campaign in recent years to trace the works and return them to the owners or their heirs. A large quantity of books ended up in Soviet hands.

> These were mostly secular books that went to Berlin, instead, and included novels by Victor Hugo, Marcel Proust, Emile Zola and Jean-Paul Sartre. There were also books on philosophy, as well as volumes by Salvador Dali and Marc Chagall. The French books were stored alongside hundreds of thousands of volumes the Nazis plundered from Belarus. That is why so many of the books ended up in Minsk.
>
> Criminals have for years sold illegal books online. Stolen art objects from the Middle East are showing up on Amazon, eBay, Facebook and WhatsApp. But the growth of social networks and e-commerce platforms, coupled with recent industrial-scale looting, has brought a stream of stolen antiquities online, often being offered to unsuspecting buyers. Law enforcement officials say the online outlets have become a vexing challenge as they battle a wave of looting that is stripping heritage sites of ancient artifacts. Revenue from the sales is often used to finance various types of terrorist and criminal groups that use trade to launder other illicit income including drug and weapons trafficking.

So many books ended up in Minsk? Where is that?

"There you are," Lance said. "I know of no names regarding criminals, but in the case of Nazi involvement, you could speak with a few of the victims, not the perpetrators."

"Why not the victims in all cases?" Fran asked.

"That's also an approach, although I'm not sure which way tells you the most. But you should definitely try to speak with victims and somehow get perpetrator names. And then, who knows, you might be lucky and get to speak with some of them, too."

Lance nodded to his cohort and said, "But we've got to go now. What I'll do is check with other histarians and call you if I find out anything worthwhile. Does that make sense?"

"Sure does. Plenty. And we can't thank you enough, Lance. Good luck in your teaching. Maybe I'll sign up for your class someday."

Handshakes were shared and Lance and Roger led the way out. Rick lagged behind and felt that the great importance of what he had just experienced couldn't be measured by the little time it took. And, in the presence of Fran, he was successful in curbing the usual mindset.

Just outside the library, he shared a thought with Fran: "So brief but so terrific."

Fran said, "That's right, but what say we call it a day and rest up? I'm tired and you look worse than that."

Rick agreed and asked, "Can we meet at my house tomorrow morning?"

"I'll be there early."

They separated and as Rick headed for his car, he remembered his days at Yale, the days on the fourth floor of Trumbull College. There were ten dormitory colleges then, and his was one of the oldest. He thought that they were simple days, simpler than now; less travel, less complex, less dangerous. He began humming, "*Those were the days, my friend,*" and after strolling through Cross Campus and by two more Colleges, he reached Woolsey Hall and his car, which was parked nearby. He had no idea why he had parked it so far from the library.

Fran was right. Fatigue to a fare-thee-well.

At home, he thought he'd deal with the underworld in some way.

His study seemed darker than outside, even with all its lights on, and he attributed it to his mood. But he tried hard to lighten both the room and his darkened emotional state. A large cup of coffee helped as he sipped and smelled the aroma. And he even swished some around in his mouth as he drained the last of it.

Then a host of things flooded his mind, headed by the underworld and the Nazi questions.

> *So it has or will be cruise ships, Mafia dons, and Nazi holdovers. One would think that these three... as clearcut as my fingerprints ... would be satisfying enough.*

But it dampened his mood even further. What he counted on was some kind of enrichment the following day.

Chapter 8

April 6

Everything seemed clearer after a good night's sleep. Rick dismissed any tendency to resurrect the conversations with Lance Beck and Chief Gomez. And even with Fran's try to comfort him.

At 7 a.m., he showered, shaved and dressed as if he were going to a wedding reception. Then he set about fixing the largest breakfast he could think of. He went to the refrigerator, removed the last two of his eggs and began frying them. Next came the toast. He put four pieces in the toaster, waited the three minutes it took for them to fall short of burning, and then plastered them with jelly atop butter. After that, he returned to the refrigerator, took out a bottle of orange juice and a few strips of bacon. He poured the juice in the largest glass he could find and began frying the bacon in a separate pan. By then, coffee was percolating so he filled a cup to its brim.

He had moved slowly as if savoring the steps he was taking, kind of like sticking a finger up at the chaos of the last 24 hours. When all was completed and arranged on the kitchen table, he began eating and drinking. He consumed everything before him, wasting as much time as he could, and realizing the slow pace was merely an attempt to nullify those 24 hours. He put a candy in his mouth and sat thinking for a moment, expecting his stomach to growl, but it didn't.

He got up, walked to the largest window in the room and looked out. The sky was blue porcelain. The sun was half-visible near a mountaintop, and feathered clouds were drifting toward it. They disappeared even while he watched.

He returned to the table and slid onto a chair an inch at a time. He flexed and unflexed his foot at the ankle. His mind was on overload. He went to his study and now, alert and determined, he called Paul.

"You're my information highway," Rick said. Then, while consulting his pad, he followed with, "How'd you make out with Fabio?"

Paul said, "I was just about to call you, Rick. I've spoken with Fabio twice, and he said that a certain mafiosi guy is willing to meet in Middletown, Connecticut. Just before the center of town there's a hotel called *Smile Awhile.* He's willing to be there at 1:20 tomorrow and will bring along a friend.

1:20? *A friend? What's going on here?*

When Fran arrived, Rick told him about Middletown and the mafioso guys they'd be meeting at 1:20 the following day.

"Imagine," he said, "not 1:15 or 1:25, but 1:20."

"They sound like showoffs," Fran said.

They spent the rest of the morning doing practically nothing - - - mostly reading magazines, watching television, and sorting out notes. In the afternoon, they decided to go to a movie. It was titled, *Rough Roads Ahead,* and they both slept through most of it, never considering its relevance to what lay ahead. They then stopped at a McDonalds for a hamburger and French fries.

Outside, Fran said, "I'll see you late morning then, and we'll go see those gangsters. I'll do the driving and just in case, don't forget your guns."

Rick returned home, not understanding why he still felt exhausted. Yet, he stayed up late, promising himself that he would awaken late the next morning.

Chapter 9

April 7

They agreed that the hotel in Middletown was among the most dilapidated they'd ever seen. The building's paint was peeling and one of its many small windows showed a streaky sign that read, *Smile Awhile.* Fran parked to the left of its shabby entrance. On the right was an unoccupied Cadillac convertible.

They checked for their guns and then simply took in the surroundings before getting out of the car.

They walked into an anteroom where, off to the right, two men were sitting on wicker chairs. One rose and said, “Hello. You must be Rick Chandler and this is ...”

“Fran Moreau.”

“Well, I'm John Rizzo. Fabio spoke to me about you. And this here is Ralph Garbaroni. He's the don for this territory.”

The don rose, bowed, and extended his hand for Rick to shake, but neither he nor Rizzo extended a hand to Fran.

Rizzo's attire was not unusual, but not so for the don. He was wearing a double-breasted black jacket, wrinkled pants, and no tie. Three fingers bore over-sized rings that hurt Rick when they shook hands. His voice was heavy and gruff.

He said, “Pleased to meet you, but we don't have much time for you, I'm afraid. Maybe about a minute or two and I apologize. You see, from here we go to Providence, Boston, Montpellier, Concord and Portland."

"That's your territory, right?"

"You might say that."

"Well, since you're in a hurry, I'll begin. I understand you're somehow involved in using stolen books for the Mafia's benefit. That you use them as ransom to cover whatever operations you handle. And I won't go into that."

"Stolen books?"

"Yes. And 'ransom' means payoffs to keep people quiet. Like when the subject is crime of all sorts: prostitution, extortion, loan sharking, drug cartels and the like. So is there anything you can do for us in stopping it all?"

Simultaneously, both mafiosos got up and the don said, "I get what you're driving at, and I'll see what we can do. But now it's off to Boston. Incidentally, you left 'terrorism' off your list of crimes. And that's what we'll be discussing today throughout my territory."

Rick and Fran followed them out, not saying another word. But Rick's positive expression showed through a thin spread of perspiration.

"Home run?" Fran asked.

"No, a triple."

Fran didn't say anything further, rather expressing his feelings aerobically.

"It was only a minute," Rick said, "but at least they saw us, and maybe something might come of it."

All four waved as they entered their cars. The mafiosos sped away, but Fran waited for Rick to take down some notes. Then Fran backed up, swerved around and nearly sideswiped a man who was lighting a cigarette. It was the man with the pock-marked face! Fran slowed down just opposite him as Rick lowered his window and, cupping his hands around his mouth, he yelled, "Up yours"!

As they were driving home, Rick commented, "That son-of-a-bitch. How does he know where we are, anyway?"

"I predict we'll find out sooner or later. For beginners: someone must be telling him."

"But who?"

"That'll come out. But meanwhile, let's not dwell on it. Just keep our guns handy and stay alert."

"Maybe it's the alert business that makes us tired," Rick said.

"That's logic, my friend. Logic pure and simple."

"And the other thing, Fran: so far, we've covered three of the quartet as well as we could. How do we know if it's paying off?"

"It takes time. You know that as well as I do." Fran's last statement was made gently and Rick was grateful for it.

"Let's not forget the Nazis," he said. "First of all, I recall receiving some reports that date back to the days of Evita; she offered asylum to some heinous Nazis. Secondly, some Nazis hid there in Argentina, changed their names, and faked a normal life. But others remained criminals in many ways, or they escaped to Belarus if they found that some Argentinians were growing suspicious of them. And third, many volumes of books were plundered by the Nazis from Belarus. Its capital is Minsk and it's a city that differs significantly from the rest of the country. That's why I think we should visit there. It would be more productive than a phone call. I'll check with our histarian, Lance. I'll even ask him if Belarus is part of Russia or not. Everything I've read about it is confusing."

Fran left for his home in Stamford after dropping Rick off at his New Haven home. There, he skimmed through all his books on Nazi Germany – mainly during World War II. It was an effort to clarify the enormity of the problem. Some of what he was skimming through was included in books he had written himself. He also added, word-for-word, material he'd saved from articles he'd read several years ago, like from *Wikipedia*. He then dictated selected sections into a recorder, expecting to play them back in due course, if needed. His dictation was fairly extensive:

> Nazi plunder refers to art theft and other items stolen as a result of organized looting of European countries during the time of the Third Reich by agents acting on behalf of the ruling Nazi Party of Germany. In addition to gold, silver and currency, cultural items of great significance were stolen, including paintings, ceramics, books, and religious treasures.
>
> Nazi gold is the gold transferred by Nazi Germany to overseas banks during World War II. The regime executed a policy of looting the assets of its victims to finance the war, collecting the looted assets in central depositories. The occasional transfer of gold in return for currency took place in collusion with many individual collaborative institutions. The precise identities of those institutions, as well as the exact extent of the transactions, remain unclear.
>
> In 1933, when Adolph Hitler became Chancellor of Germany, he enforced his aesthetic ideal on the nation. The types of art that were favored among the Nazi party were classical portraits and landscapes by Old Masters, particularly those of Germanic origin. Modern art that did not match this was dubbed degenerate art by the Third Reich, and all that was found in Germany's state museums was to

be sold or destroyed. With the sums raised, the Fuhrer's objective was to establish the European Art Museum in Linz. Other Nazi dignitaries, like Reichsmarschall Hermann Göring and Foreign Affairs minister von Ribbentrop, were also intent on taking advantage of German military conquests to increase their private art collections.

When the Nazis were in power, they plundered cultural property from every territory they occupied. This was conducted in a systematic manner with organizations specifically created to determine which public and private collections were most valuable to the Nazi Regime. Some of the objects were earmarked for Hitler's never realized Fuhrermuseum; some objects went to other high-ranking officials such as Hermann Göring; while other objects were traded to fund Nazi activities.

The Third Reich amassed hundreds of thousands of objects from occupied nations and stored them in several key locations, such as Musee Jeu de Paume in Paris and the Nazi headquarters in Munich. As the Allied forces gained advantage in the war and bombed Germany's cities and historic institutions, Germany began storing the artworks in salt mines and caves for protection from Allied bombing raids. These mines and caves offered the appropriate humidity and temperature conditions for artworks.

Approximately 20% of the art in Europe was looted by the Nazis, and there are well over 100,000 items that have not been returned to their rightful owners. The majority of what is still missing includes everyday objects such as china, crystal, silver, and famous books. Some articles of great cultural significance remain missing, though how much has yet to be determined. This is a major issue with the art market, since legitimate organizations do not

> want to deal in objects with unclear ownership titles. Since the mid-1990s, after several books, magazines, and newspapers began exposing the subject to the general public, many dealers, auction houses, and museums have grown more careful about checking the provenance of objects that are available for purchase in case they are looted. Some museums in the United States and elsewhere have agreed to check the provenance of works in their collections with the implied promise that suspect works would be returned to rightful owners if the evidence so dictates. But the process is time-consuming and slow, and very few disputed works have been found in public collections.

Rick's hand still hurt from the don's rings and now his throat hurt from all the dictation. Nonetheless, he was eager to phone Lance and did so. Rick brought him up to date and the histarian said he would speak to other histarians to get a full measure of what the next move should be.

Within the hour, Lance called back and said, "I'm not certain about this, but I think there's a former Nazi commander from Buenos Aires in Minsk. He moved to hide there, not only himself, but also his many stolen books. That turned out to be his specialty. … books, not gold or silver or valuable antiques."

"How old is he, and what does he do there?"

"Mid-sixties and he runs an auction house."

"Hmm, easy for books – steal them, then auction them. Should we go there?"

"I would … yes. Start off with their police department. I learned the chief's name. It's Boris Popov. And if you're concerned about language differences, the most commonly used and understood foreign language in Minsk is English. So it's Russian and English.

Chapter 10

The light plane to Minsk required two stops to refuel. They landed at the Minsk airport at 7:50 a.m. and were told where the police department was located.

It was so hot that Rick removed his jacket and kept it in his left hand along with his briefcase. He wanted to keep his right hand free, just in case.

Even at that early hour, they saw crowds of people inside the terminal, milling around like zombies -- wooden, listless, mechanical. None were smiling; some were bumping into one another without apologizing. And the building itself was a mess with poor lighting, ratty walls, and squeaky doors.

They agreed that they had to kill an hour or so before showing up at the chief's office, so, twice, they slowly walked around the inside rim of the terminal. At one point, they stopped at a snack bar and each man had its breakfast special: coffee, corn cereal, doughnuts and a tart-tasting liquid. They ended up outside, near a taxi whose driver said he was willing to drive them around to see some sights and explain what they were.

They passed by the Russian Orthodox church of St. Mary Magdalene, which the driver said was built in 1847; by a Jesuit college; a war memorial in Victory Square; the Railway Station Square, which he said was an example of Stalinist Minsk; and many, many parks with thick greenery.

He dropped them off before an administration building whose front bore a large sign with a list of its offices. Each was written in Russian and English. The last one was “Police Department".

Rick payed the driver in rubles amounting to 25 U.S. dollars. He included a hefty tip.

Inside, Boris Popov greeted them at his open office door. “I looked out the window, saw the three of you, and assumed you were who you are,” he said. “Rick Chandler and associates. A man named Lance contacted me and told me you'd be coming here. He also told me why, and for starters I must say that I know nothing about a Nazi commander. So do come in … come in.”

In a space that looked more like a cubicle than an office, the chief dragged three chairs to the front of his desk and said, “Do sit … do sit.”

The trio's eyes squinted as if agreeing that they should expect future repetitions.

Before sitting on the front edge of his desk, the chief extended a hand toward each man. Fran and Ansel shook it vigorously, but not Rick. He offered only his fingers, explaining that he had hurt his palm in a training exercise.

Popov was dressed like a police chief – gray shirt and trousers; black tie tucked in at the breast; blue shoulder insignias containing four yellow stars. He might have been in his mid-sixties but he moved around like a much younger man.

“So if my friend, Lance, did his job,” Rick said, “I won't be wasting much of your time.”

“Not a waste … not a waste.”

“Well, thank you,” Rick said, easing back in his chair. “Could you help out in any way? The situation is frightening everywhere and no doubt here, too.”

"I understand it's bad. That Lance man said so."

The chief said that he wasn't aware of thievery details - - - at least of its extent, but that he would investigate immediately. "And if it's real bad, and if you took the time to come here to see me personally, some arrests will no doubt be made. But how soon is a question mark … a question mark."

"I understand, chief, but let me say that we hope what we're doing dissuades others from continuing their illegal practices, or discourages still others from starting some. And it takes not only time to unfold, but also even more time for us to learn about it."

"Yes, time has to be considered," Popov said, yanking out his tie so it now flowed down to his belt.

"Well, as I said, chief … thank you. I wish you luck and much success."

"Amen," Fran said.

The three visitors got up and Rick said, "Speaking of time, we've got to leave."

"But this has been a terribly short visit. You won't wait for some tea or coffee?"

"No thanks – we must be off."

"Are you going right to the airport?"

"Yes, we are."

"Well, I'll have one of our officers drive you there."

- - - - -

At the terminal, Rick said, "If a single hotel in Middletown, Connecticut is dilapidated, from what I see here, this whole country and its people are dilapidated. It's like no one cares - - - except the chief back there. I wouldn't be surprised if they think nothing of cheating on each other, spying on each other, and who knows whatever else. They probably think they could even get away with murder. And I've come to think that I may not have to deal with the information I dictated. This could very well turn out to be enough."

But who the hell knows if and when?

He was carrying his briefcase as if it weighed a ton … as if he wanted to shove it back onto the shelf in his house. Then he asked, "So where's old Scar-face?"

Fran responded, "Oh, he's probably around, but we can't see him all the time."

"You think he'd stop stalking us if we took on a different pursuit?"

"Who knows?"

PART TWO

Chapter 11

Whenever Rick completed an undertaking, his mind neither fell dormant nor reset to something as challenging. And this was such an occasion.

He felt as though he were in a state of complete uncertainty about the immediate future until he received a phone call from a person that Paul had often spoken about – the head of an organization called, Gens de Vérité.

"Mr. Chandler," he said, "my name is Leon Cassell and I'm calling on behalf of Gens de Vérité. I've followed your career for the past month or so and have been impressed to no end. Before that, I even read all your books and know that you've lectured a lot. I understand that you're now in a relative standstill in your current investigation and am wondering if you'd be interested in taking on another assignment. I can explain over the phone what we promote – right now, in fact – or we can meet somewhere and I can do so in person."

"I see," Rick said. "What's the assignment?"

"Have you heard of the Sacco-Vanzetti case?"

"Yes, who hasn't?"

"Well, descendants of Vanzetti feel that the case ought to be reopened because they feel both men got a raw deal – that they were innocent. But on top of that, they've talked to the living relatives of some other people whose cases were controversial, and they've talked those relatives into joining them. It's become sort of a fraternity. They're joining for a common cause. Each relative has resented what people think of his family, even of only its name. They want their family names sanitized . . . to have those names removed from controversial scrutiny. They say that a discredited opinion of their family's name has lingered for decades and they want it cleared, once and for all. And get this: somehow **you've** entered the picture."

"Me? Why's that?"

"I have no idea, except that Vanzetti said he once heard you lecture about his family, but he was late for half of it. He wants to hear you again … the whole talk."

"But what exactly would I be accomplishing?"

"Giving this and other talks and in them saying that Sacco, Vanzetti and all the others don't deserve their bad reputation, and if they think the families have gotten a raw deal, it ought to be addressed."

Leon didn't give Rick a chance to comment … instead he went right on.

"And I'll mention the other families in a second. Also, we both know there's a statute of limitations and we wouldn't be able to reverse things or whatever … but we'd be satisfying the defendants, and there wouldn't be those terrible disasters they're threatening to carry out."

By then, Rick was so absorbed, he had put aside Leon's stating "all the others" and "terrible disasters".

"But how did they get others to go along with this? I can't wait to hear who they are."

"Again, no idea. Maybe through the Internet."

"And how did this guy get the notion to call your Vérité?"

"It's Mr. Vanzetti who called me, and he claimed that their group just recently heard of us. Can you imagine? A hundred-year-old organization? He said that various families have been vilified from one generation to the next, and that's why they've turned to us. He ended up giving me his phone number."

"I'm having trouble piecing this all together, but I suppose the next question should be: who are the 'various families'?"

"Sacco-Vanzetti, Charles Lindbergh, Sam Sheppard, and Phil Spector … all from America."

Funny … those first three are the
ones I wrote about two books ago!

"But the most serious thing involves what they say they'll do if certain demands aren't met. They've threatened to blow up the Eiffel Tower and Napoleon's sarcophagus in the Louvre; and the Elgin Marbles at the British Museum; and set off multiple explosions at the Arc de Triomphe as well as at the Rock of Gibraltar."

Rick suddenly couldn't contain himself, for the mere mention of the Rock grabbed at his gut. A long and threatening experience there had never left him. It occurred two years before and was the most dangerous experience he'd ever faced in conjunction with international police authorities.

But he finally said, "Christ, can you believe all this?"

"I certainly do. We just can't take a chance, Rick … uh … I may call you that?"

"Yes … and you're Leon. Okay?"

"Okay. As I was saying … we can't take a chance. And Vanzetti's relative said that he and Sacco want to meet with you and they suggest that you lecture about some of the cases you've written about. They and most of the other relatives would be there. They want a fresh take, especially on the four American cases, because some current relatives aren't sure. They only know what an immediately prior descendant has told them. So if we're talking five decades, not every single relative has heard the details."

"You mean the relatives of Sacco, Vanzetti, Lindbergh … and let's see … Sheppard and Spector?"

"Those are the ones. If their relatives know you've chosen them, they'll be in the audience. You might even talk to one or two, although you might be preoccupied with other people. I could phone Mr. Vanzetti about this."

"You know, Leon, I don't mind lecturing. Maybe it's my ego … center of attention or something like that. But I wouldn't do it four times unless I did some research."

Leon nodded, then said, "It just dawned on me that I should have started this conversation by describing Vérité and then something about myself … so you'll be clearer about this if and when you say 'yes'."

"Shoot."

"Well, we're a French organization that's been in existence since the fall of Napoleon in 1815. Gens de Vérité worked alongside the French government but had never been part of it. And still isn't. When retained at a sizeable cost, it was noted for solving worldwide puzzles related to the national security and defense initiatives of countries that sought its help. Now, it takes up causes as they develop, focusing on projects lacking any iota of political or special interest rhetoric. Membership extends throughout Europe and even beyond, numbering about two thousand."

Rick was sure Leon had given such details 1,000 times before.

"With regard to yours truly, I've been involved in law enforcement for as long as I can remember. Early on, I was captain of both the police force and the *Préfecture de Police* in Paris. Ten years later, I began teaching criminology at their *Grandes-Écoles* and, at the same time, lectured regularly at the Paris Police Museum. Currently, I'm teaching a course on Corrections, Crime and Criminology at what was once referred to as the Sorbonne and now as the University of Paris. And I can still make arrests, but only in Paris."

Now it's 2,000 times!

"You've been very thorough, Leon, but is there more I should be doing besides the lecturing?"

"I'm labeling it, *Setting History Straight*. You'd have to: one, visit the relatives of each family–as I said before. Two, give the lectures. And three, somehow increase the security at each stated blowup site."

Rick figured as much and, almost fully intrigued, he said, "That's a tall order. Increasing the security is important and I can do it. The lectures? I can give them. But the business of visiting the families? I'm not so sure about that one. And besides, it seems to me that the way I deliver the lectures would make the visiting unnecessary. So can I think about it all for a day or two?"

"Yes, by all means."

"Would you be willing to meet me in New Haven, say at the Yale library?"

"Again, yes, I would. Just give me directions before we hang up."

"Good. I think my decision will be in the affirmative, but I'd like to meet with you first. Plus I'd like to confer with my wife and with my good friend and longtime buddy, Fran Moreau. He'd be accompanying me through it all. Also our driver, Ansel Stewart."

"I totally understand. There's one more thing I should have already brought up. And that's about money. Vérité is prepared to pay you a million dollars if you accept this assignment. No matter how it turns out, it's payment for the time spent."

Rick wasted no time answering. "No, no," he said. "I wouldn't want that. I'm totally well heeled. Please donate the million to a worthy cause of your liking."

"And Fran, your buddy?"

"No, he doesn't need the money either. He's in the same boat as I am."

Leon kept insisting on doling out the money to them, but to no avail.

They ended their conversation after Leon gave Rick his phone number and received directions to the L & B Room at Yale's Sterling Memorial Library. They would meet there the next morning at eleven.

Chapter 12

Rick holed up in his study to outline what had been done and what still needed to be done, but he first phoned Angela again. He spoke about the way things were going.

"Sounds like you have everything under control," she said, "so keep it up. You want me to come home?"

"No, you'd only get in the way."

"I knew you'd say that, my darling."

"What did I say?"

"That I'd show you the way."

"I think we're both way off," he said, beating her to a loud chuckle. "But I'll keep you up to date. I figure that what lies ahead will take roughly two more weeks."

"Take your time … and I love you."

"I love you, too."

Now to the day's hard part.
The what, when, where and how.

It had been awhile since Rick had sat at his desk, and he knew that once he did, he'd be there for some time … stretching, massaging his back, looking around while thinking. Then he rose and walked out the back door -- welcoming the idea of checking on sounds he thought he heard. One minute, they were of a chirping variety. The next minute, they were sputtering sounds. He believed the chirps were made by birds. But not the sputtering. He didn't stay there long though, reentering the house after deciding all the sounds were the result of nerves.

At his desk, he sat immobile, trying to relax, to sort things out -- yet not for long. He had grown tired of writing notes to himself on a 4x6 scratch pad of white sheets. He therefore opened a lower drawer and took out a larger yellow tablet.

But before he entered anything on it, he decided, once and for all, that the proposed summit meeting should definitely be held. And that it should take place in New York City with Chief Gomez as the presiding chairman, for he –Rick – would be too busy taking notes. He would recommend having it aboard the *Seacraft*, the cruise ship that not only docked in Buenos Aires every Friday, but was also there in New York every Thursday and Friday. Also, he was sure the chief wouldn't mind flying there. Rick recalled a conversation he had once had with him about it.

Gomez had said something like: "You've done your share of traveling south. I should do my share of traveling north. Besides, I could see some of my old friends who still work at the dock there."

Rick spread out a bunch of white sheets before him and began transferring some of the contents to the yellow tablet. In the process, he thought the back of his hands looked yellow. He lifted them off the tablet and scrutinized them.

Not yellow. Nerves again.

The most immediate event ahead was the library meeting with Leon, and it headed the priority list that Rick printed on a tablet sheet:

1 — Agreeing to work with Leon and Vérité.

2 — The question of lecturing. Should schedule be announced to the public?

3 — Visiting each disaster site to recommend added security.

4 — The status of my MAIN CHALLENGES.

5 — Have never told Leon about a summit meeting. It's a *must*, so tell him.

6 — Some sightseeing but not much at disaster sites.

Then there followed a whole host of subjects that Rick slowly printed on the tablet:

1–Status of main challenges:

Identifying some looted treasures, especially famous books. Have them returned to rightful owners, if possible. Have this serve as example to others seeking to steal treasures. Prostitutes and cruise ships. Organized criminals could be of service in some cases. But is still too early to determine what the status is of any of these.

2–Who should be invited to the summit meeting?

Rick, Fran, Ansel, histarian Lance, Paul D'Arneau, Chief Gomez, Carlos, Leon and let's not forget Calderone.

3–Where?

New York City. On the *Seacraft*, which docks there. For Gomez and Carlos, flight time from Buenos Aires is about 10 hours.

4–The disaster sites:

Paris: Eiffel Tower; Napoleon's sarcophagus; Arc de Triomphe

Britain: Elgin Marbles

Gibraltar: The Rock

5–Cities of victims (according to descendants):

Sacco-Vanzetti: Plymouth, MA

Lindy: Hopewell, NJ

Sheppard: Cleveland, Ohio

Spector: L.A.

6–Proposed schedule:

Day 1– Lecture: Sacco-Vanzetti. Sightseeing.

Day 2– Disaster sites: Eiffel Tower, Napoleon's sarcophagus, Arc de Triomphe. All in Paris.

Day 3– Lecture: Lindbergh. Sightseeing. N.J.

Day4– Lecture: Sam Sheppard. Cleveland.

Day 5– The summit. N.Y.

Day 6– Lecture: Phil Spector. Sightseeing. L.A.

Day 7– Disaster site: Elgin Marbles. Britain.

Day 8– Disaster site: The Rock. Gibraltar.

Rick then made a folder that was full of copies –three pages clipped together–and put the thick folder into his briefcase. He planned on giving three pages to Leon, to Ansel, and to each of the other members of the summit team. He then phoned Fran about the library meeting.

Later on, Rick's sleep was twitchy at best, but by early morning his nervousness seemed to have evaporated.

Chapter 13

It so happened that Rick and Fran arrived at the library at exactly the same time and walked to a far corner of the L & B Room. On the way, Rick looked around for a photographer and saw none.

Seated there was an oversized man who introduced himself as Leon Cassell. He struggled up and extended a hand to both men. They nearly doubled over from the force of the handshake, but they let it pass.

Leon was well over six-feet tall, paunchy and likely a three-hundred pounder. He had thinning brown hair, a hawk nose, wide mouth and a wispy white mustache. Marked creases appeared seared into his forehead and a perpetual squint did all but hide the deep blue of his eyes. There was both a towering presence and a gracefulness about him.

After some small talk, primarily about Leon's flight over from Paris and Rick's acceptance of the job, Rick retrieved three printed sheets and handed them to Leon.

He looked them over and said, "Excellent job … says it all … and I like the idea of a summit meeting. But I have a question to ask about announcing your lecture schedule publicly. To whom?"

"Newspapers, social media and the like."

Rick had heard it before but still cringed when Leon shook his head and responded, "That would make you too much in the open. Kind of dangerous, Rick. Maybe you should have a police escort. I could arrange it for you. Would you be comfortable with that?"

"Yes, but he or she should be nearby, not by my side."

"Perhaps there should be two … one could be across the street, for example."

"And the other?"

"Driving near you in a car, and waiting in it."

"But not dressed in police clothes, right?" Rick asked.

"Right … regular clothes."

"With guns hidden."

"Hidden."

"Nightsticks?"

"Hidden."

"Tasers?"

"Light weight and hidden."

"We'll see," Rick said. "What say you, Fran?"

"I'm all for police escorts and the hidden stuff… yeah, all for it."

"What about the escorts when I'm in a building?" Rick asked.

"They'll follow you wherever you go, so don't worry, they'd be unrecognizable. They're trained to be. But let's be selective."

Leon checked the sheet again. "And about the status of things?" he inquired.

"What it says there, and I'll let you know if anything new develops."

"I'll do the same."

"What? How would you know?"

"Rick, don't disregard the fact that once we begin working together, news about it will mount by the day, if not the hour."

"I suppose that's what will happen. We live in a glass house, so to speak."

"On all sides."

"You don't think our phones are rigged, do you?"

"I just don't know. And I don't think that anything we do at Vérité remains a secret for very long, because we have so many members. And they just talk and talk and talk."

"Hmm -- secrets are passé, I guess."

"Never existed, when you come to think of it. Now let's see, what else?" Leon asked as he perused the sheet. Oh yes, your lecturing. You're familiar enough with the cases?"

"It makes no difference if I gave the lectures before, because in the book I coauthored with Dr. Henry Lee, we deal with those very cases. I can refer to the book in giving each talk. Even read whole segments. It'll be open right in front of me."

"Okay. And what do you mean by 'organized crime could be of service'?"

"I should have elaborated. I meant that organized criminals – like the Mafia – could both help and hurt our cause. *Help* when some looters compete with the Mafia and *hurt* when some mafiosos are in cahoots with the looters."

"I guess I'm clear on it."

"Should I cover everything about each case?" Rick asked.

"Yes. Relatives there want to hear everything. That's why they're there. Mr. Vanzetti told me so. I can't stress it enough. After all, you're really giving the lectures for *their* sake. So, the whole mile … whatever it takes."

"Okay, you asked for it."

"No, they did … I'd bet on it. And I'll be at each lecture."

"So that's settled. I was worried about the time I'd be spending … talking away. Next are my thoughts about visiting with who-knows-who at the potential disaster sites. It's all going to involve a lot of traveling. Fran will accompany me, and we'll also have Ansel, our driver. And there'll be plenty of time for sightseeing. I've done so much traveling in the past– with quick stops everywhere– that I rarely did any sightseeing. Maybe now I can catch up and do some, even in locations close to home."

Rick looked Leon over and came to the conclusion that the man was as knowledgeable as he could have hoped for. That the Vérité chairman not only understood questions but also had answers that made complete sense.

"Now … where would I be giving the lectures?" Rick asked, feeling like giving one right then and there.

"I'll find a place in the city where the so-called crimes took place. The local police will advise me."

Leon checked a tablet again. "Like your first one –Sacco-Vanzetti– it's in Plymouth, Massachusetts. There's got to be some kind of an auditorium there. Or near there."

One-hundred percent satisfied, Rick said, "Okay, we've really covered the landscape. You want to sleep at my home tonight?"

"No, but thanks … I've already registered at the Taft Hotel down the street. And there are two more things we have *not* covered. Who invites the summit attendees and when should it be held?"

"I'll take care of the inviting," Rick said, "and as far as when? Let's make it four or five days from now."

Chapter 14

Plymouth, Massachusetts

April 13

Leon phoned Rick at just after eight the next morning and said that the Sacco-Vanzetti lecture would take place at eleven a.m.

"I spoke with the relative last night and he said that he could pull a crowd together by eleven this morning."

"Where?"

"There's an auditorium in their mall. Seats a good four-hundred. And he guesses there will be standing room only. He and his family spent all day talking it up yesterday. And I also found out where the other three could be held. Seems that study halls at high schools are best. They all seat 200 or so, and they're available. I'll call the other three in the morning … and also some police officers who could oversee it all."

- - - - -

After breakfast, Leon said he had made the calls.

Rick asked, "Did you give any dates or lecture titles?"

"Not really. I could call them back. I know the titles, but what dates?

Rick consulted his calendar booklet. "Let's see," he said, "Todays the 13th. We'll be in Paris on the 15th, but only for that day. So arrange for the study halls on the 16th, 17th and 19th at one p.m. And the cities will be Hopewell, New Jersey; Cleveland; and L.A… in that order."

"Good. But what happened to the 18th?"

"That's the summit day. And also … tell them we realize we're not giving them much advanced notice, but to do their best in drumming up attendance."

"Will do."

"And Leon –"

"Yes?"

"I hope I haven't made it too complicated for you."

"No, no. I've written it all down and I'll handle it."

Shortly before 11 a.m., Charles Reagan, a local dignitary, introduced Rick, who stepped to the podium at the base of an auditorium that was filled to capacity. And, indeed, there was standing room only, both at its sides and near its upper railing. He smiled at three familiar faces in the front row, off to the right: Fran, Ansel and Leon. He had no idea what any family members looked like, much less the police escort, if there **was** one.

Rick thanked the attendees for being there and held up the book he coauthored with Dr. Lee – *Famous Crimes Revisited*. He clarified that he'd be either referring to it or outright quoting from it during his talk.

"I'll also have these notes I once made while writing the book."

Then he said he'd been asked to give four lectures in the next couple of weeks and that this one would definitely be the longest. And as a trick his father had taught him, he had brought along a heavy metal rod that was shaped like a pencil and he would be laying it across each page of the open book as he came to that page. Explaining that it thus freed up his hands as he lectured, he raised them a few inches above the podium, some of the notes in one hand.

"So are you ready?" he asked. There was thunder in his voice.

The reply was beyond audible and there was even some clapping. Many in the audience looked prepared to take their own notes.

"I'll be speaking minimally off the cuff and maximally off referrals to my old notes and to the book, mostly the latter. So don't be surprised if what I say sounds stilted.

"Also, I must level with you, my friends. I happen to believe that the outcome of this case was somehow rigged, as were one or two of the others I'll be speaking about in my travels to other cities. As for the remaining ones, their outcomes were indeed suspicious. I'm going to try to elaborate on what I have written here in my notes. It's a section with the heading 'Time line'. So for Sacco-Vanzetti, six subjects:

"The crimes and arrests.

"The Plymouth trial. A dress rehearsal?

"The Dedham trial.

"Witnesses and evidence.

"Ballistics magnified.

"Verdict. Whose victory?

"We'd be here all day if I covered all six, so let's just see how it goes. I hope to offer it all straight timewise … or at least, close to straight. But before all that, I must begin with an historical summary: Most people have never heard of Nicola Sacco and Bartolomeo Vanzetti. They were Italian anarchists charged with the 1920 killing of a shoe factory paymaster and his guard in South Braintree, Massachusetts. Sound like a familiar place? Their controversial trial is universally included among America's most famous, not only because of issues of ethnicity, draft evasion, radicalism and an arguably bigoted judicial system, but also because of the passion of the times. In the eyes of many, never in American legal history has public apprehension so shaped the outcome of a trial; never has one been conducted under such a shadow of ethnic hatred and political panic. And thrust in the middle of this landscape were two admitted radicals who embodied the twin threats of an unwelcome foreign element preaching a foreign political view.

"World War I had just ended and political change was rampant abroad. The Bolsheviks had finally gained a foothold in Russia, a man named Hitler was advocating an anti-Semitic policy in Germany, the Austro-Hungarian Empire had been decimated, and the entire world appeared engulfed in a surging sea of socialism.

"At home in America, an ailing Woodrow Wilson was president but would soon be succeeded by Warren Harding. Prohibition was in full force, sparking the boom of speakeasies, and F. Scott Fitzgerald wrote, 'The uncertainties of 1919 were over. America was going on the greatest, gaudiest spree in history.' Outwardly, there was little doubt that the country's mood and its aspirations were changing. The start of the decade found its youth turning into social desperadoes: daring, hard drinking and cynical. Men mocked authority and flaunted their recklessness. Women's skirts were shorter while silk stockings and bobbed hair replaced hobble skirts and flowing tresses. Those were the days of 'giggle water' and 'the cat's meow,' when a loaf of bread cost a dime and a pound of flour sold for less. People were caught up in Al Jolson, the Charleston and jazz, and they cheered loudly over Jack Dempsey in the boxing ring and Babe Ruth in the ballpark. All this was the veneer.

"For in the face of the *Red Scare* or the rise of communism, the inner mood of the country was decidedly fearful. Unlike the Vietnam War nearly a half-century later, World War I was a popular conflict as

Americans had rallied around Wilson's declaration that, 'The world must be safe for democracy.' Almost anyone who opposed the war, therefore, was looked upon with contempt.

"Despite the finality of execution, this case has never achieved closure for it was cast from the beginning into a smoldering cauldron of judicial, scientific, political and social dispute. To this day, some people believe the trial and its aftermath–six years of legal wrangling–was a travesty of legal procedure. They feel the defendants were framed, that forensic evidence may have been tampered with, and that the police investigation was slipshod at best. And this last sentence is one of the most important … if not *the* most important that I'll be setting forth today. In fact, let me repeat it: *They feel the defendants were framed, that forensic evidence may have been tampered with, and that the police investigation was slipshod at best.*

"It's principally for this last contention that I stand before you to share the story of Sacco-Vanzetti, a four-generation-old case that in many ways might be considered a prototype–the forerunner of other cases in the twentieth century whose conduct merits the slipshod label.

"And between you and me, I pray that I'm still standing halfway through all of this."

Rick hoped for and received a mixture of laughter and applause, and during it, he took out a handkerchief and wiped his nose … although it didn't need it.

"But to continue: In some fictional stories, *setting* is stressed more than in others. I did so in most of the novels I've written. Its purpose is to set the stage for the drama to follow, to anchor it in time and place. But only infrequently will such a design drive the action or otherwise influence it. Not so in the non-fictional saga of Sacco-Vanzetti. Rarely has a confluence of events – the Russian Revolution, the armistice, Red hysteria, patriotism, and journalism's focus on gangsterism – played on the emotions of an era's average citizen and on its movers and shakers alike: politicians, educators, the clergy, and all tiers of the criminal justice system. Like an unwanted foreign substance introduced into the bloodstream, Nicola Sacco and Bartolomeo Vanzetti happened upon the national scene at the wrong time.

"The Attorney General of the United States, A. Mitchell Palmer, didn't help in this regard, issuing statements to a war-weary nation, warning it of the danger of communism, socialism and any radical movement in general. In late 1919, he referred to adherents of any radical movement as potential murderers, and to their cause as criminal.

"Again, I must interject my own opinion. I wonder whether words like my last few created an early bias against the defendants and whether such words alone would have rendered the case appealable by today's standards. Any of you have an answer?"

No one raised a hand.

"So what was fueled? The activities of peddlers of hate, of those advocating anti-Semitism and anti-Catholicism, such as the Ku Klux Klan. The result was that hatemongers and pro-American fever combined to produce increasingly more nasty groups who gained influence beneath a cloud of national distrust.

"Not only were communists and socialists targeted; but avowed anarchists and those leaning toward anarchy were included as well. At the time, the popular image of an anarchist was a bomb-throwing Italian who was hellbent on overthrowing the government. In reality, anarchists favored self-government of small social units, and many Italian immigrants–because of the political conditions of their homeland–were drawn to this concept. The leading figure in the U.S. anarchist movement was Luigi Galleani, a dynamic speaker who commanded the respect of thousands of followers, including Sacco and Vanzetti. And the times shook with anti-this and anti-that.

"Sacco and Vanzetti emigrated to the United States in 1908 but didn't meet until 1917, the year our country entered the Great War, and from that point on, they would forge an alliance that would carry them to their graves.

"Their roots were at opposite ends of Italy: Sacco's in the south, Vanzetti's in the north. Both came from farming families and grew up in comfortable circumstances, but they left to seek opportunity and adventure in a democratic republic, far from the feudal society of their homeland.

"Although Sacco had dropped out of school after the third grade, he was literate in Italian when he arrived in America. As a youngster, he enjoyed helping in his father's vineyard, orchard and vegetable gardens. He was a hard worker and considered cheerful, even jovial. His mother once said that hard work would always bring a smile to his face.

"His father was a Republican, his older brother a Socialist, but neither appeared to have stirred any serious political thinking in the boy. However, after early experiences and associations in America, a hard left philosophy was to take form. This included changing views about religion as, over the years, he passed from a belief in God, through mounting skepticism, and finally to atheism. The same was true of Vanzetti.

"Some of Vanzetti's writings depict a deep respect for God, especially during his early teens, a time when two circumstances shaped his thinking. One was brought about by his father, who stated unequivocally that formal education would be a waste of time for his son. He insisted on a trade. Over a six-year span, therefore, he apprenticed the boy to several owners of pastry and bakery shops located far from home. Vanzetti worked 15 to 18 hours a day and hated every minute of it. The other circumstance was a prolonged bout with pleurisy. Bedridden, Vanzetti began to read as never before, especially the works of St. Augustine. One line would become his favorite: 'The blood of martyrs is the seed of liberty.'

"Seeds had been planted. Those half-dozen years were spent journeying alone, and they afforded little shelter to a steady onslaught of ideas from casual acquaintances who called themselves socialists. Vanzetti appeared fascinated by their doctrines, which were later to structure his life and prove to be incendiary in the United States.

"It was as if an austere father plus Vanzetti's illness drove him to the extremes of bitterness and intellectual rebellion. I believe he'd been deprived, after all, of friends, schooling, and his mother's tangible love. This at a time when he was tired, depressed and subjected to a new philosophy that appeared to offer hope.

"As for Sacco, his upbringing was more stable, but I can see that his future radicalism, though having a later onset, was just as intense.

"When Sacco departed for the U.S. in 1908, he was 17, three years younger than Vanzetti, who sailed two months later. They were short, dark men, Sacco clean-shaven and Vanzetti sporting a large bushy mustache. Sacco lived in Milford, Massachusetts. He eventually married and worked as a shoe edger. He read little and, though quiet and polite, was considered excitable. Vanzetti, on the other hand, was calm and thoughtful. He was a voracious reader and often wrote flowery, idyllic passages about nature, human frailties and philosophy. A bachelor, he at first moved around a great deal in New York, Connecticut and Massachusetts, working as an unskilled laborer. He finally settled in Plymouth, Massachusetts, as a fish peddler.

"Up to this point, my impression was that their experiences had shaped their beliefs, and certain questions should be asked. So I'll ask them. Would they have become radicals had they remained in Italy? In the United States, had they truly become hardened subversives or merely idealistic rebels, groping through webs spun by Galleani and other authoritative figures? This phase of the story is less clear in my mind than the one that unfolded, a drama whose outcome hinged on the veracity of certain details submitted in the subsequent trial. Truths? Distortions? Lies?"

Rick reached over to a side table for a glass of water. He took tiny sips slowly and on returning the glass, some water spilled. He took out his handkerchief again and mopped it up.

"Sorry," he said, looking sheepish. "I must confess that I spilled the water on purpose so I could give my voice a rest." More laughter erupted, including his own.

"Politically, neither man was a radical when he left Italy, but over the next several years, each was sharply influenced by what he heard and observed. Poverty, squalor and prejudice swayed them both, Sacco lamenting social injustice toward foreigners in general and Italians in particular.

"And what other factors spawned their attraction to an anarchistic philosophy? The friendships they forged among like-minded immigrants gave them solidarity in the face of taunts and rejections. Recent arrivals fed off each other and, in the process, repudiated anything that resembled the 'American Way', especially business, government and the military. This new segment of the population drifted further and further away from mainstream political and economic thinking and was left vulnerable to any strong alternative voice. As I mentioned before, such a voice belonged to Luigi Galleani who, with his passion, eloquence and charisma, was the champion of the anarchist cause in our country. Thousands flocked to his lectures, Sacco and Vanzetti among them, and for most, it didn't take long for a metamorphosis to occur – from uneducated greenhorns to philosophical anarchists.

"Both followed the teachings of their new leader with fundamentalist reverence. They attended meetings, distributed literature, participated in strikes and helped raise funds for the strikers' families. As an itinerant fish peddler, Vanzetti circulated leaflets fomenting an idealistic revolution that scholars have called 'noble nonsense'. At the same time, Sacco was quick to inform any willing listener that all big government should be overthrown by the force of ideas, not bombings. It was during the course of such activity that Sacco and Vanzetti first met on a picket line in 1917.

"When World War I broke out, both men fled to Mexico along with some of their friends. They had often spoken openly about their opposition to all wars. Their flight from the U.S. was an incompletely understood chapter in their story, yet was one of the compelling issues of the trial. They mistakenly feared the draft because as aliens, they were not subject to it. Of even more significance, however, was their fear of deportation for they knew that under the Immigration Act of 1917, they could be deported for their anarchist activities.

"Homesick, Sacco returned to the U.S. within a few months. Vanzetti stayed behind until the armistice. The question of deportation was not mentioned at the trial or the appeals in order to protect their friends and the escape route via Mexico. Such a route allowed them to return to Italy, if they desired, rather than to exile.

"Publicly, Sacco and Vanzetti maintained their flight was made not to avoid military service per se but to support Galleani's claim that wars enhance the fortune of capitalists at the expense of the working class.

"I must stop here, folks, because I'm feeling a bit guilty and I must level with you. It turns out that I'm reading 99% of what I'm saying. But in my own defense, I really can't improve on what I've written before … and I hope you understand. It's all original, whether I wrote it before or composed it here and now."

Once again, Rick welcomed the applause.

"So that was 'The Historical Summary'. Now to elaborate on 'The Crimes and Arrests'. Although a botched robbery in a small New England town on the day before Christmas would ordinarily have been classified as a run-of-the-mill holdup attempt, it was to assume greater significance in light of the celebrated murders four months later in a shoe manufacturing town 14 miles away.

"The place was Bridgewater, Massachusetts. The time was December 24, 1919. It was a snowy, biting morning. A Ford truck inched along an ice-encrusted road from the Bridgewater Trust Company toward the main office of a shoe company. On board were its driver, a paymaster, a local constable, and a payroll of $33,000.

"Three men leaped from a parked car, screaming for the truck to stop. When it didn't, they opened fire. One man, a heavily mustached individual, brandished a shotgun; the other two, pistols. The constable returned fire and in the brief but frenzied exchange, the driver lost control of the truck, which skidded into a telephone pole. Evidently, the bandits became distracted by this and an oncoming streetcar, lost their nerve and scampered back into the car, which sped away. An eyewitness, Dr. J.M. Murphy, picked up a spent shotgun shell at the scene and put it in his pocket. For the moment, the crime was not considered particularly noteworthy and therefore was filed. Then four months later, a more dramatic, deadly crime occurred.

"The place was South Braintree, Massachusetts. The time was April 15, 1920. At 3 p.m. on a cold damp Thursday, Frederick A. Parmenter, the fortyish paymaster for the Slater and Morrill Shoe Factories, and his guard, Alessandro Berardelli, emerged from the company's administrative building at the upper end of Pearl Street and headed down the incline toward its three-story plant some 200 yards away. They carried two steel boxes containing that week's payroll of $16,000. Berardelli, 28, also carried a .38 Harrington & Richardson revolver.

"What followed was later recounted by several workers peering from the upper windows of the Rice & Hutchins Factory. Parmenter nodded toward the gate tender as the pair neared his shanty at a railroad crossing. They stepped over the tracks, which split the road, passed a water tower and an excavation site and, 50 yards into their journey, drew abreast of two men leaning against a metal fence in front of the factory. One wore a felt hat, the other a cap. The man in the felt hat spoke briefly to Berardelli, then grabbed at his shoulder. Shots rang out, the stench of gunpowder saturating the air. It was uncertain how many shots were fired but, by most accounts, Berardelli was hit by the initial shot, dropped to his knees, then took two more rounds. One of the attackers bent over the dying guard and snatched his revolver. Parmenter, hanging onto his box, tried to flee but was shot twice and died 14 hours later. During the melee, a cap had fallen to the ground.

"A signal shot was fired and a seven-seater Buick – its driver, described as a pale and sickly man and a front-seat passenger, characterized as dark and foreign-looking – pulled up from the vicinity of the lower factory. Scrambling toward the car, the two assailants turned momentarily to scatter several shots at the workers looking out from the factory windows. Some 30 workers at the excavation site dove for cover as lead whined off a nearby brick pile. The two men gathered up the payroll boxes and piled into the Buick, as did a third who had been hiding behind the bricks. Meanwhile, Berardelli had managed to lift himself to his knees only to be shot again by one of the men who sprang from the car.

"The shiny car sputtered up Pearl Street, its front-seat passenger firing at random out its windows. At the railroad crossing, the tender lowered the gates, but one of the bandits, waving a pistol, shouted they would shoot if he didn't raise them. The tender obliged and the Buick sped away as one of its occupants tossed tacks onto the street to puncture the tires of any car that might try to follow.

"Here's where you can probably tell that I'm reading *more* than 95% from the book and where it's important to keep the chronology straight because it's tricky. Before the first crime in Bridgewater, a Buick touring car had been reported stolen. It was later believed to be the same one used in that crime and in the South Braintree robbery and murders four months later. The thefts of two separate sets of license plates occurred on December 22, 1919, and on January 6, 1920. Was this the work of political and social malcontents or of professional criminals?

"The South Braintree robbery and murders occurred On April 15, 1920, for which Sacco and Vanzetti were arrested on May 5. Then Vanzetti was indicted on June 11 for an attempted Bridgewater holdup *after* his and Sacco's arrest for the South Braintree murders.

"The official charge by the Commonwealth of Massachusetts against Vanzetti was: 'Assault with intent to murder' at Bridgewater. Its charge against both Sacco and Vanzetti was: 'Armed robbery at South Braintree and the murders of Alessandro Berandelli and Frederick Parmeter.'

"The DA arranged for Vanzetti to stand trial in Plymouth **before** the joint trial in Dedham. Judge Webster Thayer would preside at both trials.

"Next we have: 'The Plymouth Trial. Dress Rehearsal'? In what some scholars consider was a matter that would presage the conduct and outcome of the joint trial, the earlier Vanzetti trial for the Bridgewater holdup was held from June 22 to July 1, 1920. Others contend that holding a trial for a lesser crime prior to a trial for a major crime was highly unusual and, at the time, was a maneuver without precedent.

"Judge Thayer was 63, a dapper individual who bore a striking resemblance to Boris Karloff. A member of Worcester, Massachusetts' social elite, he made no secret of his hatred of foreigners. Two months before, he had gained widespread attention when he presided over the trial of a man who was charged with advocating the overthrow of the government by force. After a not guilty verdict was announced, an enraged Judge Thayer chided the jury: 'How did you arrive at such a verdict? Did you consider the information that the defendant gave … when he admitted … there should be a revolution in this country? He said to the police officers that he believed in Bolshevism and that our government should be overthrown.'

"The press had a field day as they sided with the judge who, in the following year, would also preside over the joint trial.

"Vanzetti was defended by J.P. Vahey, a prominent Plymouth attorney and political activist. The prosecutor was District Attorney Frederick Katzmann. A prosecution witness worthy of mention was 14-year-old Maynard Shaw, a high school student who witnessed the incident while delivering newspapers. Should any trial testimony be considered comical, if not ludicrous, it was that given by Shaw. And I'll read how it went:

> Shaw: No hat on and I was just getting a fleeting glance at his face, but the way he ran I could tell he was a foreigner. I could tell by the way he ran.
>
> Vahey (Defense Attorney): You could tell he was a foreigner by the way he ran?
>
> Shaw: Yes.
>
> Vahey: What sort of foreigner was he?
>
> Shaw: Nation?
>
> Vahey: Yes.
>
> Shaw: Why, European.

Vahey: What?

Shaw: Either Italy or Russia.

Vahey: Which was it, Russia or Italy?

Shaw: There I can't say exactly.

Vahey: Does an Italian or Russian run differently from a Swede or Norwegian?

Shaw: Yes.

Vahey: What is the difference?

Shaw: Unsteady.

Vahey: Both the Italians and the Russians run unsteadily?

Shaw: As far as that goes I don't know.

Vahey: You don't know how a Swede runs, do you?

Shaw: No.

Vahey: Does a Swede run cross-legged?

Shaw: No.

Vahey: You don't want to have this jury think, do you, that you can tell what the nationality of this man was by the way he ran? Do you want them to believe that?

Shaw: Yes, I do.

Vahey: Now what nationality did he belong to?

> Shaw: Let me say that I believe–well, the first thing that came into my mind was that he was an Italian or a Russian. I would not say–he might be a Mexican for what I know. I would not say he was an Alaskan or an African.
>
> Vahey: You mean by that he was not a colored man?
>
> Shaw: No.
>
> Vahey: You eliminate the African, do you, from your consideration?
>
> Shaw: Yes.
>
> Vahey: He was either a Russian or an Italian or a Greek or a Brazilian or a Mexican–either one of these?
>
> Shaw: Yes.
>
> Vahey: Or a Jap?
>
> Shaw: Might be.
>
> Vahey: Would you say he might be a Jap?
>
> Shaw: No.
>
> Vahey: You would not say that he was a Jap or a Chinaman or an African–those three are eliminated absolutely, are they?
>
> Shaw: Yes, nor an American.

"Really now: the judge allowed such testimony? I have to admit that in all my years in criminal investigation and forensic science, I'd never experienced the likes of this. The prosecution got away with it, and it stressed the prejudicial issue of foreigners.

"In terms of the defense, one witness said that someone wanted to find a scapegoat for the crimes; that Italians felt unimportant and impotent in society; and that many were terrified of taking the witness stand. No wonder: they would have had to endure Katzmann's excoriating style, for he bullied virtually all Vanzetti's Italian witnesses.

"So are you still with me?" Rick asked. The entire auditorium became filled with nodding heads, including those of his friends at the lower right.

"Then I'll present two sidebars to this particular trial. (1) Vanzetti never took the stand in his own defense and, if the members of the jury were unbiased, this may have hurt his case. If they were biased, however, it probably would not have made a difference anyway, although consensus holds that, had he testified, the issue of radicalism could not have been prevented from being raised. (2) Two days after the verdict, District Attorney Katzmann relieved Captain Proctor from the responsibility of directing the South Braintree crime. True, he had given innocuous testimony about the shells allegedly taken from Vanzetti's pocket but, by all accounts, the more concrete reason for his dismissal was that he believed Sacco and Vanzetti were innocent. After his later testimony at the joint trial in Dedham, he was overheard in the corridor saying that the Commonwealth had gotten the wrong men.

"On July 1, 1920, the jury, after five hours of deliberation, found Vanzetti guilty of assault with intent to rob and assault with intent to murder. He and his closest friends were stunned. One, a youngster who testified he had been with the defendant the entire morning of the attempted holdup, later said he hadn't realized it at the time, but the verdict was probably intended to influence the outcome of the joint trial that lay ahead.

"On its own merit, the Plymouth affair might have been considered merely another garden variety trial, albeit one with questionably orchestrated evidence and testimony. In this connection, it certainly left deep doubts about proper crime scene investigation, the integrity of scientific evidence, the integrity of expert witnesses and the ethical behavior of the legal professionals involved. These doubts will again be brought into question during the consideration of the joint trial at Dedham. No doubt about it–right?"

Again the nodding, and this time Rick wondered why there weren't more people rubbing the back of their necks.

"No matter how one comes down on the various ethical and procedural issues of the trial at Plymouth, a convicted felon emerged, one who would be serving a 15-year prison term at the time of the cause célèbre in Dedham the following year. Whether the subsequent jury could possibly have been unmoved by the Plymouth verdict is a debate that continues to rage alongside the larger question of innocence or guilt. Additionally, there are those who insist that if a verdict of not guilty had been returned in that small New England town, the joint trial might have never even taken place.

"Now for the Dedham trial. Once again the aligned chronology and relevant locations: Vanzetti's trial for the Bridgewater crime had been held in Plymouth. One year later, the trial of both Vanzetti and Sacco for the South Braintree crimes was held in Dedham, 10 miles south of Boston.

"I'd like to quote a passage from a 1960 article written by Barry Reed, a South Braintree lawyer. The words really anchored the setting for the trial with the following words:

> "On Memorial Day, May 30, 1921, proud warriors of the Grand Old Army, the last remnants of the 2nd and 20th Massachusetts Infantry, who had fought at Fair Oaks and Malvern Hill, stormed Mayre's Heights and held the line at Reseca, stood at attention with veterans of recent wars as Taps drifted over Hyde Park cemetery, the final muster for those who died at Lexington, the Wilderness, Santiago and the Argonne. It was an era of patriotism and chauvinism that this country has never seen since and perhaps will never see again. The day following, within the

dying echo of the bugle, two men, aliens, anarchists and draft dodgers, were to be tried for murder."

"There are those who state unequivocally that the most important component of any trial by jury is the jury itself," Rick continued. "At Dedham, 700 people were summoned to serve as jurors and after more than a month, only seven of the 12 required had been selected. Many had feared retaliation by the Reds or the Black Hand, as the Mafia was then known. The judge, therefore, instructed a sheriff to round up more candidates posthaste. Deputies scoured adjoining towns and also raided a nearby Masonic Lodge, picking persons they deemed representative citizens. The jury had its complement of 12. No Italians were among them."

Rick paused in order to arrive at the proper way to present his further thinking.

"I must ask," he said, "since a jury should represent a cross-section of the community, was not the selection procedure in Dedham prejudicial to begin with, at least with regard to capital punishment? Does the exclusion from juries of those individuals opposed to the death penalty produce juries more likely to execute a defendant?"

He looked at the clock on the wall to his left, then at the audience, then back at the clock, and then at his book. He had determined that he wouldn't continue with such a detailed account of the case and, instead would cut to the chase and reconfigure the balance of his presentation. He would thereby resist an urge to proceed in an all-inclusive fashion, and he so told his audience.

"You know, there was so much to criticize about this case, right from the start. I have a list of irregularities for you, and once again I should say that it may be stuff I've already mentioned but is worth repeating. In other words, it's like a summary:

One— Picking the jury. Those selected had to be in favor

of the death penalty.

Two— Neither Sacco nor Vanzetti owned a car, nor knew how to drive one. How come this never came out?

Three— The police knew the car was headed south. Why wasn't a roadblock set up? They could have phoned ahead.

Four— The important issue of Sacco's cap. It was allegedly found at the crime scene. It was three sizes too small. Had it been planted? Chain of custody, alteration of evidence, false statements—if even there was a cap lying there in the first place. If not, it was found over a day later and could have belonged to any employee going in and out of work.

Five— Four spent shells that were recovered from the crime scene. Three had a right twist. One a left twist. Planted?

Six— The head of the Massachusetts State Police, William Proctor, testified that they were guilty, but then changed his mind. Had there been collusion?

Seven— Some bullets were also recovered from the crime scene. They and the spent shells changed hands many times over a period of a full year, plenty of time for a plant. A chain of custody issue.

Eight— Nothing was done regarding fibers, hair, trace evidence, or shoe prints in a supposed getaway car or at the crime scene. Sloppy or deliberate?

Nine— Several witnesses changed their testimony during and after the trial.

Ten— Judge Thayer, the presiding judge, was heard

saying in public: "They're obviously guilty. Let's prove it now."

Eleven— Prejudicial trial issues. As mentioned, each day, the defendants were marched to court from a nearby prison. They were handcuffed to each other, under heavy guard, and were led past crowds of people. In the courtroom, they were herded into an iron cage that was placed just before the bar–in full view of everyone, including the jury members.

"After six years of appeals, they were executed. What shocked me was the length to which the Commonwealth went to convict two men. And you no doubt recall hearing about the fate of other bullets fired at the crime scene. To this I might add other irregularities, and please forgive me if much of what I say amounts to overlapping: tampering with evidence, like taking the revolver apart; deceit and withholding of evidence, like the serial number of Berardelli's gun; possible switching of the gun barrel or the bullet and shell. And how about a whole host of questions such as: What became of the boxes containing $16,000? The money was never recovered. What happened to it? The cap didn't fit, right? How many bullets were actually test fired? Any inventory of those bullets and their casings. What happened to the others in the getaway car? Any follow-up on them?

"But the most disturbing irregularity was the one dealing with fingerprints. I don't remember the exact quote, but I believe it was Justice Oliver Wendell Holmes who talked of a 'magnetic point' and said that evidence can be attracted to it or repelled by it. The state police had taken prints from the defendants and compared them with those lifted from the Buick, which had been abandoned. Then the police met with the district attorney in his office, but the subject never came up during the trial or later during the appeals. Was this an instance when evidence was repelled from the magnetic point? An instance when the prints didn't match? But why didn't the defense ever ask about it all, for heaven's sake?

"I've said it at least once before, ladies and gentlemen, but after six years of appeals, the two men were executed. Many believe they got the wrong guys–that besides being foreigners, they were political scapegoats.

"I hope I haven't dragged this case out too far. Did I leave anything out that's important? I don't think so. I've given this talk so often that if I had, my heartbeat would have become audible. And I don't think any of you have heard it. In any event, that's the lecture and thank you for listening."

Rick collected his papers and book and slid them into his briefcase. Everyone rose and the applause was deafening. He nodded toward every section. Fran, Leon and Ansel rushed to his side as he was thanking Charles Reagan for the opportunity to speak there. The triad then escorted him up the center aisle and out into a sunny late morning.

I hope the performance was as sunny as it is out here.

He shook his damp shirt loose from his shoulders.

Chapter 15

There wasn't much talk until they sat at a Friendly's and ordered lunch. Finally Rick said, "So what do you think, guys?"

"You covered a lot of ground," Leon said, "and their interest never waned."

"So repeat your approach during the next lectures," Fran said.

Rick looked at Ansel and asked, "What say you, Mr. Driver?"

"I couldn't agree more."

Rick nibbled on a piece of toast, but drank his coffee in three gulps. The others had just finished egg salad sandwiches when he addressed Leon: "But does the way it went measure up to the purpose of giving lectures in the first place?"

"Absolutely … and 'measure up' is a good way of putting it. Let's just measure up for the next ten days. I think the combination of your lectures and your speaking to disaster site people should ward off anything catastrophic."

None of them appeared anxious to leave the restaurant, as if there was more to accomplish there. In fact, they remained in their seats and continued talking to one another. When sightseeing came up, the predominant suggestion for the afternoon was that they should limit it to Boston and nearby Cape Cod.

"But first," Leon said, "why not make your invitational calls for the summit. I assume **we're** invited, but who else should be there?"

"Well, there's histarian Lance Beck; old friend, Paul D'Arneau; Buenos Aires Police Chief Joe Gomez; his receptionist, Carlos; and Fabio Calderone. He's a Mafioso-turned-good-guy. Completely trustworthy. Hmm … that's really only four calls. Joe can take care of Carlos. I thought there'd be more."

"Okay then," Leon said. "There's an empty booth across the way. Get it over with. Make the calls from there. We can wait. Then it's off for us to see the wizard … hmm, where did that come from?"

"*The Wizard of Oz* with Judy Garland," Rick said.

Leon snapped his fingers as though the question had been answered correctly.

Rick slid from their booth and headed across the aisle and Leon said, "Wait … you have their numbers?"

Rick turned and shook his briefcase. "There isn't **anything** I don't have right in here," he said. "There's even a thick folder devoted to Wikipedia accounts of world events and the like."

He returned 20 minutes later and found the other three fellows reading parts of the same newspaper.

"Well?" Leon asked.

"I can't believe it," Rick said.

"You couldn't reach them?"

"No, just the opposite. I reached each one and they'll all be coming."

Should be interesting.

Ansel arranged for a car and did the driving; Rick sat in a back seat. They left Dedham at 1:30 and figured on two hours in Boston followed by a 45-minute drive to the Cape and two hours there.

"You needn't stop everywhere, just slow up now and then," Rick said. "But is it okay for us to stop at **some** places? Look inside a building, for example?"

"Rick, the rest of today belongs to you," Fran said. "You call the shots … we're just along for the ride."

"Thanks, fellas. I'll signal when to stop."

First, they slowed down opposite Fenway Park and could tell by the crowd at its entrances and the distant roar from inside that a ball game was being played. Then they passed by Copley Square, the Museum of Fine Arts, Boston Commons and the Boston Public Library. Rick identified them all.

"Wait," they said in unison. "How did you know their names?"

Rick held up his briefcase with one hand and a small folded map of Boston and Cape Cod in another. "It even has small pictures and written descriptions and dates," he said. "I looked the map over yesterday. And I stuffed more info about Cape Cod in this briefcase of mine. Getting heavier and heavier. It's really a walking library."

It wasn't long before they reached Harvard Yard and Rick asked for a stop. Ansel backed into the only parking space he could find as Rick was commenting: "That's Wadsworth House over there. And that's the Office for Scholarly Communication, the Widener Library, University Hall, and the famous Memorial Church." He was pointing wildly with delight and the other two seemed to be enjoying his reactions.

"It's the Memorial Church that I'm really interested in. Listen to what it says here."

> The Memorial Church of Harvard University, part of a vibrant interfaith network of Harvard, is an interdenominational Protestant church in the midst of Harvard Yard that serves as a place of spiritual refuge to the entire community.
>
> "MemChurch", as it is called, stands opposite Widener Library as a visible reminder of the historical and spiritual heritage that has sustained Harvard for nearly four centuries. We have a saying at Memorial Church: "Everyone may not belong to MemChurch, but MemChurch belongs to everyone!"

Leon said, "I've heard about this church. Not only is it a place for worship but it also features a theme that changes weekly."

"A theme?" Fran asked.

"Yes," Rick said. "This week's is how a current event can relate to religion."

"And what's this week's current event?" Leon asked.

"Climate change."

"And its relationship to religion. Why's that?"

"Because the Pope commented on it just this past week," Rick answered.

"Well don't lecture us, Rick, but give us an idea what this is all about, according to your map there. You said it's got descriptions and dates. It's a map of all maps … I'll vouch for that."

"Okay. It talks here about NIMBA. That's 'Not In My Backyard'. Says that too few states have industrial wind turbines. That these turbines require no coal, natural gas or uranium to generate energy. It mentions global warming and carbon emissions as bad for health, and that something should be done about it. It also asks if climate change is something that influences ocean waters. For example, is it somehow related to the deaths of so many whales . . . from Mexico to Alaska?"

"And the Pope …"

"He expressed the same view."

"So what you're saying, Rick, is that all of this is an example of the historical and spiritual heritage that you already read to us. And it changes weekly?"

"I didn't say that. It's what's printed and, yes, it's a theme that changes weekly. But enough's enough. Let's go inside."

He led the way from their car into the church's vestibule. It was nearly as wide as the church itself and was surrounded on two sides with bright, stain-glassed windows, below which were rows of flowered plants and lighted candles. The door to the inside was partially ajar and one could see an altar, two pulpits and numerous pews half-filled with kneeling students.

Rick whispered, "I'm told that some students spend as much time in here as they do in the classrooms."

Off to the side of the vestibule was a gentleman writing at a desk. He wore dark clothes and a white collar.

"Probably the rector," Leon whispered.

"Probably," Rick whispered back, "but let's not disturb him or the students. Let's just move on."

The remaining time in Boston covered more slow-ups but no further stops. Rick pointed out the Massachusetts Institute of Technology and, during a three-mile drive along Freedom Trail, they observed many of the city's historic monuments. Then there was Boston Common … America's oldest park … the State House, the Paul Revere House and Faneuil Hall.

Rick spoke up: "Funny name … it says here … but it's known as the 'cradle of liberty'. On its fourth floor is the Ancient and Honorable Artillery Museum, with weaponry, uniforms, and paintings of significant battles."

He unfolded his map and continued: "This says a lot in a side insert, and I could go straight into boredom if I picked it apart, so why don't I just read the whole insert? And you might be interested … there's a famous American TV show mentioned at the end." There was no disagreement in the car. "The whole thing is taken *From PlanetWare."* Ansel slowed down as Rick read:

> One of Boston's most beautiful neighborhoods right in the center of the city on the south side of Beacon Hill has traditionally been the home of Boston's "old money" families, known locally as "Brahmins". Well-kept brick homes in Federal and Greek Revival styles line its tree-shaded streets, and at its heart is Louisburg Square, where homes face onto a leafy private park. Author Louisa May Alcott lived here from 1880 to 1888. The Nichols House Museum, a Federal-style home by Boston architect Charles Bulfinch, shows how Beacon Hill's upper class residents lived and is filled with collections of 16th to 19th century furnishings and decorative arts. At the western foot of Beacon Hill, Charles Street is lined with boutiques and shops that have traditionally catered to the neighborhood and are popular with visitors as well. Beyond Charles Street, facing the public garden, The Bull and Finch, established in 1969, inspired the popular television program, *Cheers.*

"So that's Boston," Rick said. "The Cape is next … about 45 minutes from here." He checked his watch. "Should arrive around four. We begin at the Cape Cod Canal and then travel the 60-mile peninsula to Provincetown. All in favor say 'Aye'." Rick answered first, a smidge before the other two. "The ayes have it," he announced as if the outcome had been questionable.

Ten minutes later, he asked, “Should we sit still and be quiet? Not much scenery out there, but this map touches on what will change in a half hour or so. Should I go ahead and read?”

Leon said, “Aye-aye, sir,” and chuckled.

“Well, it’s a *Travel Planner* version of what it’s picked out to highlight. Says it covers beaches, pretty towns, nature reserves, music, theater, and historic monuments. I’ll read, word-for-word. Then when we get there, we can see how close it came to what we actually experience. We have to allow for the fact that we’ll be driving up its center road - - - I think Route 6. And I know one place I’d like to stop.”

“Where?”

“Provincetown at the upper tip. Mainly to climb its famous tower. But for now, here we go”.

> Cape Cod has lots to see and do, but few go there without enjoying its wonderful beaches. The Nantucket Sound beaches along the southern shore and Atlantic beaches up the eastern shore offer broad swaths of sand and, in some places, good surfing. Beaches along the Cape’s northern and western shores, facing Cape Cod Bay, are less eye-catching but usually great for families and for those who prefer warmer water temperatures, less surf, and smaller crowds. There are even freshwater beaches on a number of its glacial ponds.
>
> As for the pretty towns, they are among New England’s most popular vacation destinations. The Cape is not a *modern* resort destination–it has been inhabited for millennia! The first European settlers arrived in the 1630s, and most of its towns boast historic houses, churches, cemeteries and other monuments to the centuries. In short, it’s long on old New England charm.
>
> Sandwich calls itself “the prettiest town on the Cape.” It’s certainly the oldest, and has the fine museums and historic houses to prove it.

Falmouth, with its picture-perfect New England village green, fine old town hall, library and other public buildings, has a dignity and class that's in pleasant contrast to the more commercial beach resorts.

Chatham, filled with graceful old trees, fine mansions, palatial inns, and a sturdy lighthouse, is perhaps the most refined of the Cape's major resort towns, drawing visitors from around the country, the continent, and the world.

Provincetown, with lots of sand and beach, gaudy commercial street strolling and shopping, whole neighborhoods of cozy inns, hides its history a bit, but this is where the pilgrims first set foot in the New World, as the lofty Pilgrim's Monument proclaims.

Hyannis isn't the prettiest of towns but it's the largest of the seven villages of Barnstable and, as the commercial and transportation hub of the entire Cape, it sits right at its beginning. Because of this, many refer to Hyannis as the "Capital of the Cape". It contains a majority of the Barnstable town offices and two important shopping districts: the historic downtown Main Street and the Route 132 Commercial District, including Cape Cod Mall and a hospital that is the largest on the peninsula.

Hyannis is a major tourist destination and the primary ferry and general aviation link for passengers and freight to Nantucket Island. Hyannis also provides secondary passenger access to the island of Martha's Vineyard.

And let's not forget Dennis, Brewster, Orleans, Yarmouth, Harwich, Eastham, Wellfleet and Truro. But be on the lookout for great white sharks in the latter two towns.

Next we have the Nature Reserves. These include the National Seashore, Nickerson State Park, Monomoy National Wildlife Refuge, and the Museum of Natural History.

Then there's Music and Theater. Very interesting. There's the Provincetown Playhouse that's active all summer; the Cape Cod Melody Tent in Hyannis that features top-name popular vocalists in concert; the Cape Playhouse in Dennis that has famous actors in timely productions; Cape Rep in Brewster with semi-pro productions of high quality; and the Monomoy Theater in Chatham with a stock company from Ohio University.

Finally, there are historic monuments like the Pilgrim Monument in Provincetown, near where the pilgrims first stepped on American soil, and the French Cable Station Museum where the first transatlantic telephone cable came ashore.

That should do it.

"In traveling the length of the Cape, let's see if we pass some of these places," Rick suggested.

"It mentions great white sharks," Fran said. "It should have included dolphin and whale watching. That's big-time out here."

They drove slowly and quietly up route 6 and, fifteen-minutes later, agreed that from their vantage point, all towns looked the same. They noted very few signs, very few stop signs, very few traffic lights – all of which would have given them a chance for clarity – as Rick pointed out. Nonetheless, he sat forward and looked out right and left windows.

"Not too instructive," he said. "But that's okay. Provincetown is coming up soon."

They reached its outskirts and Ansel drove even more slowly as they encountered the pilgrims' first landing park; an impressive-looking lighthouse; part of the national seashore with life-guard protection; and fishermen hard at work along a wide beach front. Across the street was the Pilgrim Monument. Ansel parked the car not far from its entrance and they all piled out.

"I'm climbing to the top. Any of you joining me?" Rick asked.

The others tugged at an ear as if on cue and Leon said, "No. We'll look over the museum at the base there. You go ahead. You're better at climbing that many steps."

"It's 116 steps and 252 feet," Rick said proudly as he watched them amble toward the museum. "And the tallest all-granite structure in the States."

It took only a few minutes to complete the climb - - - with two brief stops on the way up. At the top, he looked out and around breathtaking views of Provincetown and nearly the rest of the Cape. He imagined that on a clear day, one would be able to see all the way to Sandwich and the entrance to Cape Cod Canal.

That was enough; he did it; it was all he wanted. The trip back down was mostly two steps at a time and when he reached the triad, he said, "Well worth it. What a view! I just wanted to feel that sensation, and it was better than I expected."

In the car, Ansel said, "Now we take a commercial plane to Paris for the Eiffel Tower, the Arc de Triomphe and Napoleon's sarcophagus. That right, Rick?"

"Right. Three days there. So it's back to Boston and the Logan International Airport. There's just no other way to do it," Rick said.

"And you don't mind flying?"

"No, I like it."

"You do?"

"Sure. It's where I can catch up on sleep. Can't do it in a car. And sleep means dreams. I like that too … if they're not nightmares."

"After Paris, are you planning on three more full lectures?" Leon asked.

"No. I'll do Lindy as a full one . . . then maybe cut the other two short. Does that sound reasonable?"

"Reasonable."

They all ate filet mignon at a local restaurant, preceded by a single glass of white wine. They spoke little but each appeared anxious to fly the Atlantic and reach the Eiffel Tower. It would be the beginning of their role in disaster site security.

It was, therefore, back to Boston where they boarded a commercial plane at Logan Airport and flew a distance of over four thousand miles, landing at the Charles de Gaulle Airport in Paris. It took over seven hours. Sleep? Rick did. Dream? Rick did. But not until he satisfied what had been lingering in his mind for some time - - - a better understanding of terrorism. He opened his briefcase and, from the Wikipedia folder, withdrew four sheets of paper with the heading, "Terrorism Is Everywhere." Although he realized that the subject had nothing to do with what he was facing on a grand scale . . . not yet anyway . . . and although he recalled his long ago intention of reading about it in detail, he now felt neglectful over not doing so. Not even some of it. Also related to his current thinking was a line that an INTERPOL executive had expressed - - - that terrorist groups often band together.

Go ahead. Ease your mind. Read about
it now. Perhaps terrorism ***will*** *apply.*

It was just another one of his feelings. Maybe after reading the article, he'd come up with an answer. He had once heard the term, "analysis paralysis". Was *that* it? And would it make a difference by reading it . . . or not reading it? One thing he was most proud of was his ability to extract the essentials from long articles about nearly anything, and to him this was more than "anything". He also believed that, later on, when some essentials would require his full attention to a consideration of the Mafia and the Nazis, terrorism would have to be considered.

So he read it, extracting brief statements that dealt mostly with definitions:

- - - - -

> Terrorism is, in the broadest sense, the use of intentionally indiscriminate violence as a means to create terror among masses of people; or fear to achieve a religious or political aim. It is used in this regard primarily to refer to violence during peacetime or in the context of war against non-combatants (mostly civilians and neutral military personnel.) The terms "terrorist" and "terrorism" originated during the French Revolution of the late 18th century but gained mainstream popularity in the 1970s in news reports and books covering the conflicts in Northern Ireland, the Basque Country and Palestine. The increased use of suicide attacks from the 1980s onward was typified by the September 11 attacks in New York City and Washington, D.C. in 2001.

> There are different definitions of terrorism. Terrorism is a charged term. It is often used with the connotation of something that is "morally wrong". Governments and non-state groups use the term to abuse or denounce opposing groups. Varied political organizations have been accused of using terrorism to achieve their objectives. These organizations include right-wing and left-wing political organizations, nationalist groups, religious groups, revolutionaries and ruling governments.

> Legislation declaring terrorism a crime has been

adopted in many states. When terrorism is perpetrated by nation-states, it is not considered terrorism by the state perpetrating it, making legality a largely grey-area issue. There is no consensus as to whether or not terrorism should be considered as a war crime.

The terms "terrorism" and "terrorist" gained renewed currency in the 1970s as a result of the Israeli-Palestinian conflict, the Northern Ireland conflict, the Basque conflict, and the operations of groups such as the Red Army Faction. The topic came further to the fore after the 1983 Beirut barracks bombing and again after the 2001 September attacks and the 2002 Bali bombings.

There are over 109 different definitions of terrorism. American political philosopher Michael Walzer in 2002 wrote: "Terrorism is the deliberate killing of innocent people, at random, to spread fear through a whole population and force the hand of its political leaders."

Experts disagree about whether terrorism is wrong by definition or just wrong as a matter of fact; they disagree about whether terrorism should be defined in terms of its aims, or its methods, or both, or neither; and they disagree about whether or not states can perpetrate terrorism.

In November 2004, a Secretary-General of the United States report described terrorism as any act "intended to cause death or serious bodily harm to civilians or non-combatants with the purpose of intimidating a population or compelling a government or an international organization to do or abstain from doing any act." The international community has been slow to formulate a universally agreed, legally binding definition of this crime. These difficulties arise from the fact that the term "terrorism" is politically and emotionally charged.

A brief to the Australian parliament stated: The International Community has never succeeded in developing an accepted comprehensive definition of terrorism. During the 1970s and 1980s, the United Nations attempts to define the term floundered.

They were mainly due to differences of opinion between various members about the use of violence in the context of conflicts over national liberation and self-liberation.

Since 1994, the United States General Assembly has repeatedly condemned terrorist attacks, using the following political description of terrorism: "criminal acts intended or calculated to provoke a state of terror in the public, or in a group of persons or particular persons for political purposes.

They are in any circumstance unjustifiable, whatever the considerations of a political, philosophical, ideological, racial, ethnic, religious or any other nature that may be involved to justify them.

"International terrorism" means activities with the following three characteristics: One—Involve violent acts or acts dangerous to human life that violate federal or state law.

Two– Appear to be intended to intimidate or coerce

a civilian population; to influence the policy of a government by intimidation or coercion; or to affect the conduct of a government by mass destruction, assassination, or kidnapping.

And three–Occur primarily outside the territorial jurisdiction of the U.S., or transcend national boundaries in terms of the means by which they are accomplished, the persons they appear intended to intimidate or coerce, or the locale in which their perpetrators operate or seek asylum.

Since 9/11, there has been a five-fold increase in deaths from terrorist attacks. The majority of incidents over the past several years can be tied to groups with a religious agenda. Before 2000, it was nationalist separatist terrorist organizations such as the IRA and Chechen rebels who were behind the most attacks. The number of incidents from nationalist separatist groups has remained relatively stable in the years since, while religious extremism has grown.

The prevalence of Islamic groups in Iraq, Afghanistan, Pakistan, Nigeria and Syria is the main driver behind these trends.

Four of the terrorist groups that have been most active since 2001are Boko Haram, Al Qaeda, the Taliban and ISIL. These groups have been most active in Iraq, Afghanistan, Pakistan, Nigeria, and Syria. Eighty percent of all deaths from terrorism occurred in one of these five countries.

- - - - -

In 2015, the Southern Poverty Law Center released a report on terrorism in the United States. The report found

> that during that period, "More people have been killed in America by non-Islamic domestic terrorists than jihadists." (Some) believe that whites of European descent can be traced back to the "Lost Tribes of Israel" and many consider Jews to be the Satanic offspring of Eve and the serpent. This group has committed hate crimes, bombings and other acts of terrorism. Its influence ranges from the Ku Klux Klan and neo-Nazi groups to the anti-government militia and sovereign citizen movements.

I may read this again later–
in connection with the Mafia and Nazis.

One other thing crossed Rick's mind before he dozed off: whatever happened to Scar-face? Is he still following us? Is he aboard this plane?

He got up and walked the aisle–back and forth–and spotted neither him nor anyone else who looked suspicious.

Chapter 16

Paris, France

April 15

Their plane touched down at the airport and Ansel hailed a cab. It didn't take long to reach the Eiffel Tower. Rick had seen it before but never up close and never in conjunction with warning Parisian police about possible bombings.

Only Leon, who lived nearby, was familiar with its interior. Once inside at about 9 a.m., he volunteered to show the others around before they got down to business. He first pointed out the recently installed bulletproof glass walls and metal barriers that surrounded the Tower.

"They're three meters high and are strong enough to stop a truck on a suicide mission," he said. "In fact, the whole country is on a state of high alert since a series of terror attacks in 2015 left hundreds dead."

Rick said, "I can't believe I just read about terrorism and here's a good example of it."

"But let me show you around," Leon continued. He purchased four tickets to use a lift that led up to the Tower's three levels. And after showing identification that he was involved in police work, they received permission to stop at each level, look around, and get back on another lift. But this came after they walked through an eight-foot wide promenade that ran around the outside of the first level.

He pointed out two restaurants, including *le Jules Verne*, a gourmet restaurant on the second level; a 4-room apartment; a theater; a small auditorium; a door with a sign that read "Visitors' Office" in both French and English; two museums; some laboratories; and a champagne bar at the top level.

When they returned to ground level, Leon said, "See that closed metal door over there? Some of their security force sits in there monitoring all levels electronically. Other officers just roam around outside. I'm sure you noticed them … male and female … they wear police clothing with stripes, badges, and pistols in holsters strapped to their waists. I'm told the more visible they are, the more crime is prevented."

"So let's pick one out," Rick said, "and explain why we're here." They stopped an officer and found that he both understood and spoke English.

"I'm from the United States," Rick said, "and we're here for a reason other than sightseeing."

He then spoke of their backgrounds and gave a detailed account of the bombing threats and why they had been made. The officer didn't hesitate to record Rick's words in a hand-held device.

"So could you please pass this on and possibly institute even more protection than you already have?" Rick asked. He deliberately tried to sound as if time was of the essence.

"Monsieur … it *will* be done, and thank you," the officer stated as he shook Rick's hand and raced off.

"Some kind of Tower," Ansel said.

"Yeah," Fran added. "And it's the answer to a myth."

"What's that?" Rick asked.

"That the Statue of Liberty is the most photographed monument in the world, not the Eiffel Tower. But the truth is that *this* tower is the most photographed. Plain and simple, the statue's greater popularity is a myth."

"Hmm," Rick said, stroking his chin. "Reminds me of the talk I once composed and gave to a group of college students back home … 'The Myth of Mythology'."

"I've heard it myself and it's interesting," Fran said. "Maybe you should give it here."

"But why?" Rick asked.

"Because it will call attention to our being here. The introducer could explain that the four of us are part of a U.S. security force, and we've been dispatched here on request."

"And where would I give it?" Rick asked.

Leon entered the conversation. "Right here in their auditorium. It's where people congregate to watch a documentary or hear a lecture. It's always packed, from dawn till midnight, and I could inquire if you could give it."

"But I talk about things familiar to Americans, probably not to others. I'm not sure others would understand what I'd be saying."

"I'll bet the majority of them are from the U.S. and England, and that all of them would understand most of it," Leon said. "How long is it timewise?"

"Ten minutes . . . tops."

"You have it in your briefcase?"

"Why not? Everything else is in it."

"Good. So, no problem," Leon said. "You can give it before we leave for Napoleon's sarcophagus. I'll check at the Visitors Office."

Jeez, all I do is read articles,
read bulletins and give lectures.

Leon checked and got the immediate attention of a Joel Jantot. Leon was greeted with open arms when he explained who he was; why he and his associates were there; what Rick would be talking about; and why he'd be giving such a talk in the first place.

- - - - -

Within five minutes, Joel addressed a full house. "We have a special treat for you," he said. Reading from a card, he gave an accurate account of what Leon had said. The clapping nearly drowned him out. "So I give you Rick Chandler."

"Thank you, Joel," Rick began. He stood at the foot of a small, raised auditorium, opened a folder and glanced at the soiled first page of a manuscript he had placed on a podium.

"I'm about to take you on a ride filled with mythological information and examples. Especially examples. Almost all of what I'm about to say is what I'll read from something I wrote years ago. I titled it, 'The Myth of Mythology'. In addition to that, I took some of what I'll present to you from the words of the famous mythology writers, Edith Hamilton and Kenneth C. Davis.

"What I mean by 'The Myth of Mythology' is that there's a general misconception about myths arising simply to entertain … yesteryear's equivalent of *The Sopranos*, let's say. But that's only **part** of the story.

"Myths are older than ancient. They predate recorded history, science, and even religion. They lead us back to a time when the world was young and people had a connection with the earth and nature– with trees and flowers and hills and seas–unlike anything we ourselves can feel. In other words, through myths, we can retrace the paths from today's civilized man, who lives so far from nature, to man who lived so close to it.

"The link between myths and nature is only *one* aspect of what mythology is all about.

"The general public has, by and large, put its own spin on them–most people dismissing mythology as a pack of silly stories that were, one, made up and two, insignificant. That's only partly correct. Made up? *Yes*. Insignificant? *No*.

"For myths were explanations made long ago–before science came into vogue–to understand what people were witnessing. Things like lightning, and changes of season, and love, and hate, and death.

"And they used gods and heroes and monsters and demons and witches to tell the tales. It was the best that humans could do at the time, because they couldn't provide scientific explanations for any of this.

"Kenneth Davis once wrote, "Natural events, as well as human behavior, all came to be understood through tales of gods, goddesses, and heroes. Thunder, earthquakes, eclipses, rain, and the success of crops were all due to the intervention of powerful gods. The Greeks believed at one time that all the world's evils were trapped inside a box. When this box was opened by the first woman, all the world's misfortunes escaped before she was able to close the lid. They called her Pandora. 'Opening Pandora's box'."

"So myths can be a powerful business–and that's one reason they've been around for so long–since a time when the world was full of danger, mystery, and wonder. As if it isn't now!

"In some of my lectures to date, I've talked largely about present day mysteries, true crime and forensic science. That's to be expected because they're what I write about, too.

"But now, for what I guess you'd call a dramatic change of pace, I'd like to elaborate for just a few minutes on the *importance* of mythology … something I've always been intrigued with; never fully understood; and only recently appreciated in terms of its place in the history of civilization. And I'll confine my remarks to three areas:

–the impact of myths on our culture.

–their role in history

–and the differences between myths, legends and fables.

"So let's start with number one: the impact of myths. Not only those of Greece and Rome, but also those about Norse gods such as Thor, and Egyptian gods who inspired the pyramids. These myths and those from many other civilizations continue to fascinate millions of people, many of whom do not label the whole process as mythology.

"Some call it 'Going to the Movies.' For example, consider: *The Lord of the Rings* trilogy; *Matrix; Finding Nemo; X-Men; The Terminator trilogy; Troy; E.T.* (which was really an animated version of Hercules); and above all, *Star Wars*. All these draw on mythic themes.

"Think about this one. There are ancient tales of so-called trickster gods who were greedy, mischievous, and evil–kind of like the Joker in *Batman*, really.

"Often they took animal form, like the African Rabbit or Native American Coyote. Sounds like Bugs Bunny and his nemesis Wile E. Coyote to me!

"And it's not just the entertainment industry that's capitalized on myths. How about Halloween–a modern version of an ancient mythical celebration?

"In fact, many of the trappings of Christmas, including Christmas trees, wreaths, mistletoe, holly and ivy, are borrowed from ancient traditions of northern Europe in which the evergreen symbolized the hope for new life in the dead of winter.

"To get another gauge of the impact of myths:

(A) Check the calendar: the names of all the days and months derive from Greek, Roman and Norse mythology.

(B) Check the planets in our solar system: all except earth are named for Roman gods.

(C) Check our language, which is loaded with words from our mythic past: Do you buy books from Amazon.com? Are you wearing a pair of Nikes? How about words like panacea, panic, hypnosis, morphine, leprechaun, typhoon, hurricane?

"Myths certainly surround us in literature, in pop culture, and in our language."

Rick stopped abruptly and said, "I can tell that you're paying attention, but I'd understand if any of you might leave because things don't sink in. Or if you might otherwise take a nap." His last comment produced a series of quiet chuckles, and he couldn't remember whether or not he had made a stab at this kind of humor before.

"But let's carry on. First was the impact of myths. Now is its history. They play a serious role here. In wartime Japan, for example, they were the source of the national Shinto religion, for the Japanese emperor Hirohito was supposedly descended from a Shinto sun goddess.

"This devotion to the emperor led to the use of the notorious kamikaze pilots with their dynamite-laden planes and their suicide crashes into U.S. warships. It was a myth/religion that drove those young men–and an entire nation–with fanatical devotion to its emperor.

"Even during Napoleon's era, King Louis XVI ruled by thinking he had divine authority. His was a reign that was generally considered oppressive and that played a role in the outbreak of the French Revolution.

"And, it doesn't end there, as history has shown. How about 9/11? The notion of dying a martyr's death and gaining entrance to a paradise with promise of virgins is an enticing idea that continues to drive terrorists who strap explosives to their bodies, or drive cars filled with explosives, or fly hijacked jets into buildings. They're motivated by beliefs whose roots stretch back centuries ago–the idea of warriors gaining access to paradise through early death is certainly not exclusive to any one mythology or faith.

“We might even say that one person’s myth is another person’s religion.

“The history of myth, in other words, goes hand in hand with the history of civilization. Stop and think about ‘ancient civilization’. What does it mean? The wheel. Writing. Bronze. Glass. Fireworks. Paper. Noodles. In-door plumbing. Beer.

“These are only a few of the pleasant and delightful creations devised by the ancient civilizations of Egypt, China, Greece, India, Rome, and others.

“These civilizations also gave us astronomy, democracy, and philosophy.

“Now you’re probably thinking, ‘Wait a minute. All you’re doing is listing various discoveries.’ Yes, I am, but here’s the important point. These same ancients ‘invented’ the myths that grew hand in hand with the discoveries of their civilizations, making it impossible to separate one from the other. That is to separate out the myths from history itself.

“So while the importance of myths may seem less obvious than that of the wheel, writing, or a mug of beer, these old stories are still a dominant force in our lives today. They remain alive in our literature, our language, the theater, dreams, psychology, and various religions.

“In a way, then, myths helped *make* civilization.

“Now just a word about the meaning of ‘myth’. It’s derived from the Greek word *mythos*, meaning ‘story’. And it was Plato who coined the word ‘mythology’ more than 2,000 years ago.

“And to repeat myself but to say it in a different way: myths began so that humans could explain and describe the world they could see as well as the world they only imagined existed–that is, the world they could *not* see.

"I'm talking long before science envisioned the Big Bang. Long before philosophers reasoned or sought enlightenment. Or Jesus walked the shores of the Sea of Galilee. Long before there was a bible or a Koran. Long before Darwin proposed natural selection. Long before we could know the age of a rock and before men walked on the moon.

"They explained:

–How Earth was created

–Where life came from

–Why the stars shine at night and the seasons change

–Why there was sex

–Why there was evil

–Why people died and where they went when they did.

In short, myths were a very human way to explain *everything*.

"Finally, number three: What are the differences among myth, legend, fable, folktale, and fairy tale? They're not the same.

–Myths usually involve gods–supernatural beings who actually controlled events in the natural world.

–Legends are really an early form of history–stories about historical figures, usually humans, not gods. Most Americans, for instance, understand the story of George Washington and the cherry tree. A legend.

–Fables are simple, usually brief, fictitious stories, typically teaching a moral. In many fables, the moral is usually told at the end, in the form of a proverb. Often, they feature animals

> that speak and act like humans, as in the most famous examples–those attributed to Aesop in *Aesop's Fables*–such as 'The Tortoise and the Hare' in which slow and steady wins the race or 'The Grasshopper and the Ant' in which a fun-loving but lazy grasshopper plays while the ant dutifully stores away food for the winter.

"Related to fables are folktales, which in turn are related to fairy tales. Another famous collection is *Grimm's Fairy Tales*, which includes *Hansel and Gretel; Little Red Riding Hood; Snow White;* and *Sleeping Beauty*. Many of these were drawn from much older, mythic sources.

"So it is that the myths of every culture include all of the other 'stories'–that is legends, fables, folk and fairy tales. It's really been a neat arrangement … I believe one that's given us a sweeping and stimulating view of the world.

"Thank you all for listening."

Chapter 17

The taxi ride to the Hôtel des Invalides didn't take long. The driver chose a route along the Avenue de Suffren, then left onto the Avenue de la Motte Prequet. Leaving his passengers off, he said in broken English, "He will not answer you, but say hello to Napoleon." The comment generated loud laughter, especially from Rick, who increased the tip he had planned. But he accompanied the overall payment with a request that took the others by surprise.

He peeked at his wristwatch and said, "We have plenty of time, so before you go could you do us a favor?"

"Oui."

"The Champs-Élysées is so beautiful. I've traveled it before but I'd like to see it again. Could you drive us up there … regular speed … then turn around and drive slowly back to here? I'll pay you extra, of course."

Rick aimed a smile at the others and said, "That okay, fellas?"

The brief silence was broken by Leon who said, "Oui, good thought."

The other two nodded.

The driver agreed and as he began to drive in the direction of the Arc de Triomphe, Rick entertained fond memories of his past visit to the area. Many of the memories stood out, but just as many had become unclear. He knew that the road was a little over a mile long, ran from the

Place de la Concorde in the east, and ended at the Arc de Triomphe, the third of the sites to be visited–after the Hôtel des Invalides. He also knew that Napoleon came into the picture for two reasons: (1) the Arc was built to honor his military victories and (2) his body was housed in the sarcophagus at Invalides.

The taxi turned around and slowly headed back east. The sights were indeed impressive and, as if he had become part of the sightseeing, the driver pointed out and identified a park that contained the Grand Palais, the Petit Palais and the Théâtre Marigny. He said that the street they were on is the most famous one in Paris. That its breadth is spectacular, its sidewalks wide, and its many cafés, théâtres and shops attract thousands of people weekly. "They come to eat and shop, but also to see and to be seen," he said.

They arrived at the street's ending–Rond Point–where Rick commented on their passing by shady chestnut trees and sidewalks that were colorfully bordered by flower beds. "I can even smell the pretty flowers," he said.

The taxi driver swerved south and parked directly in front of the Hôtel des Invalides. He accepted Rick's tip, saluted each man and, in driving off, said "Good luck" as if he were an American.

They entered a door marked Dôme des Invalides and just inside began reading a plaque that was attached to a side wall:

> Hôtel des Invalides is a complex of buildings in where you are now - - - the 7th arrondissement of Paris, containing museums and monuments, all relating to the military history of France, as well as a hospital and a retirement home for war veterans.
>
> Included is this Dôme des Invalides, a large former church that contains the burial tomb for Napoleon Bonaparte.

"What's your take on Napoleon?" Rick asked Leon.

"Mixed feelings."

"That's the common opinion, but you've got to admit to various good things about him. We should discuss it some time."

"We should."

The others agreed.

They returned to the reading:

> The tomb is often referred to as his sarcophagus. It consists of a casket within and a scrolled cover, made of red porphyry, a variety of granite, rising high toward a double cupola and pendentives of the Dôme. An elaborate bronze door leading to the sarcophagus is flanked by two colossal bronze figures that bear symbols of imperial power on a cushion: the crown, the sword, the globe and the hand of justice.
>
> At the base of the sarcophagus is a multicolored, star-shaped mosaic recalling Napoleon's eight most famous triumphs: Rivoli, the Pyramids, Marengo, Austerlitz, Lena, Friedland, Wagram, and Moskowa. And circling around are twelve winged statues in Carrara marble, symbolizing victory.
>
> Within various recesses, at two levels and not far from the sarcophagus, are several paintings that evoke themes defined during the reign of Louis XIV; that celebrate the Catholic religion; that show angels holding the symbols of the religious and warrior monarchy; and that highlight a shield with the coat of arms of France.

They entered the Dôme cautiously and without invitation. It appeared that scores of visitors were trying to lower their echoing comments. Almost immediately, a young man approached them saying, “Welcome, gentlemen. My name is Chester Knight and I’m the police officer here.” His smile looked sincere.

He was neatly dressed in a gray police uniform with a revolver at his waist and a large medallion pinned to his left chest. It contained a photograph of Napoleon.

“Thank you, officer, and we won’t take up too much of your time. I’m Rick Chandler and my associates here are Francis Moreau, Leon Cassell and Ansel Stewart. We’re from the United States and we’re here on assignment . . . on an important mission.”

“The States?” Knight said while shaking their hands. “That’s where I’m originally from. New Jersey.”

“Well, I’ll be,” Rick said. “We’re headed there next … after a short stop at the Arc.”

He then detailed the background for their visit and requested increased security there and throughout all sections of Invalides.

“I’ll get right to it,” the officer said. “I’ll start by notifying my counterparts in the other sections. I do have to commend you all for taking on this responsibility. Sounds like the two ‘D’s - - - daring and dangerous.”

“I suppose both,” Rick said, “but the solution is not to think about it very often.”

At the door, he and the officer exchanged phone numbers.

- - - - -

It was 10:45 when they left Invalides and it took hardly any time to reach the Arc de Triomphe. Rick was well aware of its features and of its purpose in French history … honoring those who fought and died for France in the French Revolutionary and Napoleonic Wars. Names of all French victories and generals were thus inscribed on its inner and outer surfaces. A huge structure, it was located at the right bank of the Seine and at the center of twelve radiating avenues.

Two tall female police officers were leaning against a narrow elevated booth, and although they were about 50 yards apart, they stood at attention as the four men arrived on the scene. The officers came together and, after introductions, Rick once again outlined the necessity for adding increased security there, just as he had at the Eiffel Tower and at Invalides.

The two officers moved off to the side and whispered a few words to one another. Then returning to face Rick, one of them said - - - in only slightly broken English - - - that reinforcements would soon be there. Rick thought the word "reinforcements" was impressive. Not "increased security" but "reinforcements". He believed that such a word was more applicable to the military than to a commemorative structure. But then again, he understood that the Arc was a monument that celebrated *military exploits and victories.* This led to a further thought about a 1945 postage stamp he possessed. It showed the Arc in the background and depicted victorious American troops marching down the Champs-Élysées and U.S. airplanes flying overhead in 1944.

He had also read that beneath the Arc's vault was the Tomb of the Unknown Soldier from World War 1, and that all military parades had avoided marching through the actual arch. The route taken was up to the arch and then around its side, out of respect for the tomb and its symbolism.

That in the early 1960s, U.S. President John F. Kennedy and First Lady Jacqueline Kennedy paid their respects at the Tomb, accompanied by French President Charles de Gaulle. And that after the 1963 assassination of President Kennedy, Mrs. Kennedy remembered the eternal flame at the Arc and requested that an eternal flame be placed next to her husband's grave at the Arlington National Cemetery in Virginia.

Rick thanked the officers and asked one of them about a good place to have lunch. She said, "Every visitor asks us that. And by now, I can describe it in my sleep. You know what I mean? It's *Le Procope*. Their patrons have included Benjamin Franklin and the philosopher Voltaire, who is said to have consumed 40 cups of his favorite mixture of coffee and chocolate every day. And the young Napoleon would leave his hat there as security while he went searching for the money to pay his bill. But please don't tell any of his living relatives that I told you this."

The meals hadn't yet been served before Fran offered what a connoisseur of fine food once said to him: that of all the cuisine in all the world, the best for sure is Parisian. They couldn't verify it, for their lunch was scanty and quick by choice. It seemed that their collective minds were on something else.

Chapter 18

The remaining afternoon was upon them. It was twelve-forty. They discussed their options: take a canal trip, head for New Jersey, go see Notre-Dame, or do nothing. Notre-Dame won easily but only on condition that they wouldn't linger too long around any of its distinctive attractions. Nor would they rush things. Somewhere in-between. Leon suggested that they read as many plaques as possible, "for there won't be any guides pointing things out."

Rick found a brief description of the cathedral in his briefcase. Some time ago, he had extracted it from a broader *Wikipedia* article. He read the brief paragraph aloud:

> Notre-Dame de Paris, meaning "Our Lady of Paris," is a medieval Catholic cathedral on the Île de la Cité in the 4th arrondissement of Paris. The cathedral is consecrated to the Virgin Mary and is considered to be one of the finest examples of French Gothic architecture. Its pioneering use of the rib vault and flying buttress, its enormous and colorful rose windows, as well as the naturalism and abundance of its sculptural decoration set it apart from the earlier Romanesque style. Major components that make Notre-Dame stand out include one of the world's largest organs and its immense church bells.

They approached its main entrance and upon entering, beheld plaque after plaque on the walls – as far ahead as they could see.

“Remember what Leon advised,” Rick whispered. ‘Read them all because we’ll have no guide.’ From here, they appear concise anyway. Let’s hope so.”

Plaques surrounded them, but their immediate view took in a high-vaulted central nave looking down toward a huge transept, a choir and a high altar. Close by, a first plaque read:

> Welcome. Do visit all the numbered locations. There are nine of them. It is best to start in the side chapels.

“You all game?” Rick asked.

The others nodded.

“Then let’s do it, but stick together.”

For most of the afternoon, they dwelled at the nine remaining locations, studying what was before them. There was very little small talk.

The first of them, in a side chapel, was titled *Le Brun’s May Paintings*, and its plaque read: “This is an example of what is to follow. It is one of many paintings by Le Brun. In the 17th and 18th centuries, the Paris guilds presented such a painting to the cathedral on May Day of each year.”

Then back in the main chapel, they viewed and read the following:

1-- *South Rose Window*. Located here at the south end of the transept, this window retains some of the original 13th-century stained glass. The window depicts Christ in the center, surrounded by virgins, saints and the 12 Apostles.

2-- *Statue of the Virgin and Child*. Against the southeast pillar of the transept stands this 14th-century statue. It was brought to the cathedral from the chapel of St. Aignan, and is best known as Notre-Dame de Paris.

3-- *Chancel Screen*. A 14th-century high stone screen encloses the chancel and provides canons at prayer with peace and solitude from noisy congregations. Some of it has survived to screen the first three north and south bays.

4-- *Pieta*. Behind the high altar is Nicolas Coustou's Pieta, standing on a gilded base sculptured by Francois Girardon.

5-- *Louis XIII Statue*. After many years of childless marriage, Louis XII pledged to erect a high altar and to redecorate this east chancel to honor the Virgin if an heir was born to him. The future Louis XIV was born in 1638, but it took 60 years before the promises were made good. One of the surviving features from that time is the carved choir stalls.

6-- *Carved Choir Stalls*. Noted for their early 18th-century carved woodwork, these choir stalls were commissioned by Louis XIV, whose statue stands behind the high altar. Among the details carved in bas-relief in the back of the high stalls are scenes from the life of the Virgin.

7-- *North Rose Window*. This 13th-century stained glass window depicts the Virgin encircled by figures from the Old Testament.

8-- *View and Gargoyles*. The 387 steps up this north tower lead to sights of the famous gargoyles and magnificent views of Paris.

They left the cathedral and stopped for a dinner that was as quick as lunch, for each one admitted to varying degrees of exhaustion … Leon especially.

“I’m the oldest so I’m not *too* upset over looking the most fatigued,” he muttered.

“But you always look that way,” Rick said. “And all those antiques we just saw? You’re not from that era, are you?”

Fran and Ansel covered their smiles with their hands while Rick peered to his left and right.

“Who said that?” he asked innocently. “Thanks a lot.” He tried to stifle his own smile.

Chapter 19

New Jersey

April 16

It was a nine-hour flight from Paris to the Trenton-Mercer Airport in New Jersey. And from there, Hopewell was eight miles away. They arrived at the study hall in its only high school at around noon. A man who identified himself as the son of a Bruno Richard Hauptmann approached them.

"Hello," he said. "I'm the grandson of the man who was falsely accused of killing the Lindbergh boy. My name is Max Hauptmann and I thank you for coming here. I'm familiar with the cases you've written about with Dr. Henry Lee, including the ones other relatives have criticized. We've agreed to voice our displeasure as a unit. I assume you're Rick Chandler?"

"Yes, and I agree that your grandfather was **not** the killer. I'll be making a point of it in my talk."

Rick then introduced the others and handshakes were exchanged, after which Max led the four men toward a kitchen.

"I'll be introducing you," he said, "but before that, you've come a long way and probably haven't had anything to eat for awhile, so we prepared a few sandwiches, just in case."

"How nice, Max, and please forget the 'sir'. I'm just plain 'Rick'."

He pointed toward a corridor. “Are there many in the study hall down there, or is it too early?” he asked.

“No, it’s not too early. They began filing in long ago and it’s already filled up. How we’ll handle any other people . . . I have no idea.”

At precisely one o’clock, they walked into the room. It was as filled as Rick had ever imagined it would be. People were squeezed together in its rows of seats and atop three windowsills on each side, their legs hanging toward the floor. There was a podium at the front end of the crowd.

Max went off to a closet and returned with four chairs, which he unfolded and placed off to the side of the podium. He motioned for Leon, Fran and Ansel to sit in three of them, and indicated that he would join them after the introduction.

Rick arranged his notes on the podium, opened the book he had coauthored with Dr. Lee and laid the heavy metal rod across the appropriate opening page.

In the ensuing few seconds, he decided on three things: he would not explain the purpose of the rod; he would give the whole lecture with no humorous side remarks as he had in the Sacco-Vanzetti talk; and he would not ask Max if any of the other displeased relatives were there. It would be “talk away, then get up and go.”

Max’s introduction was as long as the applause that followed. Rick began with an expression of appreciation for the attendance there, then passed smoothly into the talk:

“I will begin by stating unequivocally that Bruno Richard Hauptmann was **not** the killer of the Lindbergh child. But let me cover the entire case, and I must admit that, for the most part, I’ll be quoting directly from a book I coauthored with Dr. Henry Lee. It contains my version of the case.

“Three months before the executions of Sacco and Vanzetti,

twenty-five-year–old Charles A. Lindbergh flew a monoplane, the *Spirit of St Louis*, from Roosevelt Field, Long Island, New York, to the LeBourget Airdrome just outside Paris. He was the first person to fly the Atlantic Ocean alone, covering a distance of 3,735 miles in 33 hours, 39 minutes. The time was May 20-21, 1927. Lindbergh burst onto the international scene as a genuine hero, was made Colonel by the United States Secretary of War, and received the Congressional Medal of Honor and the Distinguished Flying Cross. At the request of the U.S. government, he traveled widely and, on a trip to Mexico, he met Anne Spencer Morrow, the daughter of the American ambassador there. They married two years later. Subsequently, he taught her to fly and, together, they embarked on numerous flying expeditions around the world, charting new travel routes for several airlines. But Anne's first love centered on writing, and in the following years, she received critical acclaim for her poetry, memoirs and novels.

"To escape media attention, the Lindberghs built a home on a remote, 400-acre tract of land here near Hopewell. There, on a rainy Tuesday of March 1, 1932, their 20-month-old son was kidnapped from his nursery. Within hours, an unorganized horde of police and press personnel swarmed over the grounds and by morning, scores of curious onlookers had joined them.

"The child's disappearance was detected at 10 p.m., the police were called at 10:25, and at midnight, H. Norman Schwarzkopf, chief of the New Jersey State Police, arrived to take command. He was the father of the 1991 Desert Storm commander. Much of Schwarzkopf's authority was usurped by Lindbergh, since the hero in effect took charge of the investigation.

"In the wet ground directly below a second-story window to the nursery, the police discovered shallow footprints but neglected to measure them, photograph their sole pattern or cast them with plaster. Sadly lacking also were measurements and photographs of apparent footprints found inside the nursery.

"A homemade ladder lay flat on the ground, 70 feet from the house. It was built in three sections with the top section lying 10 feet from the other two. A ¾-inch chisel was also found nearby.

"Two holes were located in the clay beneath the window, and one of the troopers immediately fit the ladder into these impressions without first checking for trace evidence at the leg ends of the ladder. Nor had the holes been examined, measured or cast for future comparisons.

"Eventually, Lindbergh's attorney and family friend, Henry C. Breckinridge, arrived. They, along with Schwarzkopf and a 'crime scene man' began a detailed examination of the nursery where, on the window sill, they spotted an envelope that Lindbergh said he had seen earlier but had not touched. It was dusted for fingerprints, as were other areas of the room. No prints were found anywhere. The envelope contained a single sheet of paper upon which the following message was written in blue ink:

Dear Sir!

Have 50.000 $ redy. 25.000 $ in 20$ bills , 15.000 in 10 $ bills and 10.000 $ in 5 $ bills.
After 2-4 days we will inform you were to deliver the Money.
We warn you for making anything public or for notify the police.

The child is in great care.

Indication for all letters are signature and 3 holes.

"At the bottom of the paper was a drawing of two interlocking circles. The area within the overlap of the circles was solid red while the rest of the circles were outlined in blue. Three square holes pierced the crude symbol in a horizontal line.

"Over the next few days, authorities theorized that the theft was the work of more than one person, possibly a gang, and three possibilities emerged:

Lindbergh believed the kidnappers were professionals.

Schwarzkopf thought that the criminals were local and unprofessional because of their familiarity with the house, the location of the nursery window with its broken shutter latch and the modest ransom request.

Other investigators believed domestic employees were involved because somehow the kidnappers knew that, because the child had a cold, the family decided against their custom of returning Monday mornings to Anne's parents' estate in Englewood, New Jersey.

"More ransom notes were received, chiding Lindbergh for alerting the police and increasing the demand to $70,000. One week after the crime, Dr. John F. Condon of New York City, a retired physical educational teacher, placed an ad in the *Bronx Home News* offering the kidnappers $1,000 and his services as a go-between. The next day, he received an acceptance letter, which contained the intertwining circles with square holes and also a sketch of a box, 7 by 6 by 14 inches, in which the money was to be inserted. On the night of April 2, 1932, a month after the kidnapping, Lindbergh drove Condon to St. Raymond's Cemetery in the Bronx, the site prearranged for delivery of the ransom money in exchange for knowledge of the child's location. The money was all in gold certificates, making them easier to trace; in addition, their serial numbers had been recorded.

"Lindbergh waited in the car outside the graveyard while Condon wandered about the tombstones expecting to encounter the person who had been dubbed 'Cemetery John'. Unsuccessful, Condon returned to the car whereupon a voice called out, 'Hey, doctor, over here, over here! Condon slipped back to the graveyard and eventually confronted a shadowy figure with a German or Scandinavian accent. Condon handed over the bills and, in return, received a folded note, which he was instructed not to open until six hours had passed. But a mile from the cemetery, Lindbergh stopped the car and read the following message:

> The boy is on the Boad Nelly. It is a small boad 28 feet long. Two persons are on the boad. They are innocent. You will find the Boad between Horseneck Beach and Gay Head near Elizabeth Island.

"This area on Martha's Vineyard off the coast of Massachusetts was searched; neither the boat nor the child was found.

"Two months after the kidnapping, the child's badly decomposed body was discovered only four miles from the Hopewell mansion. He was face downward and covered by leaves and insects. Less than 24 hours later or 73 days after the kidnapping, the remains of Charles A. Lindbergh, Jr. were cremated.

"Before that, what many called a 'rinky dink' autopsy had been performed, because the county physician had suffered an arthritis flare up and delegated a funeral home director to make the actual dissections. Examination of the skull revealed four fracture lines and a decomposed blood clot. No photographs of this pathology were taken.

"Other than the boy's remains prior to cremation, the principal pieces of evidence at that point in the investigation were the ladder, the chisel and a number of notes from the kidnapper or kidnappers. There were no fingerprints or useful footprints. The ladder would later prove to be crucial.

"Early isolated spottings of the ransom bills were made in New York City, but such detection escalated when, in the spring of 1933, President Franklin Roosevelt ordered all gold certificates to be exhanged at Federal Reserve Banks, thus taking the country off the gold standard. None of the sightings could be traced. And then, a major breakthrough occurred in September 1934, when a dark blue Dodge sedan appeared at a gas station in Manhattan and the driver paid for gas with a $10 gold certificate that was on the ransom list. The attendant wrote the license number of the car on the bill, which was eventually traced to a Bronx resident, Bruno Richard Hauptmann. He was arrested the following morning.

"Once the suspect was in custody, the task of matching some of the other clues to him was undertaken. Comparisons of the ransom notes to several documents written in Hauptmann's handwriting, including insurance card and auto license applications, showed some apparent but not definitive matches. The police searched his garage and apartment, stripping the latter to its laths. An address and phone number found written on a piece of trim proved to refer to Dr. John Condon. Furthermore, several bundles of gold notes were found stashed within the walls of the suspect's garage. But could both of these have been planted?

"Perhaps the most important offered evidence linking Hauptmann to the kidnapping was the ladder found at the scene of the crime. Although he was a professional carpenter, it was crudely constructed; its rungs, for example, were placed six inches farther apart than in an average ladder. Subsequently, a part of its rails was found to match existing floorboards in his attic. There, one of the boards was missing and the rail section fit the space perfectly. But the defense was not allowed to visit the attic. Why not?

"Regarding the ensuing court sessions, the areas in and around the courthouse were swollen with spectators, reporters and police personnel–reminiscent of the Sacco-Vanzetti trial. The room resembled the one in Dedham except the witness stand wasn't a stand at all, but only a wooden chair.

"The prosecution was led by Attorney General David T. Wilentz of New Jersey, a fiery, cigar-smoking little man whose white fedora with a turned down brim reminded some observers of the gangster, Al Capone.

"Hauptmann's chief counsel was a well-known Brooklyn defense attorney and boozer, Edward J. Reilly. Many believed he was 'over the hill' and suffering from tertiary syphilis. He would become, within two years, an institutionalized psychotic.

"Wilentz based its case solely on circumstantial evidence. First was the discovered $14,460 ransom money. Hauptmann testified that a friend, Isador Fisch, had left a shoebox with him before departing for Germany in December1933. Fisch, he said, owed him $7,500, so he felt it was within his rights to spend some of the money he found in the box. Fisch died in Liepzig in March 1934.

"They called it the 'Fisch story' but, later on, reliable evidence surfaced that Fisch had been a buyer of 'hot' money. This tended to clarify some of the issues related to the 'Fisch story'.

"A friend of his was Violet Sharp. They lived across the street from each other and were often seen together. Violet was a twenty-eight-year-old Englishwoman who worked as a serving maid for the Morrow household, and on June 10, 1932, she committed suicide. An investigation was said to prove that she was not the abductor of the Lindbergh child, but many still wonder if she actually knew the truth and killed herself because of such knowledge.

"Another piece of prosecution evidence, and possibly the most damaging, was the connection of the section of floorboard from Hauptmann's attic to the ladder used by the kidnapper. The defense argued that not only was the placement in the ladder's rail disputable *but also that such evidence could have been planted.*

"The argument and the theory! Is history always repeating itself? Why wasn't the defense team ever allowed to inspect the attic?"

"Third was the issue of handwriting. The state's array of handwriting experts overwhelmed the defense's feeble two. But more recently, document examiners for the U.S. Secret Service and for the U.S. Army concluded that Hauptmann *did not* write the ransom notes.

"Dr. John Condon figured prominently both before and during the trial. He testified in court that the defendant was definitely the person who took the ransom box in St. Raymond's Cemetery and later—too late, in fact—his name surfaced once more in conjunction with his phone number written inside a closet at Hauptmann's house. Again, could that also have been planted? In fact, could *all* discoveries that seemed to implicate Hauptmann have been planted?

"Two other things were questionable here. One, Condon was

unable to identify Hauptmann in a police lineup after the arrest, yet fingered him in court as 'Cemetery John'. And two, after the trial, several newspaper reporters stated that a fellow journalist seeking an exclusive story had penciled Condon's address and phone number on the closet trim.

"Lindbergh was generally vague about his whereabouts on the day of the kidnapping, but stated he failed to keep a speaking engagement that evening. Also, one of those reporters asked the other one, 'Don't you think he would have remembered every single thing about the day his son was murdered'?"

"'Nah'," was the reply. "He probably blocked out most of the day."

"But shouldn't detectives have checked and verified his activity as they did in the Sacco-Vanzetti case?"

"They probably were too busy conducting the investigation and search of the crime scene."

"The other reporter's lips quivered before he then said, "Hey, wait a minute! You aren't suggesting that Lindy had anything to do with the killing, are you?"

"No, definitely not me--but maybe others might."

"It was universally acknowledged that attorney Reilly's behavior was shameful, his defense of Hauptmann shallow. He spent each lunch break drinking, and his lackluster afternoon performance reflected that habit."

"On the other hand, a confident David Wilentz, trying his first criminal case as attorney general, parlayed a charming smile and dapper attire with impressive cross-examinations, particularly of Hauptmann who endured 11 hours of a savage interrogation. Wilentz's summation was devastating:

> Now, men and women, as I told you before, there are some cases in which a recommendation of mercy might do, but not this one, not this one. Either this man is the filthiest

> and vilest snake that ever crept through the grass, or he is entitled to an acquittal. And if you believe as we do, you have got to convict him. If you bring a recommendation of mercy, a wishy-washy decision, yes, it is your province. I will not say a word about it. I will not say another word, once I sit down in this case, so far as this jury and this verdict are concerned. But it seems to me that you have and you will have the courage if you are convinced, as all of us are–the federal authorities, the Bronx people who were here, the New Jersey State Police who were here, the lawyers who were here, Colonel Lindbergh who was here, everybody who has testified–if you believe with us, you have got to find him guilty of murder in the first degree.

"Throughout the trial, an estimated 75,000 to 100,000 people filed into Flemington each day. After hearing 29 days of testimony, the jury retired for deliberations and returned 12 hours later with a verdict of guilty. Arguing his innocence to the end and after one year of appeals, Hauptmann was electrocuted on April 3, 1936.

"I must indicate what Dr. Lee's reaction was to the whole affair – and I agree with him. We say so in our book. As for myself, you've heard me say that I believe Hauptmann was *not* guilty of murder. He might have been guilty of something, but there were too many discrepancies and inconsistencies to say the man committed a murder. Dr. Lee made a point of stating that the kind of justice Hauptmann had been offered during a month-long process whose main characters were an international hero and an obscure carpenter was lacking a proper defense. He maintained that the defense was too tepid; that there were so many gaps and miscues and bungled opportunities to discredit the forensic evidence as well as the witnesses. That anything holding to solid forensic science, even to those techniques available at the time, was sadly lacking; that suppression of evidence was there; disregard for the laws of evidence was there; the possibility of tampering of evidence was there; and 'was there a frame-up, or did he really do it'?

"Hauptmann's execution was preceded by a year of legal appeals, and late in that process, sentiment about Lindbergh began to change. Remarkably, as the public turned more and more against the one-time international hero, doubts about Hauptmann's guilt arose across the country. The positions of the two became reversed for reasons that involved, among others, the public's perception of the prosecution team and Lindbergh's decision to abandon his homeland. He sailed for England in late 1935 with his wife and second son and lived there and on an island off the coast of France for more than three years.

"In the immediate post-trial months, those players important to the prosecution–Wilentz, Condon and Schwarzkopf among them–became transformed into unattractive personalities in the eyes of the media, principally because they were suddenly viewed as persecutors and self-promoters. Lindbergh, meanwhile, operated from his base in Europe and entered into an intense and open relationship with Nazi Germany, this at a time when the Second World War was at hand and American sympathies were being scrutinized. He made frequent trips to Germany, announced his admiration for the German *Luftwaffe* and befriended its leader, Hermann Goering.

"At home, many people labeled Lindbergh a dupe of German propaganda, a fascist, even a Nazi, and after the war had begun, he was considered an unpatriotic appeaser.

"Through the years, Anna Hauptmann, Bruno's widow, initiated several attempts to clear her husband's name. All were unsuccessful. Meanwhile, a combination of newer evidence and a reinterpretation of the old have led many to believe that Bruno Richard Hauptmann could not have been the kidnapper and murderer. Including me.

"Well that's enough about this case, except for a long list that I've put together. If I tell you ahead of time how many items are on it, you may all go home –so I won't. I've numbered them and here they are:

1. Why didn't the family terrier, *Wahgoosh*, ever bark on the evening of the kidnaping even though he was in the house? He was known to

be a high-strung dog who barked loudly at strangers.

2. The crime scene was allowed to be trampled on by media, investigators and later by curious onlookers. Guess what happened to the integrity of the crime scene?

3. No latent fingerprints were found anywhere. Modern technology for developing latent prints with lasers and new chemicals might have helped.

4. No photographs, plaster casts or accurate measurements were made of the prints in the wet ground beneath the window of apparent entrance of the kidnapper(s). No mention of whether or not the prints were similar to Hauptmann's.

5. Did ladder wood and floorboard wood come from the same tree? This could have been decided indisputably by twenty-first century plant DNA analysis.

6. How did kidnapper or kidnappers know which second-story window had a broken latch, the only such malfunctioning one among the 150 in the entire mansion?

7. How did the kidnapper or kidnappers know the height of the second-story window in order to construct a three-section ladder that reached perfectly to its height? What was its total weight and could one person carry it?

8. According to the location of the two holes made by the ladder in the wet ground, its top had to be

positioned a considerable distance to the right of the window. So there had to be a transfer of the boy from one person to another.

9. Trace evidence on the end of the ladder was destroyed by a trooper when he inserted it into the two holes beneath the nursery window. That also changed the size, depth and shape of the holes during the insertion.

10. Before the trial, the defense was never given any investigative notes or otherwise apprised of the evidence it would have to face. Thus, their own experts were not given the opportunity to inspect the evidence firsthand.

11. Once discovered, the child's body was immediately cremated. There was no legitimate autopsy, no documentation of the injuries and no possibility for exhumation for later forensic testing.

12. The defense team was never allowed to inspect Hauptmann's attic or to conduct its own investigation and documentations *before* the floorboard had been removed.

13. The defense initially had time sheets showing Hauptmann working in New York until 5 p.m. on the day of the crime, making it virtually impossible for him to travel to central New Jersey.

14. As a professional carpenter, would he have been satisfied with such a crudely built ladder?

15. Why did Defense Counselor Reilly allow the identification of a corpse in the woods to stand without rebuttal, especially when the autopsy was not professionally performed and confusion

reigned over the body's height and age? Hadn't Reilly ever heard of planting a seed of doubt? He surprised and angered even his legal associate in this regard.

16. There were no photographs or enhancements of the footprints in the nursery. These could have been compared to those found on the ground outside.

17. Were any tool marks discovered at the scene and, if so, were they made by the chisel found there?

18. Only two holes were found in the clay beneath the window, which indicates the suspect or suspects had definite knowledge of the window latch at the target area.

19. The origin of the envelope and sheet of paper found on the windowsill were never explained.

20. The ink–both blue and red–was never traced to its origin. Were any pens recovered form Hauptmann's house or, for that matter, from the Lindbergh estate?

21. Was the broken shutter latch an old or new defect?

22. Had any new chemical procedures been employed to bring out latent fingerprints on the ladder, chisel, envelope and paper? In 1932, the Ninhydrin Procedure had been introduced in the field. Why wasn't it used?

23. Had any comparisons been made between the writing, paper and ink of the first ransom note

and subsequent ones? Any tracing attempts for the subsequent paper and ink?

24. The body was wrapped in some clothing. Was any trace or transfer evidence recovered during the autopsy?

25. Were any fingerprints found on the shoebox containing the ransom money? Was any attempt made to trace the origin of the box?

"Long, eh? But in my winding down, aside from the list, I have to say that the most important items are one–the conclusion by the U.S. Secret Service and the U.S. Army that Hauptmann did not write the ransom notes, and two–the 60-year crusade of his wife Anna. She even had a website for it. And on her deathbed, she said: 'Please try to convince everyone that my husband and I were having dinner at home that night.'

"And who do I think murdered the boy?" Rick asked. "Maybe Fisch and Violet, but certainly *not* Hauptmann.

"The end," he said.

He thanked all those who stood up, including Max.

They shook hands.

The audience's clapping and waving were more than he had expected and he waved back just as forcefully. So did a man who had been the first to slide off a windowsill and now left the room through a back door. He was wearing a black cap that he pulled down over dark glasses. It was enough for Rick to check on one of his guns and, in glancing toward Fran, saw that he was doing the same. But they only hunched their shoulders.

Chapter 20

Cleveland

Rick decided not to shorten his talks about Sheppard and Spector after all. He and his triad set out for Cleveland, 450 miles away. It was mid-afternoon. Ansel had called ahead for the JBCC to have a light plane ready at the Hopkins International Airport, a maintenance base for United Airlines.

They arrived in time for a dinner special at one of its five kitchens operated by the airline company–Chelsea Food Services. The meal included free wine. Each of the triad drained a glass, but Rick had two.

Leon said that the city's largest high school–a five-minute walk away– had a study hall that accommodated 250 and that everything was all set for the talk at one p.m. the next day.

They retired early at a nearby hotel and slept late the next morning. Over the noon-hour, they had lunch and then walked to the school.

The study hall was filled to near-capacity. As Leon, Fran and Ansel took seats in a front row, a woman–Cecelia–approached Rick and said she would be introducing him. With little detail to spare, she did so. After a strong round of applause and his usual pre-talk routine, he indicated that the book before him would be very valuable–for him and for them. He lifted it up for all to see.

"I'm its coauthor," he said, "and I'll be reading directly from it. I just hope my words won't come across as too formal, or even pedantic.

"Now, as I've said in my Sacco-Vanzetti and Charles Lindbergh presentations–that they were not guilty as charged– I believe Sam Sheppard also was not guilty. His murder case, which began in the mid-'50s, has been described as the case that will not die, the story with nine lives. It spawned a popular television series, *The Fugitive*, starring David Jantzen and British actor Barry Morse; and a hit movie starring Harrison Ford.

"In the Bay Village section of your city, 31-year-old Marilyn Sheppard, four months pregnant, was found bludgeoned to death sometime during the early morning hours of July 4, 1954. An attractive suburban housewife, she was discovered in her bed in the second-story bedroom by her husband, Sam, a neurosurgeon who, even at age 30, was already prominent.

"Dr. Sam's story remained consistent through the years. The couple had entertained dinner guests at their lakefront home and after their departure, Sam fell asleep on the couch in the first-floor den while watching a TV movie. He awoke, believing he heard his wife calling his name, and dashed up the stairs and into the bedroom where he saw a figure in a light garment and then grappled with something or someone. He heard moaning before he was struck from behind and blacked out. When he regained consciousness, he was lying on the floor and, pulling himself up, saw his wife covered with blood. He felt for but could not obtain her pulse, then ran into the next room to check on their seven-year-old son, Chip. The boy was sleeping soundly. Hearing a noise below, he ran to the first floor and saw a man running out the back door toward the lake. Dr. Sam stated that the man was about six-feet three inches, middle-aged, with dark bushy hair and wearing a white shirt. He reportedly chased him across the lawn and down the wooden steps leading to the beach. He caught up to him and grasped him from the back. They struggled before he felt himself choking and again lost consciousness. After an unspecified period of time, he returned to the blood-spattered bedroom and paced. He believed he was disoriented and the victim of a nightmare, yet may have reexamined his wife and accepted that she was dead. His next move, he said, was to call a neighbor, Bay Village Mayor Spencer Houk. The mayor and his wife, Esther, arrived quickly. It was 6 a.m. on the Fourth of July.

"Following a brief hospital stay for shock and neck injuries, Sheppard was interrogated repeatedly by local authorities and by the Cleveland police who formally assumed responsibility for the investigation three weeks later. That interval was filled with massive media scrutiny and included a three-day inquest conducted by the coroner, Dr. Sam Gerber. Newspapers were emblazoned with challenging headlines like:

'Why Don't Police Quiz Top Suspect?'

'Police Captain Urges Sheppard's Arrest'

"And especially a local paper, *the Cleveland Press*, which didn't like the Sheppard family's prominent neurosurgeons and their clinic. It printed headlines like, 'Why Isn't Sam Sheppard In Jail?'

"Finally, the doctor was arrested on July 30, indicted on August 17 and brought to trial a month later.

"Once again I ask: a repeat of history? A rush to judgment just as in the Sacco-Vanzetti and Bruno Hauptmann cases? Or was it, in fact, the pressure of public opinion and the news media on law enforcement authorities to solve the case?

"The trial covered six weeks of testimony. The defendant was found guilty of murder in the second degree and was sentenced to life imprisonment. The prosecution had hammered away at allegations that Sheppard was unfaithful to his wife; that the injuries he sustained on July 4 were self-inflicted and superficial; and that it was his personal surgical instrument–the murder weapon– that had made the imprint on a bloody pillowcase, a contention advanced by Coroner Gerber. The defense introduced witnesses who told of seeing a cigarette floating in an upstairs toilet, although the Sheppards were not smokers; others who testified they had seen a man with a white shirt and bushy hair near the Sheppard home; and still others who corroborated the seriousness of Sheppard's injuries.

"That cigarette–it disappeared, you know. Poof! And, how could they have minimized the testimony of X-ray technicians; a neurosurgeon;

a radiologist; an ear, nose and throat specialist; and a dentist–all of whom verified that Sheppard had suffered a fractured cervical vertebra, massive swelling at the base of the skull, spinal cord injuries with neurological deficits, and chipped teeth? Self-inflicted? Or, he must have taken a pretty hard fall on concrete. Both hard to imagine.

"Other glaring mistakes in that investigation? There were many, such as not analyzing Marilyn's stomach contents, not making a microscopic study of her wounds, not determining whether or not she had been raped. Plus they never searched for trace evidence like semen, hair, wood, or foreign material on the sheets–or fibers such as wool and cotton under Marilyn's fingernails. They also failed to analyze a broken tooth found under the bed. Later, it could not be matched to either of the Sheppards. Today, DNA can be extracted from teeth. And how could they explain away the large amount of blood at the crime scene, yet the lack of any on the defendant's pants, shoes or socks? Lots of questions. There was no analysis of blood spatter patterns, and a proper reconstruction of the crime was never conducted. Or even a complete identification of **all** the bloodstains. Three decades later, DNA testing would show that someone other than the Sheppards bled in the bedroom. Moreover, new questions would be raised based on more recent autopsy interpretations.

"Following Sheppard's incarceration, a series of occurrences altered the nature of the case and added to its litany of human and judicial twists. For example, within two weeks of the verdict, Dr. Sam's mother died from a self-inflicted gunshot wound and 10 days after that, his father died of a bleeding stomach ulcer. Some years later, Marilyn's father committed suicide with a shotgun. The most important events, however, were the overturning of the 1954 trial by the U.S. Supreme Court and the ensuing second trial, which exonerated the suspect in the eyes of the law but not in the eyes of the public.

"Several characters, either newly engaged or held over from the first trial years, would assume key roles in the second trial and beyond:

1. Dr. Paul Leland Kirk. Criminalist from the University of California at Berkeley.

2. F. Lee Bailey. Defense attorney from Boston.

3. Ethel Durkin. Elderly murder victim.

4. Richard Eberling. Window washer for the Sheppard home.

5. Dr. Sam Gerber. Coroner, 1936-86.

6. Mayor Spencer and Esther Houk. Sheppard neighbors and first on the scene.

7. Sam Reese Sheppard … Chip. Son of Dr. Sam and Marilyn.

"At one time or another, Eberling and the Houks were suspects in the murder and, to this day, theories abound over the exact sequence of events on that fateful night, and of who could possibly have been in the bedroom.

"From the start, the first trial was a media 'carnival', not an inappropriate term, for it was the basis for the dramatic Supreme Court decision after 12 years of continuous appeals. Speaking for the Court, Justice Tom Clark ruled in Sheppard's favor because–and I quote–'The massive, pervasive and prejudicial publicity attending petitioner's prosecution prevented him from receiving a fair trial consistent with the Due Process Clause of the 14th Amendment. Despite his awareness of the excessive pretrial publicity, the trial judge failed to take effective measures against the massive publicity that continued throughout the trial or to take adequate steps to control the conduct of the trial.'

"Once more my question: Was this a
repeat of Sacco-Vanzetti and Lindbergh?

"Clark went on to say the judge should have postponed the trial or moved it to a county 'not so permeated' with publicity. He elaborated on the impact of the media upon jury members, citing the pretrial publication of the names and addresses of those called for duty. As a consequence, anonymous letters, telephone calls, and calls from friends were received by prospective jurors. They were, in effect, thrust into the role of celebrities.

"In the courtroom, the press table had been placed inside the bar, less than three feet from the jury box–and they talked and joked around. 'This,' Clark said, 'precluded privacy between the defendant and his attorneys.'

"The justice also suggested a prejudicial court. The judge was heard saying on the first day of the trial, 'Mystery? It's an open and shut case. He is guilty as hell. There is no question about it.' And a prejudicial coroner allegedly claimed at the crime scene, 'Well, men, it is evident the doctor did this, so let's go get the confession out of him.'"

The audience was showing no objection to Rick's direct and continuous reading from the book's pages. If anything, their collective silence and body language encouraged him not to change the manner of his delivery. *Such reading is smoother*, he told himself. *Ad-libbing is herky-jerky. And, after all, if it's considered 'stealing,' I'm stealing my own words because I co-wrote the book in the first place.*

"At the start of the second trial, Dr. Sam had been a free man for two years, ever since a surprising ruling by District Judge Carl Weinman in 1964. He ordered Sheppard's release from prison, stating, 'If ever there was a trial by newspaper, this is a perfect example.' The judge cited five separate violations of Sheppard's constitutional rights and wrote, 'Each of the aforementioned errors is by itself sufficient to require a determination that the petitioner was not offered a fair trial–and that when these errors are cumulated, the trial can only be viewed as a mockery of justice.'

"So chronologically what happened to this point was: Dr. Sam spent 10 years in prison, then was released, and was retried two years after that. The key years were 1954-1964 and 1966. Tough to keep it straight. But let's complicate it a bit further: In 1959, a window washer named Richard Eberling was arrested for stealing valuables from his customers' homes. When grilled by the police, he admitted he had washed the Sheppards' windows shortly before the murder and explained that he cut his finger and dripped blood as he walked to the basement to cleanse the wound. This development received little attention until 30 years later when he was convicted of killing wealthy Lakewood woman, Ethel May Durkin. During the investigation, it was learned that he had been associated with a number of women who had met violent death. Eberling thus became the leading suspect in the Sheppard case, but he was never convicted.

"One other sidebar: Sheppard had been carrying on a 'prison romance' with Ariane Tebbenjohanns, a dazzling blonde divorcee who wooed him by correspondence from her home in Dusseldorf, Germany. She eventually moved to the States and, within a week of his release from prison, married Dr. Sam. I mention this only as an item of unusual coincidence. Remember Charles Lindbergh's friendship with Nazi Germany's Hermann Goering? Well, Ariane was the sister-in-law of Nazi Propaganda Minister Joseph Goebbels!

"Judge Francis Talty was assigned to hear the second trial: the State of Ohio vs. Sam Sheppard. That he adopted the Supreme Court's objections to the first trial was reflected in his decision to drastically limit the number of reporters and spectators allowed into his courtroom.

"Sheppard was represented by defense attorney F. Lee Bailey, who had entered the case five years earlier and was instrumental in securing Sheppard's release from prison.

"The prosecution's tack was markedly different the second time around. There was no attempt to introduce evidence supporting the earlier claim of faked injuries or marital discord or a surgical instrument. In cross-examination, Bailey pressed Coroner Gerber to admit that in a countrywide search, he was unable to locate any instrument that would fit the impression on the bloody pillowcase.

"Mary Cowan, Gerber's medical technologist, testified that blood on Sheppard's wristwatch came not from contact with a wound but from spattering blood. The defense countered with its star witness, Dr. Paul Kirk who contended that:

1. Blood patterns indicated Marilyn's slayer had to be left-handed, and Dr. Sam was right-handed.

2. One bloodstain in the murder room was neither Marilyn's nor Sam's and thus must have been the blood of a third person, who was the murderer.

3. The blood on Dr. Sam's wristwatch was the result of contact with Marilyn when he had examined her.

"Dr. Kirk made his points convincingly over more than five hours of direct questioning by Bailey, thus in effect nullifying Mary Cowen's performance. The doctor had investigated all the right open questions before the trial and with Bailey's brilliant orchestration, had found the right combination for the trial. Kirk's turned out to be the last testimony of evidentiary importance in a trial that markedly contrasted with the first in terms of high drama and media frenzy.

"After 19 days of testimony and summation, the verdict buzzer pierced a nearly empty courtroom and within minutes, Judge Talty walked in; grim faced jury members filed in; and the room filled to capacity.

"The judge was handed the verdict and after perusing it impassively, he read it aloud:

"We the jury, empaneled in the above entitled case, find the defendant not guilty.

"Pandemonium erupted. It was mostly joyous and was led by Dr. Sam, who appeared to release an aching energy lying dormant for 12 years.

"But after the trial, Sheppard's life deteriorated. Severely impaired by alcohol and drugs, he encountered a series of setbacks: a malpractice suit, divorce, insolvency and, in 1970, death.

"There were still many who doubted his innocence and just as many who believed that justice had been finally served. Among the latter was his son, Samuel Reese Sheppard, the youngster 'Chip' who, in 1954, lay sleeping while his mother was slain. He took up the cause of validating the verdict in his father's retrial by attempting to establish the identity of the real killer. In the process, he became a staunch opponent of the death penalty and often spoke out against it in speeches throughout the country.

"Nearly half a century later, Sam Reese conceded to the exhumation and DNA testing of the bodies of both his parents in a quest to win a civil suit filed against the state of Ohio. It was reported that their DNA did not match the DNA of a blood spot that had been discovered at the crime scene.

"I'll end it there, ladies and gentlemen. Oh! Except for two questions: Who do I think murdered Marilyn? Eberling. And was he left or right-handed? It was never determined."

PART THREE

Chapter 21

New York City

April 18

It was back to square one regarding the summit meeting. The invitees had been asked to arrive on their own at 2 p.m. on April 18 aboard the *Seacraft*. It would be docked in New York City.

Rick arrived a half-hour earlier, however, so he could question the captain or a senior assistant about the ship's role in handling unidentified goods, if it had such a role in the first place.

But he ran into a young staff officer with purple and gold stripes on his epaulet. He identified himself as the assistant chief engineer and when asked, said that the prearranged meeting would take place in a hall reserved for passengers on the second deck. Rick decided to pursue the questioning with him.

"I'm writing a book about cruise ships," he said, "and I'm in a section dealing with what goes on below their decks–where the storage compartments are located. I'm wondering if you can help me out."

"I'll try."

"Are your storage compartments very large?"

"Very. Large and overloaded."

"What's in them?"

"Books."

"What kind of books?"

"No idea. We're just paid to ship them."

"Are the people the same as the people who ask that they be shipped?"

"No. Different ones."

Rick decided to go out on a limb and said, "Two more questions: One, can I have some of their names and addresses? And two, do prostitutes ever board this ship?"

The engineer looked evasive. "You'd have to ask the captain about that."

Rick thanked him and handed over a 100-dollar bill. The engineer took it. Then waving it, he said, "Oh, there's one more thing you should probably know."

"What's that?"

"We come from Buenos Aires to here every week. Then the books you asked about?"

"Yes?"

"They go by plane to Switzerland – and, I understand, from there to Minsk in Belarus. While that's going on, we return to Buenos Aires and do it over again. Been going on for some time now."

"Does the chief in Buenos Aires know about this?"

"I have no idea."

Rick thought he didn't.

On the second deck, the hall reserved for passenger events was as bare as an empty freezer. A large rectangular table was the only exception. Its chairs were filled with eight people whom Rick expected to see: Fran, Ansel, histarian Lance, Paul D'Arneau, Chief Gomez, Carlos, Leon, and Calderone.

Once Rick took a seat, the chief said, "I've been asked to run this meeting – so hear ye, hear ye, hear ye! And if I had a gavel, I'd be pounding it."

Everyone laughed including a usually stoic Carlos.

Gomez continued: "This meeting will now come to order. I guess we'll go around thc table and listen to what each of us has to say. Remember–the whole purpose of our get-together here is to bring the group up to date – to summarize where we stand on things; on what's been done; and on what still needs to be done. And even if you think that most of us are aware of what you might bring up, do it anyway. It's like filling a pot as high to its brim as possible, but with time to go even further. So, let's start with Rick."

Rick, who had already begun to take notes, put his pad aside and began by relaying what the engineer said a short while before. Next was the list of lectures he'd given to help appease the relatives of those with a questionable criminal past: Sacco-Vanzetti, Charles Lindbergh, Sam Sheppard and, later on, would be Phil Spector. He spoke of possible disaster cites and having visited the three in Paris to ask for greater security. Then came a list of key challenges, some done and some yet to be done: attempting to identify looted treasures – especially famous books – and having them returned to their rightful owners; having such detection serve as an example to others seeking to steal treasures of all kinds. He ended with the mention of prostitutes; of the meeting with some Mafia figures; and of a future visit to Switzerland to investigate widespread Nazi dealings and payoffs. For the first time, the name of Juan Saltanban was brought up. Rick said that upon visiting the Rock of Gibraltar, they would confer with him about the use of a magical device that might help weed out looters. He said that when he was last in Gibraltar, he had met him and was shown the device.

Lance then asked to be heard. "All I have to offer is that histarians will be available as needed."

"I echo that sentiment," Paul said. "Rick and I go back a long way, and he knows that I'm ready, willing and able to help out when asked. Off the cuff though, a good friend of mine is Walter Sparks–goes by the name of 'Sparky'. He's the criminalist/pathologist at Hollings General Teaching Hospital in Connecticut and can be of great value to us."

Fran, who himself had been taking notes, looked up and said, "Speaking of a long way in the past, Rick and I have combined on many things. In fact, I talked him into getting involved in the first place. I call it the 'looter hunt.' We've traveled together all over the place, trying to piece together who's been stealing so many valuables – like paintings, ceramics, Nazi gold, deeply religious treasures and, as you've heard, valuable books. It's really an international epidemic and we're trying like hell to cure it."

Ansel and Carlos kept gazing at one another, as if one knew what the other was thinking. Finally, Ansel said, "We're relative newcomers and can't add much to what's already been said except that–and you all know this–I'm a driver and Carlos there is the chief's receptionist."

Carlos nodded.

Attention then shifted to Calderone. "I'm afraid most of you don't know me," he said, "but I'm a former member of the Mafia. Believe me–I no longer am. And I'm not a spy of any kind. Rick can vouch for that. Right, my friend?"

"Sure can."

"So I'm willing to help out–whenever and however."

Leon next piped up. "So much has been covered, my friends, that there's not much left to bring to the table. Suffice it to say that, as the head of Gens de Vérité, I was the devil who enticed Rick over there to give his talks. Tiresome, I'm sure, but he won't confess to it. And he even gave an excellent reading on terrorism." Leon then folded his hands on the table in a 'nothing more to add' gesture.

"Can you still make arrests, Leon?" Rick inquired.

"Yes, I've never lost that authority, but I only have it in Paris."

"You pack a gun?"

"Sure do."

"And it's loaded?"

"Sure is. But why these questions?"

"Curious, that's all. Or maybe I just wanted this whole group to know how influential you are."

"Rubbish."

The chief surveyed the group of eight and said, "That leaves me, I guess. The only thing I have to inform you about–and as often as Rick and I exchange phone calls–is something I've never told him. The reason is that I just heard about it myself. But this ship we're on apparently transports valuable but stolen books from my city to here on a regular basis. Where the books come from in the first place . . . I have no idea. I haven't had a chance to investigate yet because I only learned of it shortly before I flew here."

Jibes with what the engineer said, Rick thought.

The last laugh occurred when they were about to disassemble. For all to hear, Fran said, "Good job, chief. But I don't understand why you didn't ask us to rise and sing the '*Star Spangled Banner*' before we started."

On the way out, Rick called Gomez aside and said, "If this business about books being shipped is all phony, give me a call."

Gomez, looking haggard, replied, "Yeah, just as soon as I get home, I'll have my men look into it. If books are not being shipped, I'll call you. Or do you want a call either way?"

"No. Only if it's a phony accusation."

As he expected, Rick never heard back.

Chapter 22

Los Angeles

April 19

That ended the summit meeting and Rick was happy over what had been accomplished. Exhilarated, in fact.

The next day in Los Angeles, he and his triad were ready for the Phil Spector case. The school study hall was filled to near-capacity as if tickets had been sold for the event. Off to the side, three empty seats were marked RESERVED and Fran, Ansel and Leon took them. The introducer was a local movie critic. Applause was louder than during any of Rick's recent lectures. He said so, gave thanks, and began:

"Phil Spector. Who was he?

"He was a legendary music mogul whose criminal case rocked this area and beyond. It was a case in which a jury had to decide if he had murdered a tall, beautiful movie actress. There were two trials, in fact, because the first one had ended in a hung jury.

"Throughout his career, he was variously described as:

–brilliant
–eccentric
–unbalanced
–and, sometimes, violent.

"Nonetheless, he made a mark as one of the giants in the music industry, more so as a record producer and songwriter than as a performer.

"He was once called 'a little man with lifts in his shoes, a wig on his head, and four guns.' He would flaunt firearms, including confronting performers or laughing while placing a loaded pistol at a fellow producer's head, or supposedly joking with a potential lover by inserting an unloaded gun in her mouth and pulling the trigger. Real weird!

"Such gunplay took a different turn in the early morning hours of February 2, 2003, however, when he was arrested on suspicion of murdering 40-year-old Lana Clarkson in his mansion.

"From the beginning, the death of a fading actress in the home of a reclusive music producer puzzled both the police and friends alike. Stories quickly circulated that Spector and Clarkson were drunk, engaged in playful activity and, in the process, she was accidentally shot. Another story was that she had been very depressed because she was an over-the-hill actress. She rejected Spector's sexual advances and, instead, kissed his gun and took her own life. Still another story was that it was an obvious case of murder, given the sexual rejection and his fascination with guns.

"But more about his life and career:

"He was born in 1939 in New York City; mastered piano and guitar at an early age; and when he was just 17, wrote a song titled, *To Know Him Is to Love Him*. It sold over a million copies in a month. Thirty years later, it became a hit again, this time for Dolly Parton and Linda Ronstedt. In his early 20s, he wrote hits like: *Spanish Harlem* for Ben E. King; *On Broadway* for The Drifters; and *You've Lost That Lovin' Feelin* for the Righteous Brothers. It's still cited as the song with the most U.S. airtime in the 20th century.

"So that was Spector, the songwriter. As a producer, he turned out such blockbusters as:

– *Zip-A-Dee-Doo-Dah*

– *My Sweet Lord*

– *Deep River-Mountain High*

– *Just Once in My Life*

– *Unchained Melody*

– *Ebb Tide*

– *Every Breath I Take*

– and the Beatles' colossal album, *Let It Be*.

"In fact, during 1960 to 1965, he produced over 25 Top Forty hits! Just remarkable!

"And during that period, he developed the revolutionary "Wall of Sound," a production technique that utilized a large number of musicians and their instruments to create a thunderous effect—with kind of an echo.

"He worked closely with John Lennon, Tina Turner, Connie Francis, Cher, and the Ramones.

"He won two Grammy Awards and, in 1989, was inducted into the Rock and Roll Hall of Fame.

"But before all that, during the '70s, he began to exhibit more erratic behavior and became more withdrawn. Some called him paranoid or schizophrenic. He kept a handgun in his waistband and let his hair grow longer, curlier and wilder.

"Now, what about Lana Clarkson? She was a 40-year-old struggling actress who was working as a VP hostess in a Hollywood nightclub. When she was younger, she had starred in 'B' movies, like *Barbarian Queen* and *Amazon Woman on the Moon*. She was statuesque, six-feet-tall, and still gorgeous. But there was much evidence that she'd become severely depressed over not having any film work and even in making ends meet.

"Spector met her for the first time at a nightclub and she agreed to accompany him to his home. She obviously knew he was an important man and probably still had key connections. His chauffeur drove them to his mansion, left them off near the back entrance and waited in the car–apparently to drive her home. Two hours later, he heard a shot and Spector came out the door, carrying a black handgun and saying, "I think I killed somebody." This can be taken several ways. The important thing, from the defense's point of view later, is that he didn't use the word 'murdered'. The chauffeur stated he looked behind Spector and, through the open door, saw a woman sprawled on a chair. The left side of her face was covered with blood.

"Spector was eventually arrested, the case went to trial and a mistrial was declared in September 2007. During that trial, five women testified that he had once threatened them with a gun.

"The prosecution claimed, 'Spector was a very dangerous man who has a history of playing Russian roulette with women–six women–Lana just happened to be the sixth.'

"The defense countered with, 'It was a circumstantial case. She was depressed over a recent romantic breakup and grabbed a .38 pistol from a nearby drawer and shot herself.'

"The first trial lasted 162 days–nearly six months.

"The prosecution focused on:

–sexual advances being spurned

–the key testimony of the chauffeur and of the 5 women who claimed he'd menaced them with guns

–and his previous history of gun play.

"The defense focused on:

–suicide as the manner of death

–an aging actress who was despondent over her

flagging career

–physical evidence from the death scene–like blood spatter, gunshot residue, tissue residue, and the location of the wound. I'll get to more of this in a moment.

"The defense was rather clever, I think, in stating it could produce a witness with no memory problems, no agendas, no language barriers–and that witness is called 'science'. They said they would prove that Spector couldn't have fired the shot by citing three things:

–the small amount of blood spatter on Spector's white jacket, in contrast to the large amount on Clarkson

–the small amount of brain tissue and gunshot residue on him as compared to what was on her

–that Clarkson's DNA was on the gun, not Spector's DNA.

"World renowned gunshot wound authority, Dr. Vincent DiMaio, testified for the defense and at one point commented on a list of forensic issues as if they were articles of faith–such as:

–in 38 years as a forensic pathologist, he found that people do not want to accept suicides so they will try to make suicides into murders

–that the large amount of gunshot residue on Clarkson's hands contrasted sharply with the single particle on Spector's hands

–referring to blood spatter on Clarkson's hands, he said it was the suicide equivalent of a positive pregnancy test. "It is not always present," he said, "but if it is there, it is there."

–that certain statistics supported suicide, saying

> that 90% of women who kill themselves do so by shooting themselves, and that 75% of such people fire into their heads.

"In September of 2007, the first trial had been declared a mistrial, and the second one that began in the spring of 2009 mirrored much of what went on in the first one … like I've already presented to you.

"In the second trial, defense attorney Lina Kenney Baden presented a six-hour closing argument. In it, she charged that law enforcement officials railroaded Spector because they were desperate to win a conviction against a celebrity. She said, 'They had a history of high-profile cases, like O.J. Simpson, Robert Blake and Michael Jackson, and a history of bad results.' She implied that the legendary music producer would be the first celebrity notch in the government's gun belt. She spent considerable time on the forensic evidence, which she said exonerated Spector, concentrating on the producer's dinner jacket and calling it probably the most important piece of evidence in the trial.

"She challenged the prosecution's claim that Spector was within three feet of Clarkson when the gun was fired, stating rather that the blast propelled blood and tissue from her mouth and nose 'like a bazooka.' Asserting that the sleeves of Spector's white jacket would have been heavily stained had he been holding the Colt revolver in her mouth when it discharged, she said, 'But those areas were pristine.'

"As for Spector's location at the time of the shooting, the defense attorney referred to the upward angle of the gunshot wound and said that, given the deceased's seated position in a low chair, Philip Spector would have to be kneeling between her legs to get that angle–'He's short, ladies and gentlemen, but he is not that short,' she emphasized.

"Finally, she dismissed the testimony of the five women and their claims against her client with the compelling statement: 'Stories don't trump science.'

"Summing up my personal view:

One–I don't believe it was murder.

Two–I don't believe it was suicide.

Three–I believe it was an accident. They were both drunk; he was nutty to begin with; they were horsing around; and she was shot.

Four–when all was said and done–that is, when the second verdict was rendered–'guilty with a sentence of 19 years to life'–the prosecution in California had improved its batting average."

- - - - -

Rick picked up his materials and began slipping to the side of the podium but quickly returned to the microphone and, ignoring the warm applause, said, "And I thank you all for your attendance and attention."

As the four men left the school, Rick hoped his lecturing was over and wondered if it had soothed the ire of the families of Sacco, Vanzetti, Lindbergh, Sheppard, and this one. His thoughts then drifted into the final two places that Mr.Vanzetti had labeled as possible disaster sites, places they would next visit: the Elgin Marbles in Britain and the Rock of Gibraltar. And since the visit to the last site hadn't been totally rewarding before, Rick wondered how he would react this time around.

But before long, and even though his mind was still over-crowded, other thoughts arose: the Nazis, the Mafia, Evita, Napoleon, and Saltanban.

How deeply involved will I be getting with them?

Chapter 23

London

April 20

Fran had once given Rick an article about the British Museum and its Elgin Marbles, and later the same day, one about Gibraltar. On the way to Britain, Rick located the first article in his briefcase and read it:

The "Elgin Marbles" is a popular term that in its widest use refers to the collection of stone objects–sculptures, inscriptions and architectural features–acquired by Lord Elgin during his time as ambassador to the Ottoman court of the Sultan in Istanbul. More specifically and more accurately, it is used to refer to those sculptures, inscriptions and architectural features that he acquired in Athens between 1801 and 1805. These objects were purchased by the British Parliament from Lord Elgin in 1816 and presented by Parliament to the British Museum. The collection includes sculptures from the Parthenon. Today, the Museum has grown to become one of the largest museums in the world. Greece has been hammering Britain for decades to return looted statues taken from its Parthenon that draws throngs each year to the British Museum. They are commonly known as the *Elgin Marbles* and are housed in a section of the Museum called the *Duveen Gallery.*

After landing at London Heathrow Airport, they informed a taxi driver of their interest in the Museum and were driven to Great Russell

Street, not far from the city's center. From the outside, the Museum stretched far and wide and had a Greek Revival façade with many columns. Leon counted 40 out loud before they stopped. An elongated pediment over the main entrance was decorated by allegorical figures. Inside, they passed by statues and by sections that were labeled with signs attached to adjoining walls, much like a person's identification tag: the Great Court, the Reading Room, the Enlightenment Gallery. They circled by a counter containing original Beatles lyrics; by the Magna Carta, the Rosetta Stone, and original manuscripts of iconic authors like Jonathan Swift, Henry Fielding, Charles Dickens and T.S. Eliott; by collections of early clocks, artifacts of early man and by some Rembrandt sketches.

Here and there, uniformed men and women stood like the statues inside but they managed smiles as the men passed by. They all bore a gun and nightstick attached to a leather waistband.

Eventually, the four men came upon a room with "Director" on its door. They entered and saw two neatly dressed men seated before cluttered desks. To either side were video screens depicting the activities of each floor of the Museum. They rose and greeted them warmly.

By now, Rick's routine of explaining possible disasters and thus advising additional security measures was engraved in his head. He stressed the Elgin Marbles and explained it all as if bored. But he quickly realized it, so pointing to the entrance door, he advised them to "double or triple the number of live statues you have out there." He thought he had cracked a joke, but only Ansel laughed.

It then seemed strange to Rick, but one of the security men said nearly the same thing that the four men had heard at the Eiffel Tower: "It *will* be done and thank you."

It had been some time since they had engaged in any sightseeing, so the consensus was to take in key London highlights. Only Leon had done so in the past. It was still early afternoon when Ansel rented a car and they drove off to view the many places of interest – to drive past them, or to stop and walk in and about them.

Rick hoped that the next few hours would be therapeutic, so he informed the others that while they were in London, he'd like to begin a new "order of business."

"It's not really 'business,' men, but what am I to call it – 'order of sightseeing'? You get what I'm driving at, don't you? And it would comply with a plea of taking our time."

They traveled to the elegant St. James, not far from Scotland Yard. Leon had stayed at the hotel twice before, considered it one of the finest examples of Edwardian architecture and so informed his cohorts. They then took a short walk past Buckingham Palace and St. James Park and as the sun grew brighter and the cry of circling birds became louder, they eventually came upon St. Paul's Cathedral. They didn't go inside but instead read a notice that was posted on one of its enormous doors.

> We welcome you to this historic Cathedral Church in the heart of London, a site that has been used for Christian worship since 604 AD. Our congregation comes from all over the world and from different branches of the Christian Church. We invite you to join heartily in your singing of the hymns and to associate yourself with the Choir, as it makes an offering to God on our behalf through Psalms, Canticles and Anthems.

The word that struck Rick the most was "heartily" for it was the way he began to feel as they continued on. They strolled by the Towers of Parliament, the Prince Albert Memorial, Westminster Abbey, and the famous Clock Tower as seen over the Westminster Bridge. Then to Trafalgar Square and a tube ride to Piccadilly Circus where they stopped for a quick pizza lunch. After that, they joined with others to feed some birds in St. James Park and then walked up Birdcage Drive to admire Big Ben and the well-known statue of Winston Churchill. After returning to the Palace to witness the changing of the guard, Rick breathed more heavily, for they were ready for the Cabinet War Rooms. They were located deeply underground and protected by a six-foot pad of steel and concrete.

Near the bottom of its entrance was a tripod locked by chain to a metal beam. Rick looked three doors ahead and saw a smaller tripod similarly locked. Both contained typed articles protected by glass. The first one was eloquently written by Beverly Shaver and indicated that she was a freelance writer from California. With some minor extractions it read:

War Room: Step Back Into World War II

They are not faces featured on the standard tourist circuits. They must be sought out, often in unlikely settings. But when experienced, they convey an urgent sense of a drama played out in time. Their mementos and monuments can pierce the heart and alter a visitor's consciousness in some permanent way.

London's Cabinet War Room complex is this sort of place. So that the world won't forget, the British government has painstakingly restored and opened to the public these underground headquarters where Winston Churchill, his War Cabinet and military chiefs worked. Here in the original settings, artifacts and exhibits tell the story of what happened more than 70 years ago at a nerve center of the Allied struggle against the Nazi juggernaut.

Within the complex, a continuous soundtrack chillingly recreates the ambience of London under the blitz – the day and night sirens, "those banshee howlings," the thunder of exploding missiles and crashing structures as the British people, with their backs to the wall in 1940, endured a deadly rain of destruction and death. Heard too, as one moves from room to room, is the rich baritone clang of Big Ben tolling defiance and reassurance. Visitors stop in their tracks to listen to the unbearably poignant broadcast words of Churchill, the "bulldog" leader, rallying his people: "Fill the armies, rule the air, pour out the munitions, strangle the U-boats, sweep the mines, plough the land, build the wounded, uplift the downcast and honor the brave."

This self-guided tour, aided by a map with explanatory text, begins with the steel-beamed Cabinet Room where more than a hundred meetings were held between 1940 and 1945. The critical importance of decisions and strategies arrived at in this subterranean chamber is belied by its Spartan simplicity. There on the far side of the rectangular conference table is the prime minister's broad-backed chair, doughty and emblematic beneath the world map.

American visitors find themselves swallowing hard at the glass frontage of a cubicle, one of the most important facilities in the complex. The small bare room appears a shrine-like setting for a black cult object–a cradle phone. Here was the ultimate in 1940s technology, a transatlantic hot line. From here, Churchill could speak directly by radio telephone to Franklin Roosevelt in Washington. On the wall to the right is a clock with black hands showing London time, red hands indicating Washington time. Further down the corridor is the room where the typists worked round the clock, breathing lightly of the vent-delivered air, often sleeping after late shifts in dormitories in the sub-basement. The typewriters here resemble the dusty clackety machines stored in our parents' attics, and the duplicating machine on the center table, incredibly, is turned with a hand crank.

Like all truly important museums, this War Room complex is more than a memorial and authentic setting of great events. It works in sounds, images and small telling events–the grim gas mask lying next to a shabby string purse spilling ration coupons; the quill pens and primitive little adding machines with tin flak helmets hung on pegs above them; the door to the Transatlantic

> Telephone Room with the special lock marked "Vacant" and "Engaged" taken from a toilet door; the cloudy little hand mirror in the Mess Room hanging next to a poster advising "Better Pot-luck with Churchill today than Humble Pie under Hitler tomorrow. Don't waste food!"

With the others' earphones turned on, Rick listened and read every word while they followed behind, apparently doing the same thing. But then they passed Rick, arrived at the second tripod and read its article more quickly.

In the meantime, Rick paused at each and every cubicle, taking in Churchill's bedroom, the War Room with a fan for his cigar smoke, the colossal map with its scattered pushpins, and an array of colorful phones nicknamed "the beauty chorus."

At the second tripod, Rick again digested what was written in a much smaller article by David Knowles taken from *Travel & Leisure*:

> A 21-room time capsule beneath the former Office of Works building, these Cabinet War Rooms are a far better memorial to World War II than Europe's deserted battlefields. From here, Churchill directed the British campaign. You can almost hear his shoe leather slapping against the linoleum floor. Wherever you look in this bunker-turned-museum–at the thousands of pinholes on a world map marking torpedo strikes, at the BBC microphone that the prime minister used to address the nation–the place simply resonates with the past.

Each man admitted that fatigue had set in–that this time the grouping of increased security measures with sightseeing over a most unusual span of time was enough for a day. Yet, they agreed to fly directly to Gibraltar.

Chapter 24

Gibraltar

"The Rock is straight south of here," Rick said. "We're three hours away–1,500-miles. I checked on it last night. We've got to give the usual security warning but also confer with Juan Saltanban. Remember my mentioning him? Well, his office is right next door. I've been giving him a lot of thought lately. And in conjunction with what? Two things: with what he calls his 'Synchronous Action Device' and with … are you ready for this? Histarians! Will he be willing to work with them to help us out?"

During the flight down, Rick opened his briefcase and found the article that Fran had given him a couple of days before. As Fran watched him, Rick read it:

> The Rock of Gibraltar is a limestone promontory of the British overseas territory of Gibraltar. The territory has a population of about thirty thousand. Most residents are descended from Italian, Maltese, Portuguese and Spanish settlers. Others are descended from British military personnel who were formally stationed there. Almost all inhabitants live in apartments in the town of Gibraltar, and the workers are primarily employed by its government, by dockyards or in jobs related to the tourist industry.
>
> As for the Rock itself, it is nearly 1,400 feet high and is

located off the southwestern tip of Europe on the Iberian Peninsula. It is considered crown property of the United Kingdom, forms a peninsula that juts out into the Strait of Gibraltar and borders Spain. Occupying nearly all of Gibraltar's 2.3 square miles, most of its uppermost area is covered by a nature reserve where about 250 Barbary macaques reside. These animals–the only wild population of monkeys in Europe–along with a labyrinthine network of tunnels–attract numerous tourists every year. The underground tunnels are known as the Galleries and the Great Siege Tunnels.

These underground tunnels have a unique history. They were first dug in the late 1700s. The British commander wanted to create the potential for cannon fire upon Spanish batteries in the area below the north face of the Rock. The siege lasted about four years, and during that span, the British constructed six such embrasures and mounted four cannons.

The so-called Galleries were constructed later on. Comprised of an entire system of halls, passages and embrasures nearly a thousand feet long, they too are a popular tourist attraction. From that location, visitors are able to view the Bay of Gibraltar, the isthmus and Spain itself.

All told, the Rock contains over one hundred caves. The most prominent and the most visited is St. Michael's Cave, situated halfway up the western slope of the Rock. Within it is another area called Cathedral Cave, once thought to be bottomless and therefore an underground link to Africa. This has never been substantiated. Cathedral Cave now serves frequently as an auditorium for concerts, ballet and drama presentations. The beauty of its crystallized

> surroundings draws raves from its numerous attendees. They are particularly drawn to a centuries-old stalagmite that became so heavy it dropped and landed on its side at the far end of the chamber.
>
> From a military standpoint, it was fortified by over 30,000 British soldiers and sailors during WWII, thus playing a key role in the defense of shipping routes in the Mediterranean. In 1942, during the war, the Allies launched an attack from Gibraltar against Germen and Italian forces in North Africa. And as recently as 1997, it was revealed that Britain had concocted a secret plan to hide servicemen in the Rock's tunnels in case the German's captured it. It was named "Operation Tracer" and had the radio capability to report all enemy movement. A six-man team remained undercover for over two years before they were disbanded and returned to civilian life.
>
> Such a history of sieges and military action is responsible for the popular saying "solid as the Rock of Gibraltar." Technically speaking, it is not based on the solidity of the Rock itself, rather on the action and dedication of the servicemen assigned to it.

It was 8 p.m. when they landed at the Gibraltar Airport. While waiting for Ansel and Leon to rent a car, Fran said, "Rick, I know you like to dictate some of your experiences, and I know they include a horrible one which you found hard to dictate. I've heard it once before . . . remember? I found it so fascinating. Would you be up to reading what you dictated two-years ago? I'd be all ears."

"Alright, I guess. You're very convincing, you know, but it was so hard to do last time and probably will be harder this time. Why I even keep the damn dictation with me–I have no idea. But here's what I dictated."

He found the pages stuffed in a side pocket of his briefcase and as he straightened them out, he coughed up some phlegm into a tissue.

"See," he said. "Even my salivary glands get upset."

> The following is my recollection of being held captive there. I've tried to be as accurate and complete as possible. In fact, I cannot help but remember most details. Only the dialogue may be off somewhat. Where I wasn't certain of the exact words spoken, I've inserted my best memory of them.
>
> I heard a knock on my door, rose and opened it. Four men, all tall, brawny and overly mustached, pushed me aside and burst into the room. Three of them kept their hands in their jacket pockets. The fourth identified himself as Tony and spoke fluent English. He barked at me: "Now don't say a word or make a silly move and you won't get hurt. Just come with us. Once again, no questions asked. You understand?"
>
> My first inclination was to ask a simple question or two. Wouldn't you? Maybe they had come to the wrong room. I felt my heart pounding, but still took a chance with a single word.
>
> "None?" I asked.
>
> "None. Just walk along with us to our van. We're driving up the Rock to a place I'm sure you've never seen. We'll keep you there until we receive further instructions. It might take awhile."
>
> I felt fortunate I wasn't hammered by one of them for asking a single word.
>
> Two of them grabbed me, one on each side, and the five men, closely aligned, headed down the corridor toward the back exit.

It wasn't long before the van reached the Cathedral Cave. A single taxi was ahead of us, followed by a line of others.

I was glad I wasn't blindfolded, but reasoned that my captors didn't want to alert anyone as to what was happening.

On the way, I gawked at the apes, wishing they were human enough to understand the situation and go for help.

When they reached the fallen stalagmite, the van pulled off to the side. The men waited for all the taxis to pass before squeezing out and leading me through a rusty gate that was hidden by the stalagmite. They remained outside as I stooped to enter, and I offered no resistance for fear of being roughed up. Tony then closed the door and said something like, "We'll be in touch." He then locked the gate–I don't remember how.

Right about then was when I wondered who ordered this … this imprisonment.

Through the bars, I said, "Now that I'm locked up, may I go ahead and speak?"

"Be my guest," was Tony's answer.

"Have you ever been in here?" I asked him. You see, I was already planning an escape based on my knowledge of worldwide caves and tunnels, and I figured the less they knew about the layout there the better.

"No," Tony said. He laughed and laughed, saying, "but I hear it's cool and cozy." I wished I had him alone.

Then they all disappeared. To where, I don't know.

From here on in, what I can describe has to do with what I faced without anyone trying to stop me. It wasn't easy, believe me, but I made it or I wouldn't be here to tell about it. To dictate it.

Just inside the gate, I strained to maintain my balance on craggy footing. I turned in a circle without feeling threatened, probably because I recognized the enclosure as some kind of anteroom to a cave tunnel. I reinforced my confidence by reviewing my many days of "caving", which included negotiating pitches, squeezes and –God help us–water holes, water streams and dirty ponds. But that was long ago. I stopped once I hit age 40, but before that, I'd regularly undertaken it for sheer enjoyment or for exploration as in mountaineering or diving.

This is where the term "spelunking" comes in. It refers to exploring caves as a hobby. For years I had a bumper sticker that read: "Cavers rescue spelunkers."

Even now, I can still see the lack of illumination and it got worse the farther I got, inches at a time. Soon I was enveloped in a montage of giant crystals and rock formations. I could identify most of them; the obvious stalactites and stalagmites, helicities, cave pearls and baconstrips formed from what were called dripstones and soda straws. What I could make out in the dim light, despite my experience, looked like an alien world. But the footing got better; I stumbled only once, and it became time to explore. I made out a higher landing beyond the overhang of a jagged side precipice. I found a gnarled length of wood propped against it and used it to claw my way upward, but it was a tedious process. Very tedious. Twice, I remember, I stepped on a rocky projection that split off, but I somehow managed to keep from falling by grasping others. I knew that if I did fall, it would have been curtains. And then, halfway up I guessed I was at the point of no return and wondered why in hell I'd begun the climb in the first place. Talk about being caught between a rock and a hard place!

But somehow I plowed ahead, or rather, *up*, and once on top, the light was dimmer and the air was chillier. Frigid, really. I was out of breath and coughing. What a feeling! I fell to my knees, then leaned back against–you guessed it–a large rock. I can still feel the clouds of dust worsening my cough. I was sure I had only minutes to live, and how does one feel when he's about to die? Does his whole life pass before him? Is that just an illusion or does it really happen? How would we know anyway? The person dies!

But instead of screaming, which I should have done, I ran through some of my earlier days when I volunteered to search for missing mountain climbers and was introduced to a phenomenon I'll never forget: "paradoxical undressing." It's what happens to some people when they're exposed to extremely cold temperatures over a long period of time. Hypothermia and it could lead to death. These poor souls are found in a protected location–under a bed, behind a couch, behind a boulder. I'm told that the theory is that this behavior is due to a primitive brain stem reflex of burrowing, as can be seen in hibernating animals. But it wasn't happening to me. I wouldn't let it. I recall checking my arms and found them cold, but not any different from when I was outside on a snowy night.

I squinted straight ahead and was able to make out a sloping tunnel that began far off. Not *too* far though–maybe a golfer's delight of 95 yards.

This time, I was convinced I could see a sliver of light. I pulled myself up and headed in that direction, brushing away spider webs and dodging bats flying by. As I trudged and trudged over uneven footing and still craved food–a sure sign that my ordeal hadn't wiped away my appetite–I thought how favorable it was that Tony and his goons hadn't passed beyond the gate with me. If they had, I might not have had the opportunity to climb the precipice, as perilous as it was.

The physical patterns of a whole host of caves crossed my mind as I moved along. Ones that I was familiar with: branchwork, angular network, anastomotic, spongework, ramiform. I knew, firsthand, that most were composed of carbonate rock, but even when I reached the start of the tunnel, I couldn't decide on what I'd be traversing.

One thing was clear, however: I'd be dealing with a steady stream of water, possibly with tributaries that would converge from the sides, feeding into the main current. How high the current would get suddenly became my main concern. I rolled up my pants to my knees.

Three-quarters along, I made out a gate ahead, similar to the one I'd entered before, and prayed it wasn't locked.

Throughout the entire length of the tunnel, the water came no higher than my ankles and, reaching its end, the gate opened easily. I walked out, pivoted around and gave the exit of the tunnel a sarcastic salute.

"Great as usual, isn't it?" Fran asked. "Now where are we in current life?

"Immersed in a brain-teaser just as complicated."

When Leon and Ansel returned, they left for the base of the Rock just in time to witness a changing of the guard ceremony. Leon had already commented on the regularity of it. It took place just outside an office door marked "Guard Office".

"This is the place," Rick said. "I can't wait to get it over with."

They went in and found a spacious room filled with a half-dozen men who, like the guards in London, were seated at desks and focusing their attention on video screens. All of them wore earphones and were leaning toward nearby radios while making notes.

Unlike the London office, however, one of the screens showed the quartet entering thc office. Reflexively, both Rick and Fran shrugged their shoulders to check on their guns, but then Rick said–loud and clear–"Hello … hello! May we have your attention?"

Two of the men removed their earpieces and came over. Then what occurred from that point on was, to Rick, like the remake of an old movie. He gave the same warning advice after elaborating on why it was necessary. The men, in turn, listened intently and, within minutes, stated that security throughout the Rock would be doubled within a half-hour.

Outside, the quartets' smiles would have filled a billboard. Rick said, "That's it, men. Mission . . . not impossible . . .but complete! Now for Mr. Saltanban. Get ready for something you won't forget. I haven't. Ranting and raving about telecommunications and a machine you won't believe exists."

Chapter 25

Juan Saltanban's office complex was less than a stone's throw away from the Caleta Palace Hotel, one nestled into a sheer cliff, with balconies facing the ocean, ships off in the distance, and zillions of birds chirping overhead. They stayed there for the night.

As they headed for the complex early the next morning, the stench of workers' heavy drilling at the foot of the Rock gave way to the soothing odor of Catalan Bay. Instead of what one might expect around damp and fishy docks, the air now smelled clean and raw, as if everything could start over.

Earlier, Rick had phoned Juan about a possible upcoming visit and was encouraged by a most positive reply . . . that he would be anxiously awaiting their arrival.

In addition to hearing the pronouncements of a man Rick described as brilliant, he wanted to see if the Synchronic Action Device–or SAD–might assist in their work involving the retrieval of stolen goods.

The walk to the complex was as sunny and delightful as it was in the past. Rick recalled its shabby gray exterior that had been replaced by glistening green paint that again made his eyes smart.

They opened a set of ebony doors and walked onto an elongated balcony. Just as before, a loud bell resounded throughout the balcony, though no one answered its call. Rick looked down over a railing and was more impressed than he had been the last time, for the number of interconnected rooms had tripled. He reasoned that such enlargement had been possible by extending added construction onto a nearby area of plush meadowland. Each of the rooms was occupied by a female employee who was working at a computer, never looking up, typing like a robot. Rick didn't say it, but he wondered if Juan was somehow controlling them with his SAD.

The contents of each room hadn't changed though: a beech-colored swivel chair with a waterfall seat edge and contoured backrest; teak side tables that held a computer, printer and copying machine; a large shredder; and a table with a glass top, below which a steel frame rested on cubic pillars.

Suddenly they heard Juan's voice emanating from an overhead speaker. "Welcome, gentlemen," he said. "I shall be there in a minute or two."

Rick felt it gave him the time and opportunity to explain the relationship between Juan and himself, so he motioned for the triad to take seats on a side bench and then joined them. He began:

> We first met four years ago at a scientific symposium in Berlin. He was lecturing there. I was impressed with his grasp of science and a bit intrigued with his refusal to use words that had contractions. He was the first person I'd ever met who spoke that way and I haven't met any others since. Or should I say, "I had" and, "I have not"? Anyway, when asked about his background, he stated that he was once the president of Radonia in South America but quickly gave up politics and moved to this present location because he liked the protection of the Rock next door. He even composed a song titled, "In the Shadow of the Rock."

Rick had more to say but Juan appeared out of nowhere. "Greetings," he said.

"Thanks for having us," Rick responded. He introduced the triad and all handshakes were full and prolonged.

"Come down to my studio," Juan said.

They followed him along the balcony until they reached a pair of rooms. As he led them past the first one, Rick noticed that its door had a steel beam across the front with a padlock at the end of it. They arrived at the far room–tiny and crowded with stacks of papers everywhere–on tables, chairs, the floor. The tallest stacks nearly concealed a small desk. Only a nameplate could be made out. It read, "Juan Carlos Saltanban."

Juan spread his arms and said with a touch of fanfare, "What is it you Americans say: 'Violá, my cubbyhole'."

"You said 'pigeonhole' last time," Rick said.

"Pigeonhole, cubbyhole . . . it is both."

Juan opened a closet door, dragged out five chairs and asked them to sit. They did after apologizing for not helping out.

Rick felt that Juan hadn't changed much, except that his goatee was grayer and his stoop was more pronounced. Tall and hefty, he was nearly sixty-years-old and was no doubt dying a head of curly, dense hair. He was wearing square, wire-rimmed glasses that were attached to a red and blue chain. On each finger was the expected gold signet ring, a "J" in script on his left one and a "C" on his right one. Rick recalled once asking him why there wasn't simply a "JC" on each of them and the response was, "No, no. These are for 'Juan Carlos'. Your way is reserved for someone more important than I am. Jesus Christ."

Rick also recalled Juan's reference to Radonia, and asking him how he got interested in telecommunications before the short stint in politics. Not much varied from the way he expressed it years ago. He again spoke of his interpreting smoke signals; of the Sumerians who developed the first known system of writing; the Romans who started the first newspaper; the English who introduced the first known pencil; the French who developed photographs; and the Canadians who put the first radio together. Next he dwelled on three Americans who invented the telegraph, the telephone and the phonograph: Morse, Bell and Edison.

As he said before, "The telegraph was a very important instrument during your Civil War for both your press and the armies of both sides. And it helped at your stock exchange and at your railroads."

Rick became more attentive than he expected because he'd suffered through it all before.

"You have heard enough?" Juan asked.

"No, do continue."

"How about you other gentlemen?"

"Do continue," Leon said.

Rick appeared as though he was strengthening his resolve to seek all he could from Saltanban, while Fran and Ansel looked like individuals suffering from a rare disease.

Saltanban went on: "What did I plan on next? Ah … the telephone. You know, two funny things. One, the sound a telephone makes is a bell. And Alexander Graham Bell discovered it in the late 19th century. Is that not something? And two, one never thinks of it, but at the beginning there were no switchboards. They came during the next year. Then came dial phones, service between countries, and the two things that I am most interested in. Do you know what either one is?"

"Public speaking," Rick blurted out. He paused before adding: "I am sorry … no, *I'm* sorry … but I couldn't resist. Do keep going, Juan."

"Alright then. I am most interested in … first, commercial satellites. Think of them as relay stations." He stopped for a brief moment to begin playing with a spot on the carpet with the toe of his shoe. "But I shall not elaborate here. Why have they not simply been called 'relay stations'? But I have said enough about this. Was it a mixup? I am afraid I ramble once again, and if I do not stop rubbing that spot, it will soon become a hole." It appeared that he tried to smile, but his face wouldn't cooperate.

"Some other time," he said, "perhaps I might further discuss the radio and the phonograph. So now, I hope you understand that it is all related … all these forms … and all these countries that somehow wanted to … how do you say it … wanted to get into the act. Anyway, we are now up to the second thing I am most interested in: plans about advanced telecommunications."

During all the speaking and all the listening, Rick had his mind set on the SAD in the other room. But, not wanting to rush things for fear it might disrupt Juan's eventual cooperation–and the reason for the visit–he played along.

"Meaning what?" he inquired.

"Meaning what? I must get even more technical. Bell Laboratories discovered the transistor; Xerox the copier; and Corning Glass the first optical fiber that could be used for long-range communication. Fiber optics, you know, uses a laser to send signals through glass or plastic. Sending signals? Ah! My company used to deal with fiber optics and satellites primarily, but we have more recently concentrated on cybernetics. I wanted to advance knowledge about how information is transmitted by the control mechanism of machines and the nervous system of human beings, and that is where my SAD comes in. Should we go see it now?"

"Absolutely," Rick said. "But before that, how about computers? You never said anything about them, but where do you feel they're taking us? Do you feel the same way about them?"

"Because you told me when you called that you have investigated international crime, you might want to hear about some definite thoughts I have about computers. The crime-computer link. I am concerned. The Internet with its encrypted messages can be such a tool of secrecy that crime of every kind will become electronic and will take place once the decision is made. Drug operations, fraud, embezzlement, prostitution, blackmail, government conspiracies, military coups, murder. Much is possible now, but it can get worse, all due to computers. In the matter of terrorism, for instance.

"And even in business or education or government work, face-to-face meetings may no longer occur. A computer will be a sword with a double edge. Email. The Internet–an Information Super-Highway, but one that is filled with–what are they called? Potholes? It is the secrecy that is my worry. Split second. Cheap. Yes, computers are good but can become evil. I am afraid the whole planet has an analog intelligence dealing with a digital threat. That is how I view it. End of ramble. Now let us go see my model–the SAD."

As they left for the next room, Rick nearly voiced amazement over his host's knowledge, but instead asked, "Is it bigger now?"

"No, smaller."

"Smaller?"

"Yes, smaller and smarter. Improved. The information it was feeding me was really unclear. But now–by removing a wire here, a switch there, it gives me not only clarity but also greater information. What did you say you wanted it to do?"

"I'll follow your question with a question. Can it help identify a specific criminal who's calling either another criminal or an institution or, let's say, an auction house?"

"Yes, it is how it can now work. It could do only half of that the last time you saw it, Rick. But I would need an address to begin with, and then the SAD would verify who it belongs to."

Rick thought he would speak to histarian Lance Beck about the issue. But at the same time he remembered being told of the addresses and names controversy. He so informed Juan of it.

"Do not worry," Juan said. "The SAD can handle it."

Rick didn't know how it could come about, but he didn't run it down. Instead, he rubbed the palms of his hands and said, "*Perfect.* And it's got me to thinking, Juan. We don't need you. Just lend us your model." Laughter came in tiny spurts.

Saltanban led them to the next door where he removed the padlock and lifted away the steel beam.

There, on a table in the center of the room was a box with a sliding front panel and a golden handle on top. He slid the panel aside and proudly revealed a device the size of a small sewing machine. It sported row upon row of miniature screws, nuts, bolts, washers, dials, clips, hooks, pins, needles, knobs, levers, tubing, eyelets, springs, brads, clasps, staples, hoses, chains, sprockets, cables, valves, blades, belts, bushings, drills, rods, grommets, pumps, compressors, wheels, shafts,, hammers, buttons, fasteners, discs, latches, graces, tacks, hinges, cords, locks, and plugs.

It was a toss-up as to who was the most impressed … Rick for the third time or any of the others for the first time.

"You're right," Rick said. "It's smaller."

"And do not forget," Juan added. "Smarter, too. So you think I can be of service to you? I mean me and my model here?"

"No doubt about it. I'll call you when we have some addresses."

They returned to Juan's studio, he summoned one of his workers for coffee and doughnuts, and while consuming them, the men shared a mutual satisfaction with the past half-hour. "Especially me," Juan said. "And anyone who lives through my rambling deserves my help. That is why I shall give it. There is an old saying: 'What merits help is a merit in itself.'"

At the ebony doors, Juan said, "Gentlemen, I will be waiting for the call, and I hope I can be of service."

Rick led the handshakes and said, "Juan, you're definitely the key player in our grand design."

Saltanban responded with, "But this will not be a game, so I am not a player."

"Understood, but before we leave, I'd like to ask a last question: Do you know what 'histarian' refers to?"

"Oh yes. I have worked with them before."

Rick was both surprised and heartened.

"Could you again?"

"Yes, they are easy to work with."

"I agree. And a final thought–not a question. We haven't discussed it, but your company will be entitled to compensation."

"Money?"

"Yes, good old money."

"No, no. I am aware of the fact that you do not expect to be paid for what you are doing. And neither should my company be paid. Au revoir."

On the way out, Rick wondered where and how Saltanban gets all his information.

Is there anything or anybody he doesn't know?

Chapter 26

New Haven

Now Rick had to obtain some addresses. And once again, histarians were the solution. He decided to phone Lance Beck, hoping they might meet again at the Yale Library. The histarian asked Rick how things were going and received a comment that Rick had often made: "At least I'm upright and so are my buddies."

"Hey, that's really clever," Lance said, "Not up-*tight*, but up-*right*. I think I'll use it myself."

"No need to give me credit, though. But what I'd like to discuss with you, Lance, is something that should remain confidential and that means 'in person and not by phone.' You get the gist of what I'm saying?"

"Yes and yes."

"Yes and yes?"

"I get the gist of it, and I can meet you at the usual library."

"Good, and I hope I didn't sound too flippant."

"No you didn't, and I'll be there."

Flight time from Gibraltar seemed like a wasted eternity to Rick even though he made more notes on his pad and read all the articles in a newspaper that an airline steward had given him. At one point–during a deep yawn–he thought he saw a strange man staring at him. The man was sitting up front and, for one fleeting moment, had turned his head around the back of his seat. But Rick attributed the sight to his watery eyes and set it aside. Then when the plane landed, he didn't even bother to check on it before disembarking through the rear door.

It was mid-afternoon in New Haven. As agreed upon, Leon, Fran and Ansel skipped the library meeting in favor of taking the rest of the day off. It was a day that, weather-wise, matched Rick's mood: dreary, downcast and looking as though it might storm.

Inside, Lance was seated and looking through a magazine. He stood up as Rick approached him and, after a "good-to-see-you" and a handshake, they went to the L & B room. Rick was glad there was no one else there so they didn't have to speak in a whisper.

"I know it's been only two weeks since we last spoke," Rick began, "but so much has happened since then … . more like two *months'* worth, and I won't waste your time on all of it. I've asked for this meeting, Lance, because you're an histarian and when we last got together, you implied that I could reach out to you for information. But if it's sensitive information, it can't be done over the phone. And I assure you–this *is* sensitive information."

Rick then outlined what he and Saltanban had agreed upon, and even mentioned the SAD and what it could do. "But what is needed now are addresses of known criminals . . . well, not really *any* criminals . . . but ones suspected of stealing or buying valuable goods. The criminals could have moved or even died, and the addresses could now belong to new and innocent people. But Saltanban said he could handle that. Bottom line? Do you have any addresses?"

"I don't, but some of my histarian colleagues do. We've talked about it. I could meet with them to get the addresses and then provide them for you."

"I appreciate it, Lance. Just call me. My phone is special. I'm not sure how it works, but the fact is that I can be reached *anywhere*. And for me, 'anywhere' means around the world."

"I'll be calling you then."

Rick knew of Lance's busy schedule and, as he nodded and rose from his chair, he said, "Thanks, and I'll be awaitin'."

At the front door, Rick turned around and said, "I almost forgot, but I need one more favor. Could you check on the background of a guy named Franz Kauffman? He's a professor at the Federal Institute of Technology in Zurich."

"Switzerland? That's where Evita had ties with the banks there. And the country also hid Holocaust money."

Lance stopped for some scribbling in his pad and afterward said, "I'll have the professor info too … when we talk again."

Chapter 27

At home, Rick sat at his desk with a degree of comfort that was physical, not mental. For he had a major question that needed answering: Who would he be the most comfortable with when baring his soul about what he labeled loose ends? He transferred a partial list of people, places and things from his mind to his pad. For weeks now, they had been either privately pored over by himself or kicked around by him and his friends. In the transfer, he uttered the following out loud as if he were going through the alphabet until the correct word came up: Chief Gomez, stolen art, Mafia, Nazis, Switzerland, the *Seacraft* ship, its captain, prostitutes, terrorism, Scar-face, histarians, questions for Saltanban, the SAD machine.

And the answer became obvious: Chief Gomez! He called him.

"Joe," he said, "I need to talk to you. What would it be … the umpteenth time? I need your opinion on a number of things. You could probably recite them yourself because some have come up in our conversations. I'm now lumping them altogether as my loose ends. The list is long."

"I can't believe this, Rick. I have something to get your opinion on, too. Why don't we meet halfway from here to there, say in Cartagena, Colombia? Have you ever been there?"

"No, but I hear it's nice, and I'm all for it."

"Well, I've been there several times. Good hotels, good restaurants, good sightseeing–right up your alley. Why don't you fly to the CTG Airport and it'll be just a 10-minute taxi drive to the Hilton Cartagena Hotel. You use American Airlines?"

"All the time."

"I do too, and they have flights landing there regularly, so I'll meet you 24-hours from now. If we foul up somehow, check in for a hotel room. I figured we'd be staying overnight anyway. And one last thing: you mentioned a list. Could you read it to me now so I could give it some thought before tomorrow? We're not histarians, so using the phone will be safe."

Rick read the list slowly and without comment.

- - - - -

Fran joined Rick on the flight south. They landed at the airport early the next afternoon and, as they disembarked, the beauty of the city could already be seen. Rick did some thinking.

Do we sightsee first? Should I read all signs and posters?

It was as if the plane south and the plane north had colluded, for the three of them had arrived at the air terminal at the same time! Rick considered it a good omen.

It took less than a minute for them to locate each other, and they passed over handshakes as Gomez asked, "Can you believe this?"

"It's like we flew in the same plane," Fran said.

"Exactly, and I'm glad you came along, Fran."

"Thank you, sir."

"Sir? What's that all about?"

"You're a Chief of Police."

"That I am. But in Buenos Aires, I sometimes feel as though I'm called upon for everything."

"Okay then–should I make it 'Chief'?"

"No, 'Joe' will do."

"Fellas, we're wasting time," Rick interjected. "So let's take our luggage bags and huddle somewhere to decide on what we do and when we do it." They found a long bench.

Seated there, Rick said, "I don't think this is very complicated. Three decisions: sightseeing, eating, and the meeting. I suggest in that order. You both agree?"

Fran said, "Agree."

Gomez said, "Me too, and because there's so much to see, the best way is to take a tour. The guides on the buses here are the best anywhere, including Argentina. Then if it's not too late, we can start our meeting. I'll go first and it won't take long. All I want is your opinion on how I handled something."

"The cruise ship business?" Rick asked.

"Yes. Then we do your loose ends during as much time as you need. I studied your list last night, and I have a certain approach for you."

- - - - -

The bus they chose was parked in a row of them on a main street. Each was called a chiva bus according to Gomez, and was brightly painted with vibrant murals of Cartagenian scenes. They climbed the side ladder of one with a card posted on its windshield that read, "FOR AMERICANS." They then slid across a pew-like row of seats and listened to a young microphoned guide who offered an apology for the bus's pulsating lights, tweeting horns and kumbaya dance beats blaring from loudspeakers. "It will keep you awake," he said. He wore a belly-baring crop top along with aqua-colored shorts. A nametag for "Alfredo" was pinned over his heart. He noticed many visitors checking the tag and he said, "Please just call me 'Al'." And with a full smile, he added, "And please understand that during what you'll be seeing, I'll be combining it with much history. Maybe **too** much, but I think it is important and fascinating. So let us begin."

He wore glasses but spoke without notes. "If you ask a cross-section of Americans what the word 'Cartagena' invokes in them, chances are they'll mention the movie, *Romancing the Stone*, or their fears about Colombia's long-running drug war. In reality though, the 1984 adventure-comedy was filmed in Mexico. Cocaine kingpin Pablo Escobar's mansion, located an hour off the coast, has been steadily decaying since his death in 1993, and the drug war itself, never centered here, has been steadily losing steam for a few years now.

"These days, our beautiful, safe Cartagena is an increasingly popular tourist destination for travelers from South America and the States--as you can see in this crowded but heated bus."

"Founded as an important Spanish port in 1533, our Old Town is a UNESCO world heritage site and remains largely intact behind stone walls that peer out over the Caribbean. A visit here isn't your typical beach vacation, as you might just as easily immerse yourself in history, art and theater as you can take a dip in the sea. Imagine a less crowded New Orleans or San Juan without the glitz."

Rick felt as though the sightseeing would be taking a back seat to what lay beyond it, for he was not only anxious to receive advice from Gomez but also to learn what the chief himself wanted to hear. That was the way it had been lately … a switch, not in time, but in anticipation. And there were so many things behind and ahead of him that he spent more time giving in to the barrage. Relaxation had become an effort. He understood it and, with sweat doubling over his forehead, he slipped off his loafers and opened the top two buttons of his short-sleeve shirt.

Al continued: "Old Town and Bocagrande are the two main tourist neighborhoods, but aside from being partially set beside the sea, they have little else in common."

As they passed by an open-air bar, he said, "Try to immerse yourselves in the 16th century for a couple of hours, then climb the northern ramparts to greet the sunset with a cocktail at the bar you see over there. It looks out on the sea, at the traffic on Santander Avenue and over the skyline of Bocagrande."

Still with no notes, he explained, "Designed as a mini-version of Rio's Copacabana, Bocagrande is lined with a jumble of high-rises, chain hotels, congested traffic, pockmarked sidewalks, gleaming shopping malls and casual beach-shack cafés. Its shore is dotted with umbrellas and lounge chairs as well as lawn chairs beneath canopies emblazoned with cell-service logos. You'll be finding a similar mix of new construction, scruffy local vendors and wealthy Colombians on the prettier beach at La Boquilla, a Miami-esque luxury condo and hotel district merging from one of the oldest and poorest sections of the city.

"To get a fuller sense of our era-spanning sprawl," as Al put it,they drove up to see Convento de la Popa, a huge convent built by Augustinian monks in 1607 atop the highest hill in the city. They passed by some souvenir kiosks in a dusty parking lot and headed toward a brick-paved path that ran almost all the way around the convent and were rewarded with gorgeous, wide-reaching views of Cartagena."

Al signaled for their driver to slow down and then said, "Within those convent walls, you'd find a small chapel decorated with gold– and a romantic, gently eroding courtyard rimmed with potted palms."

Rick was beginning to think that their guide had taken some classes in poetry.

Closer to sea level, there were city views of a fort that was meant to deter foreign armies and hordes of pirates during the 17th and 18th centuries. "This mega-fort took roughly 120 years to build and is still amazingly intact today," Al said. "If we stopped, you'd be allowed access to tunnels here that were designed to keep soldiers safe during battle.

"Now onto color as we go on. Our grand city isn't kidding when it comes around to red, white and blue. Did you Americans get that? And any other color, too. You would wake up your sense of *alegria*–Spanish for 'joy'–if you took a stroll past these vividly-painted Spanish-Colonial houses of Old Town." He pointed with his glasses. "They lend a little glamour to the gracefully decaying streets."

They finally stopped and all the visitors edged out. "Take your time and enjoy what you see," Al said.

On almost every street, they saw Colombian-made bags, scarves, shoes and more–all in a slew of shades. In artesian shops and galleries, they also found rainbow-hued beaded jewelry, leather goods, papier-mâché masks, and miniature versions of local scenes.

The heat was relentless and Rick opened two more buttons. So did the others, even Al.

During another stop, he said, "If you're an art lover, you'll want to visit two different spots in our Old Town. One is a house that displays huge canvasses, technicolor graphics, powerful sculptures and intricate installations by Colombian artists. Do go to this Museum of Modern Art. The other spot is a modern gallery stocked with tongue-in-cheek works by artists who largely hail from Colombia as well as South America and Europe.

"Then, across the street from Old Town's yellow Clock Tower, you can either stroll through a leafy little park or march past massive legendary horses to enter an emerging neighborhood full of artists, poets and writers that blends the charm of Old Town with the former rubble of New York's Lower East Side."

The rest of the tour was beginning to awaken Rick to a more appreciative level. He was seated next to Fran and at one point he whispered in his ear, "Outstanding, eh?"

"Yeah, but it's too long."

Gomez nodded.

They had been at it for less than an hour and the rest of the tour took another half-hour.

Temperature-wise, it was now a perfect early evening. A light breeze was blowing in off the ocean as they made their way to Gomez's favorite Colombian restaurant, *Old Town's La Teibol.* It was 5:10 p.m.

They shared a dinner of mac-and-cheese served with a blended lobster tail. There was little talk and it didn't take long, as they simply wanted to get the dinner over with and begin their meeting in Gomez's hotel room.

"I'll go first," he said. "It shouldn't take long and then we'll discuss your loose ends. Take as much time as you need."

Chapter 28

In the hotel room, Gomez turned on the air conditioner; then he and Rick removed folders from their suitcases. Along with Fran, they dragged three chairs over to a table and sat down.

Gomez made a quick study of a paper he'd removed from his folder. At the same time, Rick followed suit and even underlined a sentence or two.

"So I'll lead off," Gomez said. "I went ahead and checked on the *Seacraft*, and yes, it does ship valuable books to New York on a regular basis. From there they're taken by plane to Switzerland and then on to Belarus. I interviewed the ship's captain and learned that prostitutes are somehow used in all of this. In the end, I stopped the shipping and had the captain arrested. He's now awaiting trial. That's it in a nutshell."

"And?" Rick asked.

"And I want your opinion. Have I handled it right?"

"I don't know how you could have done any better, so my answer is 'definitely'."

"See? Short and sweet. Thank you and now for your turn."

"Okay. Fran is sick of all this, but kick in, buddy, if I'm leaving anything out."

"I'll do that, but knowing you, you won't."

Rick looked over his sheet and began: "Joe, I've talked about these things; researched them; read everything posted wherever we went; and thought about all of them until I was blue in the face. But none of them are completely settled—at least to my satisfaction. I think they're really my 'loose ends'. I know you've read over the list, so could we take them in order and try to remove each one. That is, after we come to an agreement about what to do?"

The chief's eyes never left his sheet for a full five-minute response: "First off, a lot of combining needs to be done. And here's what I mean. You have twelve things listed. I've reduced them all into seven categories.

"Number one–you're making the Nazis and the Mafia too complicated. You can't argue with history. That's over and done with. Former Nazis and current mafiosi will continue to band together no matter what you try to do about it. And now–at the present time–the only reason for investigating them is to learn their role in stealing valuable goods. You've already determined that. They *have* such a role, and arrests should be made, even if it's only one at a time. Remember the word, 'deterrent'.

"Number two–it's what I just went over: shipping of books, prostitutes, and so on. Arrests have been made.

"Number three–questions for Saltanban. His device. Fine.

"Number four–terrorism will continue. I agree with the way American political philosopher Michael Walzer summed it up. I have it written here: 'Terrorism is the deliberate killing of innocent people, at random, to spread fear through a whole population and force the hand of its political leaders.' Plus the Internet says that criminal acts will always occur. And your government will have to handle it, not you.

"Number five–your speeches have been convincing. I hear that family members of the five men who were probably innocent–as you stated during the lectures–are satisfied that bad reputations have dwindled, and that the bombing threats no longer exist.

"Number six–Scar-face and maybe others like him. That will stop once they learn of how you've torn into the other five categories.

"And number seven–Fabio Calderone. Do call him and find out how he might help.

"Now," Gomez said, finally staring at Rick: "May I act like a father?"

Rick looked more than relieved–more like an innocent prisoner who just had wrist and ankle cuffs removed. "Yes, I'd welcome it," he said.

"You've got to realize you can handle just so much. Regarding the problems, some can be eliminated from the list and some can't. It's like a neighboring police chief interfering with items in my jurisdiction. So you should let it go at what you've done so far–nothing more except following through with Saltanban. And with that Calderone guy I met at our summit meeting. To be blunt about it, Rick, I think you've taken on way too much.

"Stop being in a hurry and relax. But call Angela and have her come home. Then the two of you should travel because you like it–not because you must solve everything. And don't give up writing. End of sermon."

As Rick had expected, the meeting had taken up much less time than sightseeing there in Cartagena. But in terms of a baseball game, the meeting had scored more runs.

Chapter 29

Rick arrived home early the next afternoon and no sooner had he emptied his suitcase than he was answering a call from Lance. The histarian had addresses to give and Rick wrote them down at a measured pace: 15 minutes for 25 addresses.

Lance was late for something again, so there was little extra talk. Besides, Rick wanted to phone Saltanban with the information, and he was about to when one of Gomez's phrases rang in his ear: "Stop being in a hurry . . ." So he tossed the paper with the addresses onto his desktop and went slowly through a back door and onto a graveled walkway.

To create what he called his New Haven Rock Garden, he had spent many hours digging, smoothing, lifting and sweating. He learned that when his rocks got wet from rain, they'd be especially beautiful because vibrant color veins would pop out.

It must have rained overnight because
I can smell it and I can feel it.

After he and Angela had moved there, he believed that mulch would have been as good as what he now saw. It was then that he began thinking: *It's not just seeing, it's feeling*. Right now, his feeling was that he had become unstrapped and unhinged from challenges that had accumulated faster than he realized they would. Or could. And he next coupled that feeling with an uncertainty about deserving a friend like Chief Joseph Gomez.

This little interlude was enough to erase any hurry-up behavior, so he walked back inside–slowly. He phoned Juan Saltanban and gave him the addresses.

"That should be enough," Juan said. "I will start the process. Word travels swiftly among criminals. Almost every one of them feels so guilty that he feels like if he continues, he will be caught. So after my SAD and I do our thing, we wait. Just wait. In addition to individual arrests being made, what we have done will serve as a deterrent."

Where did I hear that before?

"And by a deterrent, I do not mean a barricade. I mean a fly in their ointment. A fly that can remain there forever because we will have cut off its wings. So again I say we wait."

Then came the last of Gomez's categories: calling Fabio Calderone.

"Fabio? It's me–Rick Chandler. I hope you're well and if you're wondering about me, I'm so-so. But I'll get right to the point. I'm calling to see if you know of any Mafia activities that might be related to what we're trying to do. Especially if they're on-going. Chief Gomez says it's the kind of thing that would pay dividends in our overall - - - let's see, how should I put it? I've used this phrase so often - - - in our 'overall scheme of things.' If you remember: at our summit meeting, we talked about where we stand on things; on what's been done and on what still needs to be done. Well, this needs to be done."

"You know, Rick–I can't believe this. It so happens that I got a call–just last night, in fact–about it's being time for another of their get-togethers. Not for a large one but for their most important people in the area. The caller said it's the most important they'll ever have."

"You get calls like that?"

"Oh, yes. They treat me like I'm a retired general in their Army. I go along with it, but I have no intention of becoming one of them again."

"And they meet regularly?"

"Yeah, usually in a bar or a restaurant. They rotate around. But this one's scheduled for the *Moulin Rouge* in Paris – for tomorrow night at seven. In a dressing room there. They said I should attend for old time's sake."

"The *Moulin Rouge!*" Rick said, half under his breath. "Maybe you should go, or maybe you could take us along and we'll have a look. That would be you, me, and Leon."

Rick then maneuvered his fingers and hands around, as if trying to figure out how they would meet. He could still recall eating at *le Jules Verne* restaurant in the Eiffel Tower, but more vivid was the recall of its spread-out lounge.

"I have an idea," he said. "Why don't we meet in the lounge of *le Jules Verne* restaurant, and then we could mosey over to the *Rouge?*" They agreed.

In the meantime, he went to his computer and read the following on the Internet:

The "Moulin Rouge" stands for the "Red Mill" and is a cabaret in Paris, France. It is best known as the birthplace of the modern form of the can-can dance. Originally introduced as a seductive dance by the courtesans who operated from the site, the can-can dance revue evolved into a form of entertainment of its own and led to the introduction of cabarets across Europe. Today, the Moulin Rouge is a tourist attraction, offering musical dance entertainment for visitors from around the world.

He landed at the Charles de Gaulle Airport the next day, then taxied to the Tower and went directly to the lounge. Both Leon and Fabio had gotten there already and Rick didn't ask them to elaborate. He was preoccupied with the success or failure of a plan he was eager to carry out. It was a little before 6 p.m.

From there, they piled into a cab and reached the Rouge in no time at all. There, Rick paused briefly to admire its red color and the windmill on the roof. Then he led the way to the back of the building where, at a main door, they were greeted by an employee who was wearing a shirt with a picture of the Rouge on its front side.

"Good evening," Rick said. "I'm an author and these are my publishers. I have a scene in the book I'm now writing that takes place right here. Not out front, but here." He then gave the man a 50-dollar bill; Leon quickly matched it; and the man thanked them while slipping the bills into his pocket.

"Anyway," Rick continued, "my main character goes inside – through a door like that one – and he comes upon not the ballroom, but a series of dressing rooms for men. I want to be as accurate as possible in writing about what's taking place in one of them and, at the same time, I don't want to alarm anyone in the room. So is there a window we can peek through … like one built with one-way glass?"

"I have just the window for you," the employee said. "There are a few men in there right now. They don't belong to our cast, and I believe they rented the room."

Rick felt as though he had just won the lottery and was tempted to scream about it for everyone to hear. Basically, however, they had arrived at the correct room and he didn't care if it was by design or good fortune.

Through the window, he saw five men: Gomez's receptionist, Carlos; Scar-face; Professor Kauffman; Ralph Garbaroni, the Mafia don; and his associate, John Rizzo. On the floor were two large cartons filled with what appeared to be 100-dollar bills. The two mafiosos were handing packs of them to the other three.

"They're getting paid for their work as informants or, in the case of that Scar-face, as an intimidator," Rick whispered.

Both he and Leon checked for their guns.

"Should we rush them?" Fabio whispered back.

"No, not yet," Rick said. "Let's wait until their pockets are completely stuffed."

It took about 90-seconds for Leon to react. As if he had seen enough, he pushed Rick and Fabio aside, rushed through a nearby door and, after flashing a badge, waved his gun at them.

Then he said, "By the authority bestowed upon me by the *Préfecture de Police* here in Paris, I hereby arrest all of you."

Rick felt a wave of relief. And he realized that within three weeks, he and his cohorts had turned a combination of intent, travel and terror into a subject for his next novel.

Epilogue

–Angela returned home.

–Because word got around about their investigations, and with the help of police authorities, many of the valuables were returned to their rightful owners.

–Rick followed most of Chief Gomez's advice regarding the "bucket list", namely:

(1) He stopped making the Nazi/Mafia issue so complicated, for they would band together no matter what.

(2) He helped in making arrests in the case of shipping valuable books.

(3) He arranged for the assistance of Juan Saltanban.

(4) He began to understand that it was the government that would deal with the ever-present issue of terrorism. Not he.

(5) His speeches had worked wonders in satisfying family members of convicted murderers regarding current reputations. Plus the bombing threats no longer existed.

(6) He assisted in the apprehension of the five informants.

(7) And finally, he stopped worrying and hurrying. Instead, there was relaxation, as he and Angela began traveling–but for pleasure only.

www.ingramcontent.com/pod-product-compliance
Lightning Source LLC
Chambersburg PA
CBHW030817310726
48980CB00006B/533/J
* 9 7 8 1 9 2 8 7 8 2 7 6 6 *